JACOB'S

PROMISE

By

Bill Heyduck

CRYSTAL
HEART

IMPRINTS

DEDICATION

The book is dedicated to
Daiva Markelis who first believed
in my beginning scribbles.

The house of the wicked shall be overthrown, but the tabernacle of the upright shall flourish.

Proverbs 14:11

ACKNOWLEDGMENTS

Without my critique group the book would still be gathering dust in some desk drawer. Carolyn Stephens, Mary Dwiggins, and Evelyn Goodrick, I can never thank you enough. A special thanks has to go to Ruth Souther who guided me through the complicated process of publishing.

.

Jacob's Promise

Jacob's Promise

CHAPTER 1

The afternoon's quiet was shattered by the sound of hoof beats galloping down the lane toward the Hesser's cabin. Katherine Hesser set aside the dress she was sewing and got up from her rocker. She walked to the open cabin door to see who was coming.

Beth Ann, her daughter, slowed her strokes of the butter churn and followed her mother's gaze out the open door.

Katherine, shielding her eyes from the slanting rays of the late afternoon sun, peered out the door and shook her head in disgust. "It's the Cooper brothers. I wonder what those four no-goods want?"

She stepped back and pulled the door closed until there was only a crack of light between it and the doorframe. "You keep on working that churn," she said as she watched the Coopers pull their horses to a halt in in front of the barn.

Katherine watched biting her lip. Anytime a Cooper showed up it meant trouble. Sam Cooper, the oldest boy, was the meanest of the lot. Even his own brothers were cowed by his hot temper.

Hans Hesser was mucking out a barn stall when he heard the horses approach. He laid aside his pitchfork and came out to see who the riders were. Stepping out of the dark barn he stopped, blinded by the bright sunlight.

Before he could see clearly, the four brothers had him boxed

1

in with their horses and began riding a tight circle round him. Quick as a striking snake, Sam lashed out with his foot and struck Hans full in the face with the toe of his boot. Hans staggered and fell to his knees, blood running from his nose and cheek.

Sam jumped off his horse and kicked Hans in the stomach. Hans doubled over and landed face first in to the hard-packed ground. As Hans struggled onto his hands and knees, Sam kicked him in the ribs. Writhing in pain, Hans was helpless to stop Sam's repeated kicks. Through eyes, blurry with blood, Hans saw the twisted smile on Sam's face.

"Pa sent me to give you a little reminder. He wants your place," Sam snarled, giving Hans one last vicious kick. "Quit diddlin around and sign the papers."

Seventeen-year-old Jacob, forking hay from the barn loft, heard the commotion outside and climbed down to investigate. As he came around the corner of the barn, he saw Sam kick his father. Without stopping he charged toward Sam.

Simon, the second youngest of the Cooper brothers, spurred his horse forward and slammed into Jacob, sending him sprawling. Toby, Jacob's dog, had followed Jacob out of the barn and stood growling by Jacob's side.

"Grab that damn dog and hold him," Simon said, pulling his rifle from its scabbard, "or I'll put a bullet in him."

Jacob, trembling with rage, hooked his hand around Toby's collar and pulled him down beside him.

Sam mounted his horse and looked down at the half-conscious figure on the ground. "Pa will be in town tomorrow to sign the papers. You best be there," Sam said spitting inches from Hans' face.

Laughing, he turned and led his brothers out of the barnyard, away from the furious barking of Toby.

Using his one good arm, Hans painfully raised himself to his knees, his hand clutching his fractured ribs. Blood ran down his battered face and dripped off his chin, making muddy red dots in the dust.

Jacob and Katherine rushed to help him, but Hans pushed their hands away. "Let me be, woman. I can stand on my own." Grimacing with pain he struggled to stand, finally clutching Jacob's shoulder for support as he limped across the barnyard and up the path and into the cabin.

Inside he sat with his drooped shoulders showing how defeated he felt. Katherine began to gently remove his sweat and blood-soaked shirt.

"Beth Ann, get me some warm water and a clean rag.," Katherine said, wadding the shirt into a ball and dropping it to the floor.

Beth Ann stared at her father's bruised body, unable to move.

"I need it now, Beth Ann, not tomorrow," Katherine snapped.

Beth Ann rushed to get a clean cloth and a pan of water from the fireplace.

The sight of his father's bloody face filled Jacob with a frustrated rage. The walls of the cabin suddenly became too confining. He stamped out of the cabin and kicked a straight-back chair setting on the small porch. "We'll make you pay," he muttered in a trembling voice. "No one can do that to a Hesser and not get paid back."

He paced up and down the porch, kicking imaginary Coopers as he traveled back and forth. His anger slowly cooled, and his adrenalin sapped body sagged down onto a bench by the cabin door.

His head popped up when he heard squeaking wagon wheels coming down the lane. The slanting rays of the sinking sun made it impossible for Jacob to make out who it was. When the wagon crunched to a stop in front of the cabin, Jacob was amazed to see his Aunt Ruth and Uncle Ralph.

He couldn't believe his eyes. Aunt Ruth had written his mother a month ago saying they would be traveling through around the end of April on their way to Oregon, but it was only the first week in April and they were here.

"Don't just stand there boy, come help me down," Ruth called. When her feet where firmly on the ground she grabbed Jacob by the shoulders and looked him up and down. "Good gracious, boy you've grown two feet since I last saw you."

She laughed, kissed him on the cheek, gave him a hug, and pushed past him. Her sunbonnet sailed off her flaming red hair as she charged up the path and through the cabin door. She flew across the room and wrapped Katherine in a bone-crushing hug.

"I can't believe I'm seeing you. When you left Virginia, I

thought I'd never see you again," Ruth said with unrestrained joy.

Ashamed of his nakedness, Hans hurriedly began to pull on the clean shirt Beth Ann had brought him.

"We weren't expecting you 'til the end of the month, but Lordy, Lordy, it's good to see you," Katherine said, wiping tears from her eyes.

Ruth spotted Beth Ann standing in the shadows, smiling shyly. "Good gracious, can that big girl be little Beth Ann? Come here girl, let me get a good look at you."

Ruth grabbed Beth Ann in a hug and then held her at arm's length, "Why, she's almost a woman. She's taller than I am. And look at that beautiful hair."

In her enthusiasm in greeting her sister Ruth had momentarily missed seeing Hans. It wasn't until she heard him give a small groan as he struggled into a clean shirt. Her hand flew to her mouth. "Good Lord, Hans, what happened to you?"

"I had a little accident." Hans tried to keep the pain out of his face.

Knowing Hans didn't want to tell Ruth about his troubles, Katherine tried to distract her. "You caught us in the middle of making supper, so make yourself useful. We can talk while we work."

Outside Jacob helped his Uncle Ralph unhitch the horses and led them to the water trough. As the horses poked their muzzles in the water Jacob turned to Ralph.

"I wish you had been here a while ago," Jacob blurted, his face burning with anger. "We could have shown those Cooper boys a thing or two."

"Whoa, slow down, boy. What's got you so sputtering mad?" Ralph gripped Jacob by the shoulders.

Jacob fought to control his voice before he could tell Ralph what had taken place in the barnyard earlier.

Ralph listened, then said in a quiet voice, "Let's get the horses in the barn and fed, then we'll go talk to your dad."

Seeing them come up the path, Ruth called, "You men wash up in the basin on the porch before you come in. We'll have the food on the table by the time you finish."

Hans was sitting at the table when they came in. He had refused to go to bed like Katherine had suggested. He couldn't suppress a small groan when Ralph shook his hand. In a show of his grittiness, Hans started saying the grace before anyone else had the chance.

Everyone was subdued during the meal, making small talk about the weather and family doings from back east. A lull in the conversation gave Katherine the opportunity to bring up what was on most of their minds.

"Hans, tell them how you got so banged up. You can't keep everything bottled up inside. Remember, we're all family."

"She's right, Hans. What the hell is going on with your neighbors?" Ralph asked.

"Tell him." Katherine twisted the front of her apron in her hands. "This feud has been going on for a month now and I didn't realize how serious it was until today."

Jacob stood up, "Yeah, Dad, I want to hear too. I didn't know old man Cooper wanted to buy the farm."

Hans bent his head as in prayer, collecting his thoughts. He took a labored breath then said, "We were the second family to settle the land out on this part of the prairie. At that time our closest neighbor was five miles east of here."

Hans gritted his teeth and struggled to sit up straighter. "We built the cabin, cleared the land, and planted a crop. We dammed the creek that flows through the south part of our land. Water is what the Coopers want to use to make us sell our land."

"Can't you get the law to help you?" Ralph asked. "We passed a town four or five miles east of here, don't they have a lawman there?"

"The only law in these parts is under the control of a judge, and the judge is the cousin of Tom Cooper's wife. He's the reason the Coopers moved here in the first place."

"I can see where that puts you in a tight spot." Ralph stood to stretch the kinks out of his back from the day long buggy ride. "So, what choices does that leave you?"

"We're staying right here. No damn money bags from back east is going to run me off," Hans growled. "Now let's finish supper."

When supper was over, Hans grudgingly took Ralph's arm as they made their way to the front porch. While clearing the table, Ruth asked, "What are you going to do, Katherine, if they force you off the farm? Where will you go?"

"I'm worried sick," Katherine confessed, wiping her hands on the dishtowel. "Hans has made up his mind that he will not give up the farm. Mr. Cooper is a rotten old man who uses his overgrown sons to bully everyone into doing what he wants."

She sat down on the bench by the table wringing the dishtowel in her hands. The sons are all as big as horses." She pushed a stray hair from her face and continued. "I'm worried about Jacob. He's such a stringy little guy with too much grit and determination for his own good. If his dad doesn't fix this problem, I'm afraid Jacob will go and do something foolish."

"He's hardly tall enough to see over a cow's back and can't weigh much more than a couple of sacks of feed," Ruth said. "Surely he wouldn't pick a fight with the big boys you described."

"He's skinny, but he's a dead shot with a rifle and a shotgun," Katherine said with some pride in her voice. "He's killed most of the meat we've eaten in the last couple of years."

"I hope you don't think it's going to resort to the use of guns?" Ruth waited for a moment then said. "You know you could always sell out and come with us out to Oregon. Ralph could always use him in the store we plan to open there."

"You don't know how stubborn Hans can be. He'd never agree to that." Katherine hid her face in her hands.

CHAPTER 2

The next morning, Jacob led the horses out of the barn and helped Ralph hitch one team to the wagon and tie the spare horses to a lead rope on the back.

Hans sat on the porch, wrapped in a blanket, and watched Ralph and Jacob work with the horses. He was still in so much pain it was difficult for him to move.

Jacob and Ralph came to the porch to scrub their hands before going in to the cabin. After Jacob dried his hands, he waited patiently for his father to struggle to his feet, leery about offering any assistance. He waited until his father placed his hand on his shoulder, then slowly walked with him in to breakfast.

The room was filled with the welcoming aroma of fried pork and fresh biscuits. The fire from the open fireplace had chased the morning chill away and pleasantly warmed the cabin. After the last amen of the blessing and the first few bites of food, Ralph said, "I sure hate to leave you folks in your time of need, but we have to be in St. Louis by the first of May to catch the boat to Independence.

"We've already paid a fee to the trail guide, and if we're late we could miss our wagon train west. We're afraid that if we hit heavy rain between here and St. Louis it could make us late. That's why we're here so early."

"There's no need to worry about us," Hans said. "Once the Coopers find we can't be bullied, it'll all blow over, and they'll

7

give up."

"You know we feel bad about leaving." Ralph pulled on his jacket "But wagon trains don't wait."

"I don't want to seem nosey, but you never did tell us what you're going to do when you get to Oregon," Hans said, trying to ease Ralph's discomfort.

"I thought Ruth told Katherine in her letter. I plan to open a general store to sell goods to settlers and trade goods to trappers. You know, Hans, I could always use another hand in the store if you change your mind and want to come out to Oregon."

"I intend to stay right where I am," Hans said emphatically. "Have Ruth write Katherine a letter once you're settled so we'll know just where you are."

"It's time we got on our way, Ruth," he called through the door. "Say your goodbyes and come on out. I'll wait at the wagon."

Ruth hugged Katherine and Beth Ann, kissed each on the cheek, and hurried out the door before they could see her tears. She patted Hans on the shoulder as she passed by.

"Take care of that family of yours," she called over her shoulder as she fled down the path to the wagon. At the wagon she hugged Jacob and then let him help her up on the wagon beside Ralph.

Katherine watched Ruth and Ralph wave as they turned out of the lane and on to the road heading west. She wiped away her tears and turned to hide them from her husband. A great sadness filled her. Her sister was headed to Oregon, and this was probably the last time she would ever see her.

She regained control, shook her head to clear it, and chided herself for crying. She was losing a sister, but she still had a lot of blessings. She had a good husband, good kids, and they lived on the choice piece of Illinois farmland. What else could a woman ask for?

Later that day Jacob dragged in logs from the woods to be cut up for firewood, while Hans, a blanket pulled tightly around his shoulders, sat on the porch and watched. He was fretting about not being able to help. This was the first time in his life he was unable to do his share of the work. It galled him to have to ask his 17-

year-old son to do work that he should be doing.

There was seed corn that needed to be shelled and sacked, harness checked for cracks, and the plow point repaired from the rock he hit while plowing last fall. Kindling had to be split, the stock fed, and fences built. All that work was now on Jacob's shoulders. Hans knew that if his ribs were broken, and he feared they were, the work was going to fall to Jacob for a long spell.

After a light noon meal Jacob went out behind the cabin and started sawing on the tree trunks he dragged in earlier. The long afternoon of sawing caught up with him at the supper table, and he fell asleep while eating. Katherine gently shook him awake and guided him to the ladder that led to his bed in the loft.

The next morning, Jacob pulled his aching body out of his warm bed, quietly dressed and climbed down the ladder to the floor below. The sun was not yet up, and he had to feel his way around in the dark cabin. He added wood to the fire before slipping on his coat and heading for the barn to feed the animals.

When he opened the barn door, a sharp wind blowing through the barn hit him in the face. Somehow the horses had forced open the back doors and escaped into the pasture.

The last thing he needed was to have to round up the horses before he could start his chores. He pulled down some hay from the loft for the cow and returned to the cabin in a foul mood.

His mother was up and had breakfast started when he got back to the cabin. Her smiling face and the smell of bacon helped cheer him up. He hung up his coat and gave his mother a good morning hug.

"How's Dad doing?" he asked.

"He had a restless night, but finally fell asleep a couple of hours ago. Try to be quiet. He needs the rest."

A sleepy-eyed Beth Ann climbed down the ladder from the loft in time to help her mother serve the breakfast.

Jacob gobbled down his food and pushed back from the table. "The horses are loose, and I need to bring them in before I can start the other work," he said as he grabbed his hat and coat and rushed out the door. His dog, Toby, was waiting for him and began dancing circles around him the minute he stepped outside.

At the barn he picked up a bridle. He planned to ride one of the horses back when he found them. A light frost overnight made the weeds snap and crackle under his feet as he made his way through the pasture. He cussed the horses with every freezing step he took.

A north wind was at his back as he headed out, and he dreaded the thought of having to ride back facing it. He hadn't gone far before Toby kicked up the scent of a rabbit and chased off into the brush. Jacob wished he had brought a shotgun with him.

The thought of fried rabbit sounded good. It also occurred to him that with the Coopers acting up, it might be a good idea to start carrying a rifle when he went out to cut wood. He didn't share his father's belief that the trouble with the Coopers was over.

He was shaken out of his daydream when he saw the horses standing in a depression where the pond used to be. There was a hole in the dam and most of the water had drained away. The horses were drinking from the shallow water of the creek now running through where the pond had been.

Jacob's anger reached the boiling point. He remembered the backbreaking work he and his father had done in building that small dam. His dad was going to have a fit when he heard about this.

The horses were skittish at first, but Jacob dug some oats out of a small sack he carried and approached them with his hand out. They stood stiff legged eyeing the oats he offered. One of the plough horses was the first to approach, and the riding horses soon followed.

He got the bridle on one of the riding horses and started herding the others back to the barn. After the horses were inside the lot, he closed the gate and hurriedly fed them, anxious to get to the cabin and report what he had found.

After Jacob had gone, Katherine got Hans up and sat him on a stool to take off his old bandages. "Another day and I think you won't be needing a bandage." Katherine finished putting a new bandage on his head. "The bump on your head is more of a raw bruise than an open wound, but I think your nose is broken."

"It's not my head or nose I'm worried about, it's these doggone ribs that are killing me. You have me bound up so tight I can hardly breathe. How's Jacob going to be able to handle the plowing and the other chores if I'm still in this condition when the weather warms?"

Jacob's Promise

"Hans Hesser, you know I can handle a plow as well as any man," Katherine chided. "And I'm sure that Jacob and I together will do quite well."

Entering the cabin Jacob heard what his father said. "Don't you worry, Dad. Mom and I can handle anything that needs to be done until your ribs heal." Jacob hesitated a few moments before adding, "I was just out at the dam and found out the Coopers have punched a big hole in it. Are we going to let them get by with that?"

Hans knew he was in no shape to do anything until he healed, but he needed to calm Jacob before he did something foolish. "Don't get too worked up about it, Jacob. We can fix it. The creek will have enough water to take care of the stock. There'll be a time when I'm more able to help."

"Is that all you're going to do?" Jacob asked.

"What do you want me to do?" Hans gritted his teeth. "Look at me, sitting here with my ribs all stove in and more work to be done than you can handle. You know the law won't help, and we couldn't prove anything anyway." Hans paused.

"We just have to be patient. The Coopers will get tired of playing their dirty little tricks when they see we won't budge from the place. But I think it might be a good idea for you to take one of the horses and ride out along the fence line to make sure they didn't knock any of it down when they came in to mess up the dam."

Jacob left to do what he was told, but he wished his father would get a little more fire in him and go with him to confront the Coopers. At the barn he picked up the shotgun his father kept there to shoot varmints. If he caught a Cooper on their land, he might use it.

11

CHAPTER 3

Each day, Jacob saddled a horse and rode the fence line before he started his regular chores. Today just like every day this week, he found another place where the fence rail had been taken down. Toby accompanied him on these trips and always ran off following some animal trail when Jacob stopped to repair the fence. Jacob called him when he was ready to return home, but Toby, as usual, was too interested in the chase to heed his call.

The next morning when Jacob left the cabin, he was surprised Toby wasn't at the door to greet him. He couldn't remember a time when Toby hadn't been there to dance at his feet when he walked out. Worry creased Jacob's brow when Toby hadn't appeared by the time he finished saddling the horse. At the south end of the fence line, Jacob found the reason for Toby's disappearance. Lying beside a broken place in the fence was his body, a bullet hole through his side.

"Damn the Coopers," Jacob muttered through tears of anger. Frustrated in his inability to do anything to avenge Toby's death. He climbed down from his horse, wiping the tears from his eyes, and knelt beside Toby's lifeless body. He gently smoothed Toby's ruffled fur, then picked him up and placed him in front of the saddle for the ride home.

Jacob's parents had given him the ten-week-old puppy on his eleventh birthday and Toby had been his steady companion ever since.

Hans sat quietly as he listened to Jacob's story about his dog and the ruined fence. He knew he needed to have a face down with old man Cooper, but his ribs were still too sore.

He wouldn't be able to mount a horse, much less challenge anyone. When he again suggested patience, Jacob turned and stomped out of the house. Hans struggled out of his chair to follow him outside. He found Jacob taking out his frustration by furiously splitting kindling by the woodshed behind the cabin.

"Jacob," Hans called.

Jacob looked up at his father, his cheeks wet with tears of anger and frustration.

"Listen, boy," Hans said, "I know what's been happening is not right, and I do intend to do something about it, but can't you see I'm in no shape to confront the Coopers right now?"

Jacob hung his head. He did understand, but it didn't make it any easier to accept.

"Just give me a little more time to heal, son," Hans pleaded, "I promise we'll make it right when I'm my old self again."

Jacob nodded his agreement and went back to chopping until his fury was finally spent. He left the woodpile and faced the unpleasant task of burying Toby.

After supper, Jacob sat on the porch with his father planning what work needed to be done the next day. "First thing tomorrow, you and your mother need to go to town and trade for some supplies," Hans said. "Your mother has some young chicks she hopes to trade for some sugar and flour, and you need to take that broken piece of harness in to see if it can be fixed. You better pick up a sack of oats for the horses."

"Do you want me to charge it or pay cash money?" asked Jacob.

"Take some of your mother's leftover blackberry jam in to trade along with the chicks. Try to hold any charges as low as you can. Old man Johnson may not want to trade for much, but if his wife's there, she'll make him. She loves your mother's blackberry jam."

Katherine came to the doorway wiping her hands on her apron and took a deep breath of the cool damp April air. "Oh, that air smells so clean and fresh after being cooped up in the cabin all day." She settled in next to Hans on the split log bench.

"That sliver of the moon sure doesn't shed much light. I can barely make out the barn from here. This'll be a good night for the coons to tear something up, now that Toby's gone."

"Sit down and rest a while, honey." Hans reached for her hand.

Katherine hesitated, but sat. "I need to go to bed and you two should come, too. Beth Ann headed for the loft the minute we were done with the dishes."

Jacob joined her, his eyes drooping. He was anxious to crawl into his own cornhusk stuffed pallet in the loft. Hans and Katherine sat a little longer enjoying the soft spring night before Katherine got to her feet.

"Come on, husband," she said. "We both need to get to bed." Hans didn't object when she helped him to his feet and led him inside.

The Cooper brothers, standing at the tree line bordering the barn lot, watched Hans and Katherine enter the cabin. After the last lamp in the cabin went out the four brothers dismounted and led their horses up behind the barn and tied them to the fence rail.

They untied five-gallon cans of coal oil from each of their saddle horns and moved into the barn. Sam Cooper pushed the front barn door open just enough to make sure all the lamps were out. He knew the Hessers went to bed early. He had watched the cabin from the woods for the last four nights. But tonight, he wanted to be doubly sure everyone was asleep before he made a move.

"Killing that dog was a real stroke of luck, Sam," Willie, the youngest brother, said. "Without him here barkin' his head off, a whole troop of cavalry could ride through here without anybody wakin' up."

"That may be," Sam answered, "but I want everyone to be quiet and do what I say. Understand?" Sam couldn't see them, but he knew they had nodded their agreement. "Remember to start countin' the minute you step out of the barn door."

He held them in the barn for another half hour before opening the door and sending them out. Each crept out to their assigned side of the cabin, carrying a can of fuel, counting to five hundred as they went. A five hundred count would give each of them time to get into position.

At the end of the count, each doused a log wall of the cabin with coal oil. Sam took the front of the cabin, slipping open the front door and splashing coal oil on the floor outside Hans and Katherine's bedroom door.

When the cans were empty, they each struck a match and tossed it on the fuel-soaked logs. Their matches flared within seconds of each other and flames shot up the sides of the cabin. Carrying the empty cans, they dashed to their horses. They untied the horses and led them to the end of the pasture before mounting and riding away.

The fire raced up the cabin walls and ignited the tinder dry wooden shingles of the roof. In minutes the cabin was engulfed in flames. The crackling and popping sound of the advancing flames woke Katherine from a sound sleep.

She lay for a moment trying to sort out why she was hearing the crackling noise and seeing a flickering light. It was then she saw the flames dancing outside the bedroom window.

"Hans," she shouted, "The cabin's on fire!" Hans sat up with a jolt and nearly passed out from the sharp stab of pain that shot through his side.

"We need to get the kids and get out," she screamed. She jumped out of bed and ran to the door, while Hans struggled to his feet. She jerked the door open and was met by a wall of angry flames. Her hair was singed and the hem of her nightgown ablaze before she could slam the door shut.

"We're trapped," she cried, as she stumbled back, beating the smoldering flames on her gown.

"We can get out the window," Hans yelled. "But we'll have to jump through the flames."

Ignoring the pain in his side, he picked up the three-legged stool from the end of the bed, lifted it over his head, and threw it at the window with all the force he could muster.

The bedroom door had not fully latched when Katherine slammed it against the flames and when the window shattered a violent draft whipped the door open. A sheet of searing flame flashed through the room, igniting their night clothes and searing their lungs. The rush of heat knocked then into the flaming covers

15

of the bed, instantly ending their struggle to escape.

Jacob thought he was dreaming when he awoke to the smell of smoke. Forcing his eyes open, he saw light flickering on the rafters and shingles above the entrance to the loft. A raw pain in his throat brought him fully awake. It was smoke he smelled. He crawled to the opening and peeked over the edge.

A blast of heat hit his face and singed his eyebrows before he could jerk his head back. Flames were already licking halfway up the ladder to the loft. He scooted over to Beth Ann's pallet and shook her awake. "Wake up! The cabin's on fire and we must get out of here! Follow me!"

The flames had advanced farther at the end of the cabin where his mother and father had their bedroom, so Jacob led his sister to the other end.

Jacob stumbled over the extra tools his father had stored in the loft where it was drier, and less likely to rust. Blinded by the smoke, Jacob frantically searched through the stored tools. A crosscut saw was the first tool he found, but a saw was of little use.

Reaching past the saw, he felt around until he found the double-bladed ax. He grabbed the ax and started chopping at the shingles above him. Splinters and dirt rained down in his face as the dry shingles began to give way. Smoke, dirt, and splinters blinded him, but when he judged the hole big enough, he boosted Beth Ann through and clambered out behind her.

Safely on the roof, he led Beth Ann away from the hole they had escaped through and over to the side of the cabin where there were fewer flames. A lean-to had been built on one side of the cabin to protect the firewood from the weather. The lean-to had blocked the flames from a small portion of the roof.

Jacob, squinting through smoke-burned eyes, found the lean-to, and eased over to it. With Beth Ann in front of him they slid down the lean-to's rough shingles to the ground and stumbled away from the flames.

The second Jacob's eyes cleared he charged around to the front of the house. He kicked open the front door, but flames drove him back. He ran to his parent's bedroom window and yelled their names. A faint smell floated out of the flaming window, a smell he would never forget, the scent of burning flesh. He turned his back on the searing heat and staggered away from the cabin and fell to his knees, crying.

Beth Ann followed him and saw the flames shooting out of her parent's bedroom window. Feeling faint, she fell to her knees next to Jacob, tearing at his clothes in her anguish.

Jacob fought to control of his emotions when he saw his sister's pale face, twisted with grief. He wiped his eyes, put his arm around her, trying awkwardly to comfort her. They knelt together for some minutes, weeping. The wind shifted and Jacob become aware of another smell mixed in with the smoke. Coal oil.

The scent of coal oil slashed into his brain like a knife. He suddenly knew how the fire started and who started it. Grief gave way to a seething anger, a cold, vengeful anger, anger like nothing he had ever felt before. He made a pledge to himself.

The Coopers would pay and pay dearly. Rage clouded his thinking for only a moment before reality set in. He was one against four. How was he going to face down four almost grown men? All of the Cooper boys were bigger and stronger than he.

A cold, wet wind suddenly blew out of the northwest followed by a clap of thunder. Seconds later a gentle rain began to fall, sizzling as it splashed onto the burning timbers of the cabin. The rain grew heavier and slowly began to turn the flaming logs into steaming embers.

Their scorched nightclothes were soaked before Jacob was able to rouse Beth Ann and get her into the barn out of the rain. In the barn he pushed her up the ladder into the small, cramped loft, and buried her in straw to keep her warm, then crawled in beside her.

He curled up next to her shivering body and held her while she cried herself to sleep. Jacob lay awake all night, thinking of revenge. Thoughts of vengeance dwindled with the sudden realization that he and Beth Ann were orphans. Their only relatives were back in Virginia or on their way to Oregon.

CHAPTER 4

The Cooper brothers headed for a raised knoll about a half a mile from the Hesser cabin. At the top they stopped and turned to admire their recent handy work. Sparks swirled upward into the low hanging clouds from the roaring flames of the cabin.

"Looks like they're having a hot time in Hesser's cabin tonight," Simon said with a snicker.

"Yeah, I think we roasted a few Hessers," Sam laughed.

"You think anyone will see the fire, Sam?" Willy, the youngest brother asked.

"Nah, we're their closest neighbor, and I'll bet you can't even see it from our place."

"I don't know Sam, with these clouds so low, there might be a reflection that can be seen from farther away," Willy said.

"What farmer do you know that would be up at this time of night?" Sam said. "Come on. Let's get home and tell Pa how easy it was."

Their father was sitting on the porch, smoking his pipe, when they rode up. Tom Cooper looked nothing like his sons. He stood five feet six, had a barrel chest, with thin arms, and legs that didn't look like they belonged to the body.

None of his boys stood less than six feet tall, nor weighed less than two hundred pounds. Sam was the biggest and toughest of the bunch, but even he was afraid of his father's temper.

"Hi, Pa. You waitin' to hear how your boys cooked a few Hessers tonight?" Sam asked with a chuckle.

"Yes, I was worried. I could see the red on the bottom of the clouds over that way and knew you had the fire going. But when it started raining, I was afraid it might have doused it."

"The rain was too late to do the Hessers any good. They were dancin' in the devil's own hell afore we were out of the barnyard." Sam clapped his hands with joy. "We stopped on the knoll just south of their place and watched it burn. No rain could put out that ball of fire."

"That's good to hear," Tom said. "With the Hessers out of the way, it'll be easy to make up a bill of sale for the farm. Having a brother-in-law as the local judge doesn't hurt either," Tom chuckled. "The place is as good as ours."

"How are you goin' to get Hesser's name on those papers with him fried in that cabin," Sam asked.

"Why, Sam, you're going to be Hans Hesser for about two minutes while you sign his name," his father answered with a smile.

"How're you goin' to explain the burned-out cabin happening just when you end up with those legal papers?"

"I'll date the bill of sale a week earlier. I'll say he sold the land to me because he wanted to return to Virginia and he probably burned the place before he left just to spite me," Tom continued.

"We'll go down in a few days, when the embers are good and cool to bury the bodies out in the woods where no one will find them. If someone else happens by and finds the bodies, I'll say it was a tragic accident and that I am truly saddened by it."

"You sure make it sound easy," Sam said. "But we'll be in a hell of a lot of trouble if people in town don't buy your story."

"By God, if my brother-in-law, the judge, says it's legal, then who within fifty miles can say it isn't?" Tom growled. "Some might have their suspicions, but they'll see that Tom Cooper is not a man you want to cross, and they'll keep their mouths shut."

"You just make sure you keep your mouths shut, for God's sake. And keep away from the Hesser place until we go down there together. The last thing we need is for someone to see one of us nosing around.

"Now, wash the coal oil off your hands and pile your smelly clothes out by your mother's washstand before you go to bed. As a reward for doing the job, I'm going to let you all have a day in town tomorrow. And wash up. I don't want you going in there smelling like coal oil."

Before light Jacob grew uncomfortable with the straw sticking him in a new place every time he moved. He carefully got up and searched until he found a piece of canvas to put on top of the straw to hold in Beth Ann's body heat.

He paced up and down the length of the barn, flapping his arms to keep warm. His thin nightshirt didn't offer much insulation against the early morning chill. A million thoughts tumbled through his head. His parents were dead, the cabin in ruins, and he and Beth Ann had no one to turn to for help. He had to figure out a way to keep the Cooper brothers from knowing he and Beth Ann had survived the fire.

He stood at the barn door, looking at the smoldering ruins of the cabin. He needed to find out if anything in the cabin was salvageable. If all their clothes had burned, they were going to be in a real fix. The rain had slowed to a sprinkle and the flames had died away and become smoldering, gray ashes. Wisps of steam came up as raindrops hit some of the remaining hot spots.

He shuddered when he looked at the ruined end of the cabin where his parents had slept. With a lump in his throat, he turned toward the other end and was surprised to see about a fourth of the cabin still had some of the roof and a fragment of the scorched walls still standing.

He approached the cabin and started pulling rubble away from where the front door had once stood, but hesitated before he stepped in. He was bare foot and didn't want to step on any hot coals. The first weight he put on the burned planks of the floor broke beneath his foot.

He grabbed what was left of the doorframe to keep from falling head first into the cabin. He tore part of the doorframe off and laid it over the charred floor before he took any more steps.

Using the piece of wood as a cane, he edged along the wall on the door frame. He hadn't traveled far before he saw the big wooden trunk the family had carried with them from Virginia. The front of the trunk had deep scorch marks, but it didn't look like the fire had reached the interior. Jacob brushed the collected ash from the top of the trunk and carefully opened it.

Everyone in the family had two sets of clothes. They wore one set for a week, then changed to the other while the first set was washed. His mother insisted they needed a third clean set for special occasions and to have in case one of the everyday sets was damaged beyond repair. The extras were stored in this trunk.

He found a pair of pants and shirt for himself and a clean dress for Beth Ann, but there weren't any extra shoes. Lack of shoes was going to be a problem. Going bare foot wasn't a big handicap in the summer.

He and Beth Ann usually went barefoot every summer to save their shoes, but it was early April, and his feet weren't callused enough to walk about with any comfort.

Hanging on pegs at the very end of the cabin were two ponchos made of oiled canvas that he and his father wore during wet weather. The bottom third of them had burned off, but they could still keep the biggest part of the body dry. He wrapped the clothes in the ponchos and started back to the barn.

Edging his way back to the cabin door, he couldn't keep his eyes from traveling to the bedroom containing his parents' bodies. Grief suddenly struck him with a force he wasn't prepared for.

He fought to control the sobs that shook him but failed. He buried his face in the clothes he was carrying and let the tears flow. When his sobbing finally stopped, he wiped his eyes. He couldn't let Beth Ann see how helpless he felt.

At the barn he found Beth Ann sitting in the straw, bent over with her face in her hands. She had the canvas wrapped around her and Jacob watched her body shake with each sob. When she looked up, he saw her red pleading eyes. "Oh, Jacob, what are we going to do?

"First we are going to have to find something to eat. I was just in the cabin, and I didn't even think of food," he said. "Wait a minute and I'll go out to the root cellar and see what I can find."

In the root cellar Jacob found a few dried-up apples, some jars of green beans, 10 jars of blackberry jam and some sauerkraut. There was no use taking blackberry jam if they didn't have any bread to put it on. He stuffed a couple of the apples in his pocket and returned to the cabin. He remembered his mother had a cabinet where she stored dry beans, dried fruit and baking supplies.

But when he got to the cabin, he found only a scorched wall and a pile of black ashes where the cabinet had hung. Digging through the rubble he found part of a slab of bacon, covered with ashes He brushed it off and put it under one arm as he dug through the ashes looking for a pan to fry it in. He uncovered a skillet, a spatula, and a knife with the wooden handle burned off. On the way out of the cabin, he used the spatula to pick up a hot glowing coal and put it in the skillet so he could start a fire to cook the bacon.

Beth Ann had gotten dressed, but her eyes were still red rimmed from crying. "I did a little food searching of my own while you were gone," she said, proudly holding out five eggs she had gathered.

Beth Ann complained about eating breakfast in the barn with the smell of hay and manure, but Jacob said the smell of the burned cabin would be worse if they ate outside. He didn't want to mention the smell of burned flesh.

He had made up his mind about what they needed to do while he was in the root cellar, but didn't say anything to Beth Ann. He cautioned her to stay in the barn and out of sight.

"The Coopers will be after us if they know we survived the fire." He didn't tell her, but he wanted to be gone before the sun came up tomorrow morning.

There was one thought driving most of his thinking. How was he going to get even with the Coopers before they left the farm? He had a special revenge in mind but wasn't at all sure he would be able to carry it out. His plan might just end up with him dead.

He had to be careful and not let his hatred of the Coopers make him do something foolish. He had Beth Ann to think of. He wished there was some lawman he could depend on, but he knew the Coopers had that under control, too. It was his problem, and he had to decide how he was going to handle it.

CHAPTER 5

Jacob ate breakfast in silence, dreading the gruesome job that lay ahead of him. When he couldn't put it off any longer, he got up and walked to the back of the barn. He picked up a shovel and took a length of rope off a peg by the door. He threw on one of the half-burned ponchos and called hoarsely to Beth Ann. "I need to go dig a grave for mom and dad."

"Wait. I'll come with you," Beth Ann said.

"You stay here, there's no use in both of us getting wet, it's still sprinkling. I'll come get you when I finish."

It was going to be hard enough for him to face the job ahead and having her with him would only make it worse. He hurried away, carrying the shovel and a coil of rope before she could offer any objection. He wanted to shield her from what he knew he'd find at the end of the cabin. He hoped he had the stomach to do the job.

At the collapsed wall at the end of the cabin he stopped. A lump grew in his throat at the sight of the charred roof rafters, and shingles scattered over the bodies of his parents. An overpowering stench hit Jacob and he had to fight to hold down his breakfast. Stiffening his backbone and his resolve, he moved out beyond the logs of the fallen wall and started digging.

Shoveling the heavy rain-soaked earth soon sapped his strength and he gave up after reaching a depth of about three feet.

He laid the shovel down and returned to the cabin and pulled aside the burned timbers covering his parents.

He found it hard to accept that the black twisted forms in front of him were his parents. With trembling hands, he looped the rope around the limb of one of the burned shapes. Suddenly overcome with grief and nausea he turned and fled from the cabin. He fell to his knees behind a scorched bush, racked by the convulsive contractions of his stomach and his sobs.

He slowly regained control and forced himself to return to the gruesome job he had started. This time he concentrated on the rope and not the limb he tied it to. He uncoiled the rope and using his peripheral vision to guide him, pulled the blackened body to the edge of the grave. With his head turned to the side he untied the rope and used the shovel to lever the burned hulk into the shallow grave. The sound of it hitting the bottom of the hole sent a shudder through him.

Fighting to keep control of his emotions, he returned for the other charred shape. With both bodies in the grave he threw the rope in. He knew he would never be able to use that rope again. Trying not to look down he began shoveling the muddy soil in to cover them.

He packed the dirt down, scooped ashes over the raw earth. And then pulled some burned timbers over that to make it more difficult for any animal to dig up the bodies. The job finished, he called for Beth Ann to join him.

Beth Ann opened the barn door and saw the burned cabin for the first time in daylight. Her eyes traveled along the crumbling walls and then fell on the flowerbeds her mother had so lovingly tended. The twisted shapes of the scorched tulips and daffodils reflected how she felt inside. At the corner of the cabin she saw Jacob and walked to join him.

They stood silently for a few moments before Jacob started saying the Lord's Prayer. Beth Ann joined him, quietly weeping. With the prayer finished, Jacob didn't let Beth Ann linger at the grave. He took her arm and guided her back to the barn where he sat her down on a three-legged milking stool and explained to her what they had to get done before the day was over.

"You know we have to leave here, or the Coopers are going to kill us," he began. "We know they killed mom and dad, and they aren't about to leave us alive to tell anyone. To get away we'll need money and supplies."

"Where can we go?" Beth Ann asked, her tear streaked face nearly breaking Jacob's heart.

"We'll pack up and head back to Virginia. We have some relations there," he lied. Jacob had no intention of heading east, but he didn't want to take the chance Beth Ann might let the cat out of the bag if she knew what he had planned. "Right now, we need to get everything we can sell, or trade loaded in the wagon and get into town. I want to make some legal arrangements about the farm."

Jacob told her to gather up all but four of the laying hens and bring them to him. He left to hitch the workhorses to the wagon, then led the two riding horses out of the barn and tied them to the back.

They would have to use the riding horse to pull the wagon home after they sold the work horses. The two bare foot orphans, ponchos pulled tight around their shoulders, and bathed in the acid smell of smoke, headed for town.

Their first stop was the livery stable where Jacob sold the team of plow horses for a lot less than they were worth. He realized the liveryman saw a green teenager anxious to have some money and took advantage of the situation. After the sale, Jacob hitched the riding horses to the wagon, thankful his father had had the foresight to train them to the hitch. He drove the team to the back of the general store and hitched them to the loading dock.

Mrs. Johnson, the wife of the storekeeper, a pudgy red-faced woman, greeted them with a big smile as they walked in the front door. "Good heavenly days, what has happened to you? You look like drowned rats."

"We feel like drowned rats, Mrs. Johnson," Jacob said fighting the lump that grew in his throat. "We've had a tragedy out at our place." Jacob had to clear his throat before continuing. "Our cabin burned, and our parents were killed in the fire."

Beth Ann suddenly burst into tears and Mrs. Johnson rushed to embrace her. "Oh, my lands!' She exclaimed. "You poor children are left out on the burned farm all alone. What in the world are you going to do? What can we do to help?"

"That's why we are here," Jacob said. "We can't stay in a

burned cabin with no food to speak of, so we brought in a few things to trade for supplies. We hope to get enough to carry us back to our relatives in Virginia."

"Let me get my husband. I'm sure he'll want to do what he can to help."

Jacob was able to trade for a few sides of bacon, flour, salt, molasses, and beef jerky, but had to pay cash for the other items. He bought blankets and oilskins to roll the blankets in to keep them dry, wool coats and raincoats. He also purchased four pairs of pants and four shirts, two for Beth Ann and two for him, plus two pair of heavy shoes and felt hats for both of them.

"I don't want pants," Beth Ann objected. "I'm not dressing like a boy. I want dresses."

"We're not going to a church picnic," Jacob snapped. "We have a tough road ahead of us and pants will be better than dresses for travel."

Beth Ann was shocked into silence by his cutting reply. She turned away and pretended to look at some bolts of cloth on the counter behind her, fighting back tears.

Jacob didn't intend to be so sharp and quickly added. "Sorry how that sounded, Beth Ann, but we can't start arguing when we have so much yet to do."

Mrs. Johnson gave Beth Ann a teary hug and followed them to the front of the store. "Isn't there someone you can stay with here in town?" She asked. "I'm sure the good people on farms around here would welcome you into their families. Everyone knows what good workers you both are."

"Thank you, Mrs. Johnson, but we think it best if we head back to our relatives in Virginia as soon as we can," Jacob answered as he walked out the back door to the loading dock.

Jacob helped Mr. Johnson unload the wagon and reload it with the supplies he had purchased and traded for. He shook hands with Mr. Johnson and thanked him for being so generous with the trade goods.

Taking Beth Ann's hand, Jacob guided her out of the store and down the street to Samuel Clark's law office. Samuel Clark had been his father's lawyer when he bought the land for their farm, and Jacob trusted him above all others in the town.

When Jacob and Beth Ann entered the office, Samuel looked

up from the papers he was studying, "Well, what brings the Hesser children into town on a gray rainy day like this?"

"Mr. Clark, we need to sell the farm," Jacob said a quiver in his voice.

"Sell the farm. Shouldn't your father be the one to make that decision?"

"My father's dead and so is my mother," Jacob said, fighting back tears.

"Dead! My God, Jacob. When did this happen?" Samuel asked.

Jacob hesitated a moment to get his emotions under control before answering. "They died in a fire while we were all asleep. I suspect the Coopers set it in the middle of the night, but I can't prove it. Beth Ann and I barely got out alive."

"You need to tell this to the law and let them handle it," Samuel said.

"Mr. Clark, you know the judge is Tom Cooper's brother-in-law, and the judge appointed a marshal that does whatever the judge tells him to do. We don't want the law involved. We just want to get away from here, and back to Virginia."

Samuel thought for a moment then said, "What is it you want me to do?"

"I want you to sell the farm. If Cooper wants to buy it make sure he pays an extra high price for each acre. You can keep the extra for your trouble. I want you to hang on to the money until you hear from me or Beth Ann. We'll write you where to send it."

"I'll write up a contract and you can come back later and sign it."

"No, Mr. Clark, just let us sign the bottom of a blank sheet of paper. You can write the contract above it later." Jacob said stopping to catch his breath. "We have to trust you. We need to get out of here before we're seen by the Coopers."

Jacob and Beth Ann signed the papers, and with Jacob leading the way headed for the town's only café. He felt they deserved a hot meal after what they had been through today. At the café he picked a table by the front window and nervously ate the first meal he had ever eaten in a public place.

He was finishing his last bite of apple pie when he looked out the window and saw the four Cooper brothers ride by. He pressed the side of his face against the window glass to watch them ride down the street and hitch their horses to the rail in front of the saloon.

"Hurry up and finish eating while I pay the bill," Jacob whispered. "The Cooper brothers just rode by, and I don't want them to see us."

They slipped out the front door and hurried down the street to the back of the general store. Jacob untied the wagon, jumped up to his seat, and headed the horses for home.

CHAPTER 6

The Cooper brothers entered the saloon in high spirits. They were happy to get away from under the thumb of their father for a day and looked forward to being able to have a beer away from the scolding eyes of their mother.

Their dad said it was a reward for the work they had done at the Hessers' place and they intended to stay in town all day. They intended to stretch out their freedom for as long as they could.

In the saloon they each ordered a mug of beer and eased back in their chairs savoring the foamy drink. They took their time drinking two beers while they joked and flirted with the barmaid. The beer finished, they wandered down the street to the café to order steak dinners.

The waitress taking their orders said, "You just missed seeing your neighbors."

"What neighbor was that?" asked Sam.

"The two Hesser kids were in here not over an hour ago."

"The Hesser kids?" Sam looked around the table at his brothers.

"They stopped in here to eat after they picked up supplies at the general store. Said there'd been a fire out at their place and that both of their parents had died. Told me they were headed back to Virginia."

When the waitress finished taking their orders and left the

table, Sam said in a low voice, "How in the hell did they get out of that fire alive? You all saw that cabin. The whole place was covered with flames. We watched it from the hill."

"We gotta let Pa know," Eddie, the second oldest brother said.

"I'm not riding all the way back to the farm to tell him and spoil my day in town," Sam snapped. "He can wait until we get home tonight to hear about it."

"Yeah, why spoil our day off to fret about the Hesser kids? If they're headed east pulling a wagon, we can catch up with them in a couple of days if Daddy wants us to," Eddie said.

Willie, the youngest, wasn't so sure they should wait until night to tell their father, no matter what Sam said. But he kept his mouth shut.

The boys spent over two hours eating and talking. Eddie set down his coffee cup, pushed away the empty plate that had held his second piece of apple pie, and said, "I don't know about you, but I want another beer before we call it a day and start for home."

"Okay, one more, but that's all," Sam said. "If one of us comes home drunk, Mom'll throw a fit, and then Pa will keep us on that farm the rest of the spring."

They stayed in the saloon nursing their beer for as long as they could to extend their day. When the last of the beer was gone, Sam announced, "Time to head for home. It'll be dark by the time we get home, with cows to be milked and stock to be fed when we get there."

Simon and Eddie got up from the table and had to help Willie walk to the door. He wasn't used to that much beer. Staggering and laughing they finally got him into the saddle. Sam wasn't too worried about Willie's condition; he knew Willie would be almost sobered up by the time they rode the five miles home.

They got on their horses and were riding past the front of the general store when Marie Hays and her cousin Tillie walked out. Sam had met Marie at a wedding in the Methodist Church about six months ago and had taken a fancy to her.

They had shared a glass of punch and had even danced a few dances together. He reined in his horse and turned toward the board walk where she was standing. The other brothers stopped, too. Sam removed his hat and said, "Hello Marie. What brings you to town?"

Jacob's Promise

"Hello, Sam. My cousin, Tillie, and I've come in to pick up some material my mother ordered a couple of months ago."

"Would you and your cousin have time for a cup of coffee before you start back home?" Sam asked.

"No, Sam. We need to get back before dark or Mother will be worried to death," Marie said.

"There's no need for her to worry, me and Eddie will be happy to ride along with you to make sure you get home safe."

"Sam, that's nice of you to offer," Marie said. "We'd enjoy having you along for company, but we need to start now."

"Willie, you and Simon go on home. Me and Eddie will be along as soon as we've escorted these ladies safely home," Sam said in his usual commanding manner.

Sam and Eddie jumped down from their horses and helped the young women into their buggy and unhitched it from the rail. The two younger brothers lingered long enough to watch the buggy, a brother riding on each side of it, reach the end of the street, and turn the corner out of sight before they kicked their horses in the ribs and started for home.

"Just like Sam to leave the dirty work to us. Now we're left to tell Dad about the Hessers," Simon said.

"Maybe if we ride real slow Sam and Eddie will catch up with us," Willie said.

"I'm in no hurry to get home either, but there's no way Sam is going to catch up with us. It's three miles out to the Hays place. It'll be dark before they get back into town. We'll be home by then."

CHAPTER 7

Jacob kept the horses at a trot all the way back to the farm. He wanted to get there and out of sight in case the Coopers found out they'd been in town and decided to start looking for them. He watered the horses, then drove them inside the barn. He didn't unhitch the team, but he did get two feedbags, filled them with oats, and tied them over the horses' heads.

"Beth Ann, I have a few more things I have to do before we leave, and I have some things I want you to do."

"We have all our supplies. Why didn't we just leave from town? I don't understand why we came all the way back to the farm."

"You forgot that we still have the cow and the rest of the chickens to take with us. I still have some things I have to do here before we leave. You'll need to milk the cow while I'm gone, or she'll be bawling her head off. And change into those clothes we bought. I plan to travel all night to get as far away from here as fast as we can.

"I don't want to dress like a boy," she complained. "I don't know why you bought those clothes for me, and the shoes are so ugly. And why are you running off and leaving me?"

"Beth Ann, please do like I say," Jacob barked. "We're going to be traveling on some very lonely trails, it will be safer for you if people think you're my brother."

Jacob's Promise

Beth Ann knew her brother was probably right, but her emotions were so overwrought she couldn't help but argue. She had been nine years old when they left Virginia, and she remembered how long the trip had been. She was fearful of what the two of them might run into on the long trip east. The thought of leaving the farm filled her with sadness.

Out of Beth Ann's sight, Jacob unwrapped an oilskin from one of the blankets and spread it on the ground. He went to the storage room and got the double-barrel shotgun stored there. His father had said he didn't want to have to run to the cabin to get it every time he needed to shoot some varmint, so he kept the gun handy in the barn. Jacob loaded the gun and then rolled it up in the oilskin.

It was still drizzling rain, and he didn't want the powder in the shotgun to get wet. He had a plan that he hadn't mentioned to Beth Ann. He put on a raincoat, tucked the shotgun under his arm and picked up a shovel. Before going out the barn door he shouted back at Beth Ann.

"After you milk the cow and change clothes, try to get some sleep. Once we get started, that rough riding wagon will make sleep impossible."

He closed the barn door before she could answer and started trotting off toward Riley's Ford. The ford was about a mile away through the woods that bordered the Hesser and Cooper property. There was a deer path he could follow most of the way, and he was glad because he was still barefoot. He didn't want to get his new shoes wet and muddy.

Just before he reached the ford, he stopped to make sure no one was crossing it or on the trail. Satisfied no one was around he leapt up to the ford to inspect the ground, looking for recent horse tracks. He saw muddy tracks headed toward town, but none returning. This was the ford the Coopers used when they went to town, and this is the way they would come back.

He moved back to a small clearing in the woods behind a dense growth of blackberry bushes. He laid the shotgun wrapped in oilskin on the ground. and picked up the shovel. He moved farther back in the woods, pulled off his rain coat, and started digging a hole.

He dug like a man possessed, swearing oaths of vengeance with each shovelful of dirt. Tonight, he was going to even the score. He was going to shoot as many Cooper brothers as he could.

He dug a six-foot by six-foot shallow hole in the soggy ground, where he planned to hide the bodies. He knew it wasn't very deep, but he didn't care if animals got to them. All he wanted was to hide them long enough for him and Beth Ann to be well away before they were found. If he was lucky, they'd never be found. Let old man Cooper know what it was like to lose someone close.

He finished digging and was sitting on the edge of the hole when he heard horses. He ran back to the clearing and kicked himself for not having the shotgun unwrapped. In a panic he unrolled it and stuck two percussion caps in place and rushed, quietly as he could, to the ford. He didn't know how he was going to reload and shoot all four brothers, but he was going to try. For Beth Ann's sake, he hoped he could do it without getting killed.

By the time he got to the ford the riders had already crossed and were well down the trail. It was too dark to see them, but he only counted the tracks of two horses.

That meant he hadn't missed all of them. In some ways that was a relief, now he would only have to deal with two. Just enough brothers for the two barrels of his shotgun.

His sweat-soaked shirt suddenly chilled him, and he began to shiver. He returned to the hole he was digging and put on his raincoat. He found a fallen tree behind some bushes next to the trail and sat down to wait. He didn't intend to be caught by surprise again.

He had almost nodded off to sleep when he heard laughter. He jerked to his feet when he heard horses splashing through the ford. He moved toward the creek and waited until both horses came out on to near bank of the creek.

With the shotgun trembling in his hands he stepped out onto the trail. In a squeaky voice, he yelled, "You killed my mom and dad and you're going to pay."

Eddie saw how frightened Jacob was and yelled down at him, "Put the gun away, Hesser, or I'll sprinkle some coal oil on your tail and send you off to meet your folks."

The mention of his dead parents sent a bolt of anger through Jacob and his trigger finger jerked back as if by its own accord. Pellets from the shotgun ripped through Eddie's face and out the back of his head. His horse jumped away from the flame and noise of the blast throwing Eddie out of the saddle.

Sam Cooper let out a low growl as he turned his horse and started frantically digging in his saddlebag. Jacob saw him reach for his saddlebag and immediately pulled the trigger firing a wild second shot. Sam fell off his horse, moaning on the ground, with a hole blown in his side just under his left arm. At only ten feet the powerful blast from the near miss had left a big hole with their grouped pellets.

Sam lay in the mud dead, still gripping the reins of his horse, his dead hate-filled eyes staring up at Jacob. Jacob dropped the shotgun and fell to his knees, heaving up his last meal.

After some time, he struggled to his feet, staggered over to Sam, and pulled the reins out of his dead hand. He tied the reins to a bush and then turned to make cooing sounds in an effort to calm the other horse. The horse finally relaxed at Jacob's soft sounds and let him approach. When he had the reins firmly in his hand, he removed the coil of rope tied to the horse's saddle and led the horse over to Eddie.

He looped one end of the rope around Eddie's feet and tied the other end to the saddle horn. He stopped and took a trembling breath. He was thankful he found the rope and didn't have to drag the bodies to the hole by himself. The horses made the job a whole lot easier.

He mounted the horse and dragged Eddie down to the ford and then turned up the creek. He didn't want to leave any drag marks leading into the woods. He waded the horse up the middle of the creek for about forty feet before turning into the woods.

He pulled Eddie up beside the hole, untied the rope and returned for Sam. Sam lay with his dead eyes open, staring at the night sky. The staring eyes upset Jacob so much he had to turn away. He looked up at the sky and started counting stars, trying to clear Sam's dead face from his mind.

The rain had stopped, and the first quarter of the new moon was beginning to shine through the thinning clouds. He had hoped the rain would last a little longer so all the tracks would be washed away.

He took a deep breath and approached Sam. Without looking at his face he tied Sam's feet together with the rope, then drug him along the same route he had taken Eddie.

With his face turned away and a guilty lump in his throat, Jacob went through the pockets of both brothers. He found three dollars in Sam's shirt pocket. There was no use burying good money, it wasn't going to do the brothers any good where they were going.

He leveraged both bodies into the hole with the shovel and scooped wet dirt over them. It was a relief to see them disappear under the muddy soil.

Finished, he sprinkled wet leaves over the raw earth and then pulled logs and tree branches over the leaves. He stood by the graves, satisfied that he had done as much as he could to hide them. He thought the graves were far enough off the beaten track that no one was likely to discover them.

He was still shaking as he rolled the shotgun in the oilskin and tied it and the shovel to the saddle of Sam's horse. Leading Sam's horse he mounted the other one. He guessed that after what he had just done, he would never be able to return to this part of Illinois. The thought of never seeing his parents' grave or the farm again filled him with sadness, but he also felt a certain amount of satisfaction in avenging his parents' murder.

CHAPTER 8

Beth Ann was awakened by the sound of galloping horses. The hoof beats stopped at the barn, and the doors were flung open. She burrowed deeper into the straw, fearing the Coopers had returned.

"Beth Ann, where are you?" Jacob called.

"Jacob, you scared me to death. Where have you been?"

"There's no time to explain now," Jacob said. "Just go get the cow while I back the wagon out of the barn.

Outside he took the saddle off Sam's horse and tied the horse to one side of the wagon. He took the cow from Beth Ann and tied it to the back of the wagon. "I wish we didn't have to take that dang cow," he said. "I know she'll slow us down, but we can't leave her here to starve."

"Why are you in such a rush?" Beth Ann asked. "You left me here all evening doing nothing, now you're suddenly in a big hurry."

"Beth Ann, we need to get out of here as fast as we can. I'll tell you all about it after we're on the road. I want at least eight or ten miles behind us before the sun comes up. Please don't argue, just get on the wagon."

"Alright bossy, I'm coming." She climbed onto the wagon and waited for Jacob to get on with her. Instead of getting on the wagon he climbed onto one of the horses. "Why are you getting on that horse and where did it come from?" she asked.

Jacob answered, "I'm going to ride and you're going to have to drive the team."

"I've never driven a team all by myself. Dad let me drive sometimes, but he was always right here beside me if I needed help. I'm scared, Jacob."

"I'll be riding right beside you to tell you what to do. If you get into trouble, I'll jump on the wagon and help you out."

Beth Ann picked up the reins, slapped them on the horse's rumps, and started the wagon down the lane away from the farm.

"Turn left when you get to the end of the lane," Jacob shouted.

"Left? I thought we had to go through town," Beth Ann corrected him.

"We aren't going back to Virginia. I just spread that rumor while we were in town so the Coopers would be sent off in the wrong direction if they started looking for us."

"You lied to me."

"I'm sorry, Beth Ann. I was afraid if I told you, you might let it slip while we were in town. I know how guilty you look when you tell a fib."

"Don't you ever lie to me again, Jacob Hesser. Remember, we're in this together, and you're going to have to trust me."

"Here's the truth," Jacob confessed. "We're heading for St. Louis to try to catch Aunt Ruth and Uncle Ralph. I know they'll let us go with them to Oregon. St. Louis is a lot closer than Virginia anyway."

The rain clouds that made Jacob so uncomfortable in his wait by the ford began to move off to the east. The first quarter of the moon slowly peaked out from behind the clouds and a few stars made an appearance. Jacob let out a sigh of relief. They were finally on their way and he took the clearing April sky as a good omen for what lay ahead.

The two youngest Cooper brothers got up Saturday morning and noticed Sam and Eddie's beds had not been slept in. "Do ya suppose Sam and Eddie stayed out at the Hay's place last night?" Willie asked as he pulled on his shirt.

"I don't know, but if they don't show up in time for chores, Pa is going to skin 'em alive." Simon rolled out of bed and sat rubbing his eyes. "Ya know, I think maybe we should've told Pa about the Hessers last night instead of waiting for Sam to do it."

"I didn't have the nerve to tell him last night, neither did you. He was mad enough about Sam not comin' home, besides, Sam's the one who always wants to be the big shot," Willie added pulling on his pants.

Simon stood up stretching the sleep kinks out of his body. "Well, we're stuck with the job now. We can't wait for Sam."

"Come on let's get up to the house and get some food in our bellies," Willie stood by the door.

Simon pulled on his boots and followed Willie out of the bunkhouse their father had relegated the boys to live in and walked over to the main cabin. The smell of frying ham and baking biscuits seeping through the door hurried their steps. Tom Cooper was sitting at the table and looked up as they entered,

"I didn't hear any horses come in late last night. When did your brothers get home?"

"They didn't come home," Willie answered. "We don't know where they spent the night, but it wasn't here."

"They said they'd come home after they escorted the girls out to the Hay's place, at least that's what Sam said," Simon added, sliding onto the bench at the table beside Willie.

"Damn that boy. Lollygagging around after some girl when he has chores to do here. Taking Eddie with him makes it that much worse. I'm going to rip the back sides of both of them when they get home," Tom roared.

"There's somethin' else you need to know." Willie bowed his head so he didn't have to look his father in the eye. "While we were in town, we heard the Hesser kids had been there just ahead of us. They were buyin' supplies. Said they was headin' back to Virginia."

"What?" Tom snapped. "I thought you said no one got out of that cabin alive."

"Pa, that fire looked like hell on earth," Simon whined. "I don't see how anyone could have got out."

"Well they did, didn't they?" Tom grumbled. "Damn! I give you a simple job to do and you can't do it right. Monday we'll go to town and talk to the judge."

A smile spread across Tom Cooper's face. "We'll have him

sign legal papers showing we bought the place last week. Eat and then get out there and get the milking done. You have double the chores to do until your brothers decide to straggle in here."

Tom Cooper sat brooding after the boys left to do their chores. How much did the Hesser kids tell folks in town about how the fire started? If they were in Virginia, how much trouble could they cause him? Damn! Why couldn't they have burned like they were supposed to? He hoped his no-good brother-in–law could give him some answers on Monday.

By the time the sun peeked up over the eastern horizon Beth Ann had fallen asleep and sat slouched sideways on the wagon seat. The reins had fallen from her hands and were about to fall on the ground behind the horses. Seeing her about to fall, Jacob called out, "Whoa!" stopping the tired team in its tracks.

Beth Ann's eyes popped open, and she gasped, "What happened?"

"We'd better stop before you fall off the wagon and crack your head open. We need to eat some breakfast and rest the horses. Pull the wagon over in that grove of trees. I don't want us to be seen by anyone who could carry news back to the Coopers about the direction we're headed."

Jacob climbed down from the horse and found he could hardly walk. The inside of his thighs burned from rubbing on the saddle. He knew how to ride, but it had been a long time since he had spent so many hours on a horse. He staked the horses and cow out in a grassy spot to let them graze.

"Beth Ann, why don't you try the cow and see if she has any milk while I round up some wood and start a fire."

An hour later the fire had burned down, and the meager meal prepared They sat on a log in front of the glowing coals and began eating fried bacon and eggs and drinking warm milk.

"What should I do with the left-over milk?" Beth Ann asked. "We really don't have any way to carry it."

"Dump it out. It'll just spoil if we try to keep it. We can always get more as long as we have the cow."

"I fed some corn to the chickens, but I'm not sure they'll be laying many eggs the way the wagon bounces them around," Beth Ann said.

Jacob's Promise

"There's something I need to tell you." Jacob avoided her eyes. Scenes of the shooting flashed through his head and his hands began to tremble. Finally, he looked up and blurted out, "I shot Sam and Eddie Cooper last night down by Riley's Ford. That's where I got the extra horses."

Beth Ann stared at him in disbelief, "You shot them? Where were Willie and Simon?"

"I only saw Sam and Eddie. When I confronted them, Eddie said some nasty things about coal oil and then started laughing. I shot him before I realized I'd pulled the trigger. Sam reached for a gun he had in his saddlebag, so I shot him too."

The words flooded out until his emotions got the better of him and he had to stop and clear his throat. "I don't feel good about killing them, but when Eddie said with a little coal oil I could burn too and laughed, I went blind mad. Talking about it still makes me a little shaky."

Telling Beth Ann lifted a weight off Jacob's shoulders and his trembling stopped.

Beth Ann sat quietly She couldn't imagine her gentle brother killing anyone, not even the Coopers. "So that's why you were in such a hurry to get away before daylight."

Jacob didn't think she needed a reply and changed the subject. "I don't think we should use our real names until we're past Vandalia. We can stop using Hesser and start using mama's maiden name, Klaus"

"If I am going to be a Klaus, I 'll just take Mother's first name too, I'll be Katherine Klaus until Vandalia."

"I'm afraid you can't do that. Remember you're supposed to be a boy, so you have to pick a boy's name," Jacob said. "You need to start tucking your hair up under your hat, too."

"I don't like dressing like a boy. But if I must, I guess you can start calling me Jimmy. I kind of like the sound of that."

Jacob couldn't believe at how quickly Beth Ann had accepted their situation. She was only fifteen going on sixteen, but her sudden understanding of the danger they were in surprised him.

"We'd better try to take a little nap if we can," he said. "The horses need to rest, and we don't know how much farther they can go before we have to stop for the night. These muddy roads have made the going tough on them."

Bill Heyduck

At first Jacob was too worked up to sleep. He sat with his back against a tree watching the road, half expecting to see the Coopers come charging down it. But weariness and the warm spring sun soon had him nodding off. He woke with a start and found the sun high in the sky. He shook Beth Ann awake and went to get the horses.

He tried to hitch the Coopers' horses to the wagon so their team could rest, but the horses bucked and shied away from the wagon so violently he gave up. Angry, he tied the horses to the side of the wagon while muttering under his breath that the damn Cooper horses were as dumb and worthless as the rest of the Cooper clan.

By the time he had the old team hitched Beth Ann had the cooking utensils loaded and was sitting on the wagon ready to leave. He stiffly pulled himself into the saddle and headed west. He hoped they could put another five miles behind them before they stopped for the night.

CHAPTER 9

Tom Cooper was an unhappy man and unloaded his unhappiness on Willie and Simon. He'd fumed all weekend. It was Monday, and Sam and Eddie still hadn't come home. At mid-morning he decided to go to town.

He had the boys hitch the horse to a buggy and saddle their own horses. Just before they left, he told the boys, "When we get to town, I want you two to take the road east out of town and check with all the farms along the way.

"Stop anyone you meet on the road and ask if they've seen the Hessers or if they've seen Sam and Eddie. Sam may have heard about the Hessers and decided to follow the road east to see if he could catch up with them. Don't come home until you know one way or the other. Your mother is going to ride with me in the buggy. You boys can go on ahead."

Willie and Simon crossed Riley's Ford without taking notice of the tracks on the creek bank. The rain had washed away some of the evidence of the struggle that had taken place two days ago.

In town Tom stopped in front of the general store and jumped down from the wagon. He left his wife to struggle down without offering any help.

"I'll meet you at the café in about an hour. I have some business with the judge over a legal matter I had him look into," he said. He kept his wife ignorant of all his business dealings.

The judge was busy going over some papers with his bailiff when he heard someone enter the room. He was surprised when he looked up and saw Tom. "Hello, Tom. It's unusual to see you in town on a weekday. What drug you in here?"

"It's that legal problem we talked about a few weeks ago."

The judge nodded his understanding and said to his bailiff, "Frank, take these papers over to the sheriff, and then go by the general store and see if any mail came in on those freight wagons that passed through yesterday."

When the bailiff had gone, Tom leaned forward and put both hands on the judge's desk. "I'm here to tie up that Hesser business we talked about. I understand the Hesser youngsters have headed back east and that ought to make everything move along a lot faster."

"Tom, you have a real problem there. Before the Hesser kids left town, they made Sam Clark the administrator of the farm. He came by last Friday to register the papers at the courthouse."

"Why didn't you stop it. You're the judge," Tom roared.

"Tom, I can only do so much," the judge said. "It's bad enough that Hans and Katherine have suddenly died in a fire and the kids seem to be running for their lives.

"But to ask me to destroy court documents that a lawyer has filed is going too far. It's your problem, and if you want that farm, you're going to have to deal with their lawyer. I refuse to get involved in this or anything to do with the fire out at the Hessers."

"Keep your voice down," Tom said in a whisper. "Who said I did anything out at the Hessers? You can't blame me for an accidental fire that started in that cabin."

"Don't fool with me, Tom, and don't say anything else. I don't want to know anything. If you want that farm, go talk to their lawyer."

Tom stomped out of the office in a huff, slamming the door in frustration as he left. He stalked down the street to Sam Clark's office.

Sam had his nose buried in a stack of papers and didn't look up until Tom had pulled a chair up to his desk and sat down. "I understand you're handling the sale of the Hesser farm," Tom said.

"Yes, I've been contracted to take care of that. Are you interested? I better warn you, they left instructions that if you came in to buy it, the price was to be $3.00 an acre."

"$3.00 an acre," Tom yelled. "That land isn't worth more than $1.25 an acre,"

"I didn't set the price; I'm just following my clients' instructions. There's eighty acres. Are you still interested?"

"I'm going to have to chew on that for a while," Tom said as he got up and stomped out of the office.

Tom's business in town had lasted less than twenty minutes. He joined his wife in the general store and helped her load the things she'd purchased into the buggy. Then they stopped to eat in the café before they headed for home.

In the café he asked some of the shopkeepers at nearby tables if any of them had seen his sons on Saturday or Sunday. One merchant said he thought he saw them late Friday evening headed in the direction of home, but it was getting dark and he couldn't swear it was them.

Back on the farm Tom unloaded the buggy, unhitched the horse and stood thinking. If the boys were headed home late Friday, why hadn't they shown up? With Willie and Simon gone, Tom was forced to milk the cows and feed the horses. He couldn't relax after milking and paced back and forth across the porch.

He stayed outside waiting for the boys until his wife called him to supper. After his wife went to bed, he sat on the front porch, smoking his pipe in the darkness. A few minutes before ten o'clock, he heard horses coming up the lane.

The boys saw the glow of his pipe in the dark and rode up to the porch to report what they had found.

"We must have talked to every person living within three miles of town," Willie complained. "And no one had seen hide nor hair of Sam and Eddie. Mrs. Franklin, out about two miles east of town said she saw a wagon go by Friday afternoon with two people on it, but she couldn't make out how old they were. We went all the way out to that fork in the road before we stopped."

"Sam and Eddie couldn't just disappear into the thin air," Tom growled. "Something bad has happened. I just feel it in my bones."

Jacob and Beth Ann had gone only a mile down the road after their rest before they ran into their first real obstacle of the trip. A stream too big to be a creek and too small to be a river, filled with swift moving water confronted them. Jacob saw wagon ruts running down the bank and up the other side so he knew it was a ford but couldn't tell when the last time a wagon had crossed.

If a wagon crossed before the last rain, the water would probably be deeper now. He was worried about the wagon getting carried downstream. He stopped Beth Ann on the bank and slowly waded his horse into the stream and started across.

It was deepest near the side where he entered and got shallower as he neared the other bank. He rode back for the other horse and led it across. He came back again for the cow, but she balked at the water's edge.

She planted her hooves on the sloping bank and refused to move. Jacob wrapped the rope around the saddle horn and started pulling. The cow's neck stretched out until it looked as if her head might come off.

The cow's angry bellows were more than Beth Ann could stand. "Stop, Jacob! You're going to choke the cow to death."

"That stupid cow has a choice. She can choke herself to death or she can go into the water," Jacob shouted. "We have to cross, and if that cow is going with us, she has to cross too." Jacob kicked the horse in the side. The sudden move caused the cow's rear hooves to slip out from under her and she tumbled into the water with a splash. When she hit the water, she acted like a bolt of lightning had hit her. She jumped up and in frenzied leaps headed for the far shore. Laughing, Jacob tied the trembling cow next to the horse and crossed the stream again.

"You're going to have to drive the wagon across, Beth Ann."

"I don't want to. I'm afraid I'll do something wrong and drown."

"Come on, the water isn't that deep. I'll tie a rope to the side of the wagon and hold it, so it isn't swept downstream."

Jacob's horse had trouble getting a firm footing on the muddy bottom of the stream and when the current hit the side of the wagon, his horse almost fell. The straining team took up the slack just in time for Jacob's horse to regain solid footing.

Jacob rode out of the water, coiling the slack rope as he came. The wagon, water pouring from every seam, lumbered onto the safety of the far shore and stopped. "We'll let the team take a breather before we move on," he called to Beth Ann.

Jacob's Promise

While the team rested the sun did its work and dried some of the muddy road. The horses didn't have to work as hard, but the dry ruts caused Beth Ann to have a bumpier ride.

In the late afternoon the horses started to lag, and Jacob knew they had to stop. He saw a grassy spot up ahead on the right side of the road and guided Beth Ann over to it. The lush grass was just what the tired team needed, and there was a small brook running at the edge of the woods bordering the open space.

They were halfway across the open space before Jacob saw another wagon at the edge of the woods. A tall, lanky man and a short stocky woman were standing by the wagon waving to them. Behind the wagon were four ragged children standing around a cooking fire.

"Hello there," the man called out.

Jacob groaned. He didn't want company and if he had seen them sooner, he wouldn't have stopped. But it was too late to ignore them now. He waved and pulled up beside their wagon.

"There's plenty of space and grass, why don't ya join us? We ain't seen any other travelers on this road for three days. Where you headin?" the man asked.

"We're headed for Vandalia," Jacob answered. "You headed west?"

"No, we're headed fer Springfield. We hope to get there afore the week's out, that's if this blessed rain don't flood all the creeks and slow us down."

Beth Ann pulled the wagon past the other one and stopped. She climbed down and had trouble getting her stiff legs to move.

"I see ya got a cow," the man said. "Ours died two weeks ago and the kids have been complaining about not having any milk ever since. I'll make a deal with ya. Ya share yer milk with the kids, and Mom'll use some to make milk gravy to go with the biscuits she's bakin in the camp oven. You can eat with us."

"Sounds good to me," Beth Ann said before Jacob could stop her. "We have some blackberry jam that will go with those biscuits, and maybe an egg or two if the hens have laid."

"Ma name's Elmer Tucker and that's ma wife Sally," the man said extending his hand to Jacob. "Could I offer ya a little advice? I see your wagon forded a deep one. Ya better check the grease on those axles or it could mean a peck of trouble down the road.

"Thank you, Mr. Tucker," Jacob said, and before Beth Ann could speak, added, "My name's Jacob Klaus and this is my brother Jimmy."

Jacob felt a little more relaxed when he found out the Tuckers were headed north and away from the Coopers. He had almost forgotten how nice it could be to be around good folk. Just like his family.

When the meal was finished, Beth Ann joined Sally in cleaning up, and drying the dishes for her. When they were finished Sally looked Beth Ann up and down and said, "You're no boy, young lady. Why are you trying to fool us? No boy would offer to help with the dishes and besides you don't move like a boy."

Beth Ann hung her head in shame, "I didn't mean any harm, mam, my brother made me dress this way. He thinks it's safer while we are traveling if people think I'm a boy. I'm sorry."

"Don't be sorry, girl. I think your brother is a smart boy," Sally said.

"I wonder how smart we are to be running out on the prairie in the wild hope that we can find our aunt in all this empty space," Beth Ann muttered under her breath.

CHAPTER 10

Elmer and Sally were still packing up their wagon when Jacob and Beth Ann pulled back onto the road to Vandalia. The road had dried out, and the wheels of the wagon bounced along in bone-jarring jolts over the ruts.

They were able to travel a little faster, but Beth Ann suffered every jolt up through her spine from the hard-wooden seat. Jacob was thankful they hadn't met any travelers. They'd passed a few isolated farms, but he refused to stop at any of them. He was still afraid the Coopers might come this far looking for them. He didn't think he would begin to relax until they were past Vandalia.

After the long hours of travel without seeing people, the wide-open, flat prairie became mind numbing. Jacob found himself occasionally nodding off as he rode along, but always managed to catch himself before he fell out of the saddle.

He noticed that it was affecting Beth Ann the same way. The first day on the road they were both rather talkative, but as the trip wore on, they became silent, lost in their own thoughts.

Clouds began to build and turn black in the southwestern sky as the day wore on. Jacob saw rain approaching off near the horizon and noticed how the black clouds were tumbling and rolling suggesting a strong wind. Distant lightening flashed and seconds later, the rumble of thunder rolled across the prairie.

The thunder convinced Jacob it was time to pull off the road to find shelter. He guided Beth Ann behind a low hill topped by a line of trees. If there was a strong wind with the rain, the hill and trees would help shield them.

He turned the horses to face away from the wind and told Beth Ann to break out the raincoats. They had just crawled under the wagon as the rain hit. The clouds opened and great sheets of cold rain made a deafening rattle on the wagon. The swirling, wind driven rain had them both soaked in a matter of minutes.

The pounding rain suddenly slowed to a light drizzle and then stopped altogether. The clouds began to break up and the sun was soon shining as brightly as it had been before. The ruts in the road were now filled with water and large ponds had formed in the low places in the fields around them.

The sun may have returned, but it would take hours for the road to dry. Once again, they had to face the slow muddy progress, as well as a wagon full of wet belongings.

On the afternoon of the fifth day, they came over a small rise in the road and saw a line of eight wagons stopped facing a lake. Jacob wondered why a road would lead straight to a lake. The road they'd been traveling had joined this road about five miles back so this had to be the road to Vandalia.

Beth Ann stopped behind the last wagon in line. Jacob dismounted, tied his horse to the wagon, and walked up to a group of men sitting by a small fire.

"Is this the road to Vandalia?" he asked.

"More like the lake shore of Vandalia," laughed one of the men.

"What you see, son, is the Kaskaskia River pushing out of its banks.

"How do we get across to Vandalia," Jacob asked.

"You don't, unless you're a fish," The first man chuckled. "You sit here and wait until the water goes down enough that you can get to the ferry. If it doesn't rain anymore, it'll be low enough to cross in two or three days."

"There isn't enough grass here for animals to feed. You better do what I'm going to do and go back half-a-mile or so and find a grassy spot to camp and wait it out."

"Thanks," Jacob said. "But I think I'll find a place to camp where we can keep an eye on the water level." Jacob wasn't about to move back half-a-mile.

He found a low hill with enough grass for the stock and made camp. Standing on the wagon he could watch the line of wagons and the river. He wanted to be able to move the minute he saw wagons loading on the ferry. He couldn't do that if he was half-a-mile away.

Each day Jacob rode down to the water's edge to check on how much the water had receded. On the morning of the third day he saw the wagons begin inching forward. He hurriedly hitched up the team. "Beth Ann you ride the horse, I'll drive the wagon," he yelled. He slapped the reins on the horse's back and raced down to get a place in the line of wagons.

It was late in the afternoon before it was their turn to board the ferry raft. The ferryman told Jacob the fare was $2 and got mad when Jacob tried to dicker with him about the price. "It's either pay the $2 or get out of line and let the next wagon on. I want to make four more trips before it gets too dark and you're holding me up.

Jacob reluctantly paid the $2 and guided Beth Ann as she drove the wagon up the ramp onto the ferry. As usual, the cow became balky and wouldn't go up the ramp. The ferryman threatened to leave in two minutes whether the cow was on or not.

Jacob pulled off his coat and wrapped it around the cow's head. Once blinded, the cow allowed herself to be led aboard. As the ferry rolled and swayed in the current of the river, Beth Ann clutched the wagon seat in a death grip, terrified that they were all going to be dumped into the water. She didn't let go until Jacob led the team down the ramp and onto solid ground.

After they landed, Jacob led the extra horse off the dock and up the main street of Vandalia. Beth Ann stayed close behind him on the wagon. The shouts of drivers and the creaking of wagons wheels filled the humid air of the narrow street. Beth Ann kept her eyes glued to Jacob's back trying to block out the noise and ignore the wagons crowded around her.

Jacob's eyes scanned every side street they passed, searching for a livery stable where he could board the horses and cow. At the third intersection they came to he saw a livery sign and turnoff the main street. He stopped in front of the stable and called to a man standing by the barn door, "Got room for our animals?"

"Plenty of room," he answered. "And a place to park the wagon too."

Jacob unhitched the team and took the saddle off the riding horse before leading the horses into the barn. The liveryman had them park their wagon by the corral and put the cow in a pen behind the barn.

"I'd like to sell the two riding horses and the cow," Jacob said. "If you know of any buyers, I'd appreciate you telling me. I have a couple of saddles I can sell, too. Try to get the best price you can."

"I'll be glad to see what I can do, but there'll be a fee if I sell them," the stable man said.

"I understand. Anything you can do will be appreciated. Is there a rooming house near here?" Jacob asked. "We plan to be here over night and need a place to stay."

"It isn't any of my business, but how far are you planning to travel in that rig of yours?" the stableman asked.

"We plan to take it to St. Louis. Why?"

"Most people have a cover on their wagon so they can sleep dry. You're gonna have a soggy trip ahead of you between here and St. Louis. April can be a mighty wet month. I got a man does that work if you are interested," the stableman said.

Jacob looked at Beth Ann, who was shaking her head up and down vigorously, before saying, "I guess we could stand a little more comfort. How much money are we talking about?" Jacob asked.

"Cheapest we can do for this rig would be about ten dollars."

Jacob blanched at the expense, but the frown creasing Beth Ann's face convinced him to take the offer.

"I'll get the man right on it," the stableman said. "To get to the rooming house, just turn to your left when you leave here, and you'll find it at the end of the street."

Beth Ann stood silently while the two men talked, but as soon as she and Jacob reached the street she said, "I'm hungry and I intend to stop at the first place we pass that offers food. We can find a room once our bellies are full.

Jacob laughed at his sister's sudden demand. She had been so quiet and undemanding the whole trip that he was a little surprised at how forceful she sounded.

"Yes, ma'am, whatever you say." Jacob realized that this was the first time he had laughed since they had started on their journey. He guessed it was the relief he felt when they put the Kaskaskia River between them and the Coopers.

They found a rooming house that served meals and for fifty cents and even had facilities for a hot bath. There was a laundry down the street where Jacob took their muddy, smoke-contaminated clothes to have them washed. He was reluctant to spend the money, but he felt he wasn't spending it foolishly.

They spent two nights in Vandalia waiting for the wagon repairs to be finished. The nights in the soft hotel beds helped them recover from the nights they spent sleeping on the hard ground. Free during the day they wandered around the town, taking in the sights, smells and sounds of Vandalia. Both aware they were living a rather spoiled existence that would end once they started out on the trail again.

On the morning of the third day, they went to the stable to get their revamped wagon. The liveryman had sold the horses and saddles, but no one was in a market for a cow.

Jacob received the money for the horses, less the stable boarding fee, and paid the carpenter for the wagon repairs.

"Have either of you heard anything about the condition of the road between here and St. Louis?" Jacob asked.

"Travel this time of year is tricky," the liverymen said, "It depends on how much rain we get and how high the streams. There's a stage comes here out of St. Louis once a week and it's already two days overdue. You just never know what you might hit. There are a lot of creeks and streams between here and St. Louis."

"We'll manage," Jacob said. He turned and started to help Beth Ann up the seat on the wagon but caught himself. He had to remember Beth Ann was supposed to be a boy and a boy wouldn't need any help, even from an older brother.

CHAPTER 11

Jacob and Beth Ann left Vandalia that afternoon. Jacob was anxious to get moving again and didn't want to spend any more money staying in the boarding house. By leaving in the afternoon, they could get five or six miles of driving in before it got dark.

Jacob said it was a jump-start on all the wagons that would be leaving the next morning and they wouldn't have to fight the muddy ruts those wagons would churn up. Wagons pulled by oxen were slow and Jacob didn't want to get stuck behind one of them.

He finally stopped worrying about the Coopers once they'd left Vandalia, but a new worry replaced it. Would they get to St. Louis in time to catch their aunt and uncle before they left for Independence? If they missed them, Jacob didn't know what they were going to do.

They had enough money from the sale of the horses to buy supplies and outfit the wagon in Vandalia, but he wasn't sure they had enough for supplies to get all the way to Independence. In the last week and a half, they had spent more money than either of them had ever seen in their lives.

It frightened him when he realized how much it would take to finish the trip if they didn't catch their aunt and uncle. Jacob tried to keep his worries about money from Beth Ann, but she was aware of their situation.

Carrying all the cash from the sale of the horses was another worry and Jacob was constantly feeling in his pocket to make sure it was still there. After supper, the first night out of Vandalia, Jacob asked Beth Ann if she could sew something for him.

"Have you torn something, too," she asked.

"No, I want you to sew some money in a pouch that can be tied around the waist under our clothes," Jacob said. "I want you to make two of them, one for you and one for me. That way with the money divided we'll never lose all of it."

Beth Ann was thrilled that Jacob was ready to trust her to take responsibility for half the money. She quickly rummaged around in her sewing basket and pulled out some scrap material. "I think I have some material that'll work."

Was Beth Ann suddenly more mature or had he just failed to notice? Now as he looked at her, he saw a handsome young woman. Her auburn hair framed an oval face with full lips, a straight nose, and sparkling blue eyes.

His mother often said Beth Ann was going to be a beautiful woman, but Jacob had paid little attention to his mother's words. He guessed most brothers never thought of their sister as good looking. They were just sisters.

"You've really changed since we left home," Jacob said a big smile on his face. "Back on the farm I would have never thought of making you responsible for handling money. I guess I didn't really know my own sister. Besides, don't you know what day this is? Happy birthday Miss sixteen-year-old."

"Oh, my goodness, it is my birthday. With all we've been through this last week and a half, I don't even know what day of the week it is any more," she said.

"I saw a calendar while we were in Vandalia that reminded me or I would have missed it, too. To celebrate I bought you a present." He handed her a little brown sack, twisted together at the top and tied with a red ribbon.

Beth Ann untied the bow, looked inside and then put the sack up to her nose, "Horehound candy, my favorite candy in the whole world, and a red ribbon to wear in my hair."

"Whoa. No ribbons. Don't forget you're supposed to be a boy. Try to remember you can't offer to help with dishes or any other woman thing. I was thinking it would be a good idea if you cut your hair until it was a least as short as mine. You wouldn't have to worry about it falling out from under your hat if you did that," Jacob suggested.

"No, I'll not cut my hair," she exclaimed. "You can give some orders, but that one you can just forget. My hair is just fine stuffed under my hat. You've made such a big thing about me acting like a woman, but I only forgot once."

"What if your hat blows off or gets knocked off while you're working?"

"The answer is still no, so don't ruin my birthday by saying any more about it. I've heard all the suggestions and criticisms I need for the day. Stop suggesting and go tend the horses while I make us some money belts."

The next morning Jacob divided the money and handed one of the money belts to Beth Ann. "Tie this under your shirt and make sure you keep it out of sight."

"I'm not a baby, Jacob. You don't have to keep telling me how to do everything," Beth Ann said as she tied on the belt and pulled her shirt tail over it.

The road was dry, but rough, easier on the horses than it was on the two riding the hard bench of the wagon. The roads could flood one day and be passable the next, changing with the April weather.

The road to St. Louis became a busy one. Wagons seemed to come from every side road they passed. At one side road Beth Ann watched a big covered wagon pulled by four oxen turn in ahead of them.

"I'll bet that wagon's headed for Oregon," she said.

"You say that about every wagon you see," Jacob laughed.

"Looking at the wagons and guessing where they're headed is better than just staring at the back of the horse's rumps all day."

Near the middle of the afternoon a muffled quiet settled over the countryside. The crunch of the iron rims of the wagon wheels bumping over the ruts and the horses' hooves striking the ground were the only sounds. The birds had stopped singing, and the wind that usually blew across the prairie was not even whispering. The sky took on an unnatural yellow-green glow that made the grass and trees turn a funny color.

Jacob's head snapped up with a start from his half dream state. The unnatural quiet had suddenly made the hair on the back of his neck stand on end. Jacob stood up to search for what had disturbed him and saw angry black clouds boiling out of the southwest toward them.

One look at the churning mass was all Jacob needed before he began frantically looking for a gully, a creek bed, or anyplace to shield the wagon. The swiftness of those clouds rushing toward them made it evident violent winds were headed their way. Suddenly the day turned black and lightening slashed at the ground as the storm swept closer.

Up ahead on the side of the trail Jacob saw an eroded gully angling away from the road and turned the horses toward it. "Hang on this may be a rough ride," he yelled.

Beth Ann grabbed on to the rough wooden seat and held on for dear life. Jacob cracked the reins across the horse's rumps and recklessly drove the team down the gully and brought them to a skidding stop just before they crashed into trees blocking their way.

Beth Ann, shaken by their wild ride, stared at the fast-approaching black clouds. "Jacob, that storm is going to kill us," she screamed.

"Stop talking and break out the rain gear while I tie the horses to the trees," he yelled, "We're in for a big blow, and we don't have much time before it gets here!"

The roar of the wind grew so loud it made talking almost impossible. Trees and bushes along the top of the gully danced and twisted to the storm's whistling concert.

"Get under the wagon, Beth Ann," Jacob yelled. "It'll be safer there."

"I'm not getting under that wagon," she shouted, shaking with fear. "That ditch is going to fill with a foot of water. I'm staying up in the wagon." She crawled over the seat and curled up on the wooden floor of the wagon. She pulled a blanket over her head to try to block out the roar of the storm.

Jacob jumped in front of the wild-eyed horses and took a solid grip on their halters. In a sing-song voice he began talking softly to them, doing his best to calm them so they wouldn't bolt.

Lightening flashed with a snap and then cracked with a boom of thunder that sounded like a canon being fired. The horses reared and danced around, fighting to get free. Jacob was jerked around like a mad puppeteer was jerking his strings, but held tight.

A loud bellowing from the back of the wagon made him realize that he had forgotten about the cow. He watched helplessly as she bound away across the meadow, bucking like a wild bronco. A swirling finger of the black cloud reach down and followed her as she disappeared into the blinding rain.

Another twisting funnel churned across the meadow toward the road, tearing chunks of sod and uprooting every bush it touched. When the black edge of the spinning winds reached a grove of trees, not a hundred yards away, the trees were sucked out by their roots and flung about like seeds from a dandelion. The menacing finger of destruction bounced from one side of the trail to the other before changing course and heading straight for Jacob and Beth Ann.

Jacob knew they were doomed when he saw it coming. Saying a prayer, he locked his grip on the halters and waited to be ripped apart by the violent wind. He ducked his head and squeezed his eyes closed as the first stinging chunks of sod and mud pelted him.

The roar became so intense the wagon shook, but the wind suddenly died. In disbelief Jacob opened his eyes and looked up to see the black finger of terror sail back up into the cloud.

His arms dead from fatigue, he watched the terrible roaring monster pass over them and continued along its meandering path. It seemed as if the twister had torn a hole in the bottom of the clouds because water poured out of them in such great torrents.

Prying his aching fingers from his death grip on the horses, Jacob became aware that he was standing in two feet of water just as Beth Ann had predicted. With the horses now calmed he left them and went to the wagon to check on Beth Ann.

He didn't hear a sound coming from the wagon and feared Beth Ann had been hurt. The covering of the wagon was torn, but not destroyed. He found Beth Ann curled into a tight ball, her knuckles white from gripping the blanket tight over her head. Her world of terror ended when Jacob put his arms around her and told her it was all over.

It was still raining when Jacob backed the team out of the gully and approached the quagmire that had once been the road. After just one look he decide to save the horses and camp at the little mound of high ground a few yards off the road.

Jacob's Promise

He moved the wagon and was ready to climb down when he remembered the cow. He stood on the wagon seat and searched the prairie. About a hundred yards out he saw the cow's brown body covered with big splotches of mud and grass. He knew she must be dead. He jumped off the wagon and started digging through the kitchen supplies. When he found the knife, he was looking for he looked up into Beth Ann's pale face and said, "I guess we'll have steak with our mush tonight."

CHAPTER 12

Tom Cooper was beside himself. It had been four days and there was still no sign of Sam and Eddie. How could two grown boys and their horses disappear off the face of the earth without leaving some trace? Someone had to have seen something.

That night, as the family sat at the supper table, Tom told Willie and Simon he had a job for them. "I want you two boys to head out east of town tomorrow and see if you can find anyone who saw your brothers. At the same time, you can ask if anyone has seen the Hesser kids. They're somehow mixed up in all this or they wouldn't have slipped out of town the way they did."

"Jacob Hesser couldn't have stood up to Sam for a second. Sam woulda broken him in half," Willie said.

"Damn it, Willie, I know how tough Sam is. But that kid might have done something sneaky, maybe shot them in the back. That's why I want you to go east out at least twenty miles. Stop at every farm and talk to anyone coming from the east. If you come to a group of houses or a store, stop and ask at every one of them. Do you understand?"

"Yes, Pa," they answered together.

After breakfast the next morning, Willie and Simon tied bedrolls behind their saddles, filled their saddlebags with food their mother had prepared, and set off for town.

When they arrived in town, Willie said, "It's useless to ask about our brothers or the Hessers in town. Pa's already asked everyone here. No use us asken, let's just ride on through."

"I'm with you. I think this is all a wild goose chase anyway," Simon said. "There ain't that many cabins on any of these roads, and I know we'll get the same answers we got the last time we asked. I can only think of one other town within ten miles, and it only has a general store and a blacksmith."

They headed east out of town and at the fork in the road, Willie turned on to the left fork and turned back to Simon. "We'll meet back here tomorrow about noon," Willie called as he trotted away. He made sure he took the left fork because he knew Marie Hays, the girl Sam was sweet on, lived on this road. He didn't get much of a chance to talk to girls with Sam around, and he didn't want to miss an opportunity.

When Willie got to the Hays' house he found Marie sitting on the front porch making butter in an oak churn.

"What are you doing out in this neighborhood?" Marie asked when she saw Willie.

"Pa sent us out looking for our brothers and last we heard Sam was with you."

"Lord, Willie, that was almost a week ago, and Sam left here for home before it was dark."

"That's what I figured," Willie said climbing down from his horse. "He probably met some of his old buddies and is off fishing somewhere. He'll do anything to dodge work."

"I'll bet you're thirsty from your ride," she said. "If you'll take over this churn, I'll go to the cistern and pull up the can of cold buttermilk and get you a glass."

"That's a welcome thought," Willie said. "I could use something cold and wet."

Marie gave him a shy smile and set off to get the buttermilk while Willie worked the churn. He was taken by her pretty smile and dark curly hair. He also didn't miss her swaying hips as she crossed the porch and headed for the cistern. He just might come to see more of her if Sam didn't show up.

He bet Sam and Eddie had either run off to get away from their father or they had gotten themselves killed in a fight somewhere. Either way he didn't think Sam would be seeing this girl again.

Willie sat visiting with Marie for two hours, long after the girl had taken the butter out and worked it into a ball. She told him that Sam and Eddie said they were heading for home when they left her place. "Said they were worried your dad would be mad for them taking so long to get home."

Mrs. Hays, a dumpy little woman with flour on her cheeks came to the door and called to Marie, "You've visited long enough, young lady. I have work for you in the kitchen. Willie's welcome to stay for lunch, but he'll have to wait out here while you do your chores."

Willie wanted to stay longer, but remembering his father's wrath, didn't dare stay for the noon meal. He'd have to hurry if he was to cover twenty miles by nightfall. That was as far as he was going to go whether it was twenty miles or not.

He left the Hays' place and rode, stopping at every farm, until the sun was half hidden by the horizon before he stopped and unsaddled his horse. He gathered some firewood, spread his blanket on the ground and when the fire was lit, warmed the food his mother had packed for him.

He sat sipping coffee and thought about the wild goose chase they were on. He had talked to every person he met, and none of them had seen any men fitting Sam and Eddie's description, nor the description he gave of the Hessers. It would be nice to know where Sam and Eddie had run off to but running all over the country looking for the Hessers seemed to be a waste of time.

Willie resigned himself to the fact that his Pa would never give up until he had some answers. If the Hessers had anything to do with Sam and Eddie's disappearance, they'd pay dearly. As darkness settled in the bird songs were slowly replaced by the chirp of tree frogs and crickets. Willie put one last log on the fire, rolled into his blanket and fell into a deep sleep.

Simon took the right fork in the road and, much like Willie, found that no one had seen his two brothers or two young people traveling alone. He reached a small town just about the time he figured he'd traveled twenty miles. He saw a tall lanky man riding toward him on a mule and asked him what town it was.

"Blue Stem," the man answered. "Just like the grass out on the prairie."

Jacob's Promise

It was late afternoon when Simon arrived in town and he spent the rest of the day stopping in stores asking his usual questions about his brothers and the Hessers. His last stop was at a saloon that served food.

He decided he would have a real sit-down meal instead of the one his mother packed for him. Besides, here he could enjoy a beer or two with the meal. He felt free of his older brother Sam, who was always setting limits on what he could and couldn't do.

He was beginning to enjoy the fact that Sam wasn't around. Lately, Sam had begun sounding more and more a pain in the butt.

The tables in the part of the saloon that served food were filled and the room buzzed with many conversations. Simon found an empty table and ordered a big meal. After eating, he pushed his plate away and ordered his third beer. He was taking his first sip of beer when a stranger approached his table.

"I notice you're alone and all the other tables are filled. Would it be a bother to you if I sat down?"

"Nah, sit down, I could use some company," Simon said. "I've been riding alone all day and I don't know anyone in town so your company's welcome."

The man dropped into a chair and let out a sigh of relief. "I've been in the saddle all day too and I'm beat. I think I've ridden about thirty miles." He stuck out his hand and said, "My name's Jake White."

"Hi, Jake. Glad to meet you. I'm Simon Cooper. Which way are you headed?" He asked.

"I'm coming from St. Louis," Jake answered. "I been working on river boats for the last year. The last one I was on caught fire and sunk and I damn near drowned. I'm done with the river. I'm headed for the good, solid ground of Ohio."

"I've never been on a river boat, but I've ridden a couple of ferries and that didn't seem too bad," Simon said.

Jake laughed, "There's a lot of difference in going up and down a river than just crossing it." Jake leaned back in his chair and studied Simon. "You said you didn't live around here. Are you headed east?"

"No. I'm headed west. I live about twenty miles west of here," Simon answered.

"What brings you to a little dinky town like this? I'd think you could get supplies someplace closer to home."

"I'm lookin' for people, not supplies," Simon said.

"There aren't a lot of people around this part of the country so you shouldn't have any trouble finding who you are looking for."

"The people I'm lookin' for don't seem to want to be found. They left town sort of sudden like. My two brothers, Sam and Eddie, have disappeared and a couple of kids, a boy and a girl, left town after their parents died in a fire.

"My father is interested in buying their farm, but he can't find them. The boy is about seventeen or eighteen and the girl is fifteen or sixteen. I thought sure someone would have seen them on the road. It's a little unusual for two kids to be travelin' alone out here, but so far I've had no luck."

"I haven't met anyone named Sam or Eddie, but what did this boy and girl look like?" Jake asked.

Simon described Jacob and Beth Ann as best he could remember and then added that they probably would be riding in a farm wagon. "If they had passed you on the road, you'd think someone would remember them?"

"Are you sure they went east," Jake asked. "I passed a couple of kids that looked something like you described, but they were heading west. Out on the other side of Vandalia I ran into a covered wagon with two kids in it. They were both dressed like boys, but the younger one sure looked more like a girl to me."

"Did you get their names?" Simon asked.

"No. I didn't talk to them much. A big storm had just passed through and they were busy getting their wagon straightened out. They're the only two I saw that come close to the pair you've described."

"Thank you, Mister. I think you just solved the mystery of why we haven't found them." Simon paid his tab and went out to his horse. He couldn't wait to get started back home. He finally had something to tell his father.

He rode two miles outside of town before he stopped to camp for the night. He was up at first light and headed west again before the full sun had cleared the horizon. Reaching the fork in the road, he headed up the left fork to meet Willie.

He was too excited to wait for Willie to come to him. When he saw his brother, he set his horse into a gallop. Reaching Willie, he rode round and round him yelling, "Have I got news for you. I think I've found out where the Hessers went."

He stopped circling and rode up beside Willie and repeated what he had heard in the saloon.

Willie was as surprised as Simon had been about where the Hessers had gone. Anxious to tell their father the good news they put their horses into a fast trot and headed for home.

CHAPTER 13

As Jacob and Beth Ann traveled the next morning, they saw the result of the tornado's path. The prairie was marked with twisted trees, bits and pieces of wagons, and dead animals. The funnel cloud had skipped back and forth, from one side of the trail to the other, for more than two miles.

"I hope I don't see any more storms like that for the rest of my life," Beth Ann said when she saw torn canvas and parts of a wagon wheel scattered along the trail beside them.

The farther they traveled the more wagons they saw stretched out before them.

"How will some of those people ever make it," Beth Ann asked. "I saw two small wagons go by with whole families pulling it like they were horses. People working like animals."

"We're lucky to have horses," Jacob said. "But don't get too comfortable. If we lost a horse, we'd be walking too."

They hadn't traveled far before they caught up with four wagons pulled by oxen. Jacob was impatient with the oxen's slow pace, but there were too many of them to pass. Reluctantly Jacob fell into the line and followed along at a slow pace.

Reaching the Mississippi River, they joined a line of wagons half a mile long. The ferry closed at nightfall and they had to sit in the line overnight. It was late the next day when their turn came to pull onto the ferry.

Jacob's Promise

Awed by the width of the river they stood by their wagon and watched the ferry work its way across the muddy waters. The foul odor of dead fish mixed with smoke from the river boats hung in the air over the water like liquid dust.

Beth Ann was filled with excitement as she watched the frenzied activity on the river and saw the many buildings of St. Louis on the far shore. Warehouses lined the river's edge, with boats blowing black smoke and maneuvering for a place to dock.

Arriving at the dock on the far side of the river, Jacob and Beth Ann were met with a volume of noise far louder than anything they had ever encountered. There was the babble of voices, shouted orders to stevedores, boat whistles, shrieks of frightened animals, and the pounding from buildings being constructed.

The stench of animal waste joined the fish and smoke odor they had encountered out in the open water. Beth Ann held tight to Jacob's arm as they pulled onto the dock and onto a bustling city street.

On the crowded avenues, fancy buggies with prancing horses mingled with the large lumbering covered wagons pulled by oxen. On the boardwalks, pale women with big hats and silk dresses rubbed shoulders with sunburned women in gray wool dresses and men with muddy boots and sweat-stained shirts. Black faces, red faces, white, powdered faces, and the red-brown, wind weathered faces of those traveling west mingled, but ignored each other.

Seeing the swirling mob of the city, Jacob knew it would be an expensive place to stay. He hated to spend what money they had staying in a boarding house, but he needed to be in town while he searched for information that might help him find his aunt and uncle. He worried about his tired horses, they could use some rest and the pampering at a stable.

On the ferry Jacob talked to the ferryman about camping outside the city. He told Jacob that the west side of the city was crowded with wagons and most of the land over grazed. Hearing that, Jacob decided he had to spend the money and stay in town.

At the first boarding house, Jacob stopped the team and left Beth Ann holding the reins while he went in to get a room. Inside he met a portly gentleman smoking a big cigar.

"I need a room for a couple of days," Jacob said assuming the gentleman was the owner. "What do you have available and how much is it?"

"I'm filled to overflowing and so is every rooming house in town," The man blew smoke rings over Jacob's head. "I have whole families living in one room and three men sharing beds in all my other rooms."

Dejected, Jacob returned to the wagon. "There are no rooms here and the owner told me it would be the same in every rooming house in town. We're going to have to go out west of town after all. We'll have to ride into town every day to take care of our business here. I don't like it, but it's the best we can do."

He climbed back up on the wagon and turned the team west out of the congested city. When they reached the last scattering of houses past the edge of town, Jacob saw a wagon pulling out from the back lot of one of the houses. He jerked back on the reins, almost throwing Beth Ann out of her seat with the sudden stop.

"What in the world?" Beth Ann started to say but stopped when Jacob jumped down from the wagon and ran up to the door of one of the houses. When a woman answered, Jacob asked excitedly, "I just saw a wagon leave the back of your house. Do you rent camping space?"

"I've rented the little shed back there to a couple of fur trappers, but you can camp there if you aren't afraid of being next to an Indian," the woman said.

"You can put your horses out in the pasture, but I expect you to clean up your campsite before you leave. It'll cost you 50 cents a night, paid in advance," and held out her hand.

Jacob dug two coins out of his pocket and handed them to her. He was so happy to find a place to stay near the city that he didn't even think of the cost.

He pulled the wagon on to the back lot behind the house and unhitched the team while Beth Ann unpacked cooking utensils and food for their noon meal. Once the horses were turned into the pasture, Jacob went to the nearby woods and gathered wood for a fire. As he was coming back, he saw two men standing by the shed waiting for him to approach.

One was a white man with a slight, but well-proportioned build. He wore buckskin pants and a shirt with fringe dangling down the length of the sleeves. He had a short blond beard, and long hair that matched it. The other man was a tall broad-shouldered Indian with his hair pulled into a ponytail and tied with a bright red ribbon.

The white man's piercing steel-gray eyes took Jacob's measure before he stepped forward and said, "Hi, young man. I see you're camping at the Edward's place, too."

"Yes, sir," Jacob answered.

"I'm Joe Adams, and this is my brother-in-law Two Bears."

Jacob looked at the big Indian standing beside Joe Adams and was surprised to hear Joe say the Indian was his brother-in-law. He set down the wood he was carrying, hoping the surprise he felt didn't show in his face and shook hands with both men.

Jacob immediately sensed that these men knew all about the trails going west and he needed that information. "Would you two like to join me and my brother for supper?"

"That's real generous of you. We have a little mending to do on some equipment, but it won't take long. Then we'll come over," Joe said as he and Two Bears turned to leave.

Jacob picked up the wood and returned to where Beth Ann was waiting for him to start the fire. "I just met our neighbors and invited them to eat with us."

"You know we only have mush, bacon and eggs to offer them, I hope they won't be disappointed," Beth Ann said.

"You should see the size of the Indian with Joe Adams. Believe it or not he said the Indian was his brother-in-law."

"Does that mean Joe is married to some wild Indian woman?" Beth Ann frowned and gave a little shiver.

"I don't know how wild she is, but she's an Indian," Jacob said.

"You invited them so start slicing some bacon for your new friends," Beth Ann said as she tossed the side of bacon she was holding to Jacob.

The same morning Jacob and Beth Ann's ferry docked at St. Louis, a paddle wheeler from New Orleans pulled into the wharf a short distance up the river at a different landing. Two passengers, Mr. and Mrs. Henry Lafarge, disembarked, followed by two rough looking men carrying the Lafarge's luggage. A buggy was waiting for them and when the baggage was loaded, the four climbed in and turned up Walnut Street to Barnum's Hotel.

Henry Lafarge was a distinguished looking man, with coal black hair, a thin mustache and a small pointed beard. He wore a tall gray hat, blue cut-away coat, ruffled pale blue shirt, gray pants and spats covering his shiny shoes.

His wife, Alice, matched him in splendor with a shimmering purple silk dress, trimmed in white lace and flared by numerous petticoats. She carried a pink parasol, her lace covered hands gripping its handle.

The pair traveled to St. Louis each year and were well known and accepted into St. Louis social society. They spent lavishly when they came to town, as fitting a man who owned one of the largest clearing houses for freight from sea-going ships and river boats plying the Mississippi.

What wasn't known by most folks in St. Louis was that the Lafarge's also owned one of the highest priced bordellos in New Orleans, and he and his wife came to St. Louis on recruiting trips to keep the bordello supplied with new young faces.

Lafarge's method of recruitment was to have his two employees scour the wagon trains for young girls, who were either unhappy with the life on the trail or felt lost because a parent was sick or had died. Lafarge enticed these frightened girls with promises of a big paying job.

Once securely on the boat, they were locked in their cabin until the boat was well on its way to New Orleans. This was the Lafarge's second trip to St. Louis this year. Their grand plan was to open a second bordello.

That meant they were going to have to double the number of girls they usually picked up. Mr. Lafarge did not rule out the possibility that his men might have to kidnap a few young girls to fulfill the quota he had set. Finding enough vulnerable candidates and convincing them to come to the boat might take too long.

Lafarge owned the cargo boat and had it captained with a man he paid handsomely to keep his mouth shut. As a special favor he allowed the captain to pick one of the girls as his cabin mate for the trip down the river.

It was a way to blackmail the captain and make him less likely to say anything about how the girls were recruited. The boat was a lumber carrier and the only passengers were the girls and Mr.

Jacob's Promise

Lafarge's employees.

CHAPTER 14

Willie and Simon had intended to be home by early afternoon with their good news, but a heavy rain had washed over them and made a quagmire out of the road. They had to hold their horses to a slow walk. They passed through town and were half way home when Willie held out his hand signaling Simon to stop.

He put his finger to his lips and pointed down the trail. Trotting toward them was a lone coyote carrying something in its mouth. Their mother had ordered the boys to shoot every coyote they saw because coyotes had been raiding her chicken house.

Simon drew his rifle out of its case and carefully charged it. He took aim at the coyote's chest and squeezed the trigger. The coyote saw Simon point the rifle and turned, but the bullet got there first. The coyote dropped in the mud and lay still.

"Nice shot, Simon. I thought sure you'd missed him," Willie said.

Simon rode over to the coyote and looked down. "I'm gonna cut off his tail so Ma can hang it on the fence with the others we've shot."

Simon drew his knife, climbed off his horse and started sawing through the boney tail. While he was squatted down working on the tail, he looked over to see what the coyote had in his mouth. One quick look and he dropped the knife, jumped to his feet and backed away.

"Jesus save me, that coyotes got somebody's arm in its mouth. There's a hand with a part of a sleeve on it."

"That damn coyote's dug up someone's grave," Willie said.

"Ain't no cemeteries around here," Simon said backing away "The only cemetery around is four or five miles from here."

Willie climbed down beside Simon for a closer look. The heavy clouds had grayed the light to the point it was impossible to see clearly. "Get a match, Simon. So, we can get a better look."

"I'll get the matches, but you know damn well everybody around here wears the same kind of work shirt." Simon got the matches and bent down by Willie before striking one. The match flared, and they examined the shirt in the flickering light. "See, I told you the shirt wouldn't tell you nothin. It's the same kind we're both wearin."

"Strike another one and let's look again," Willie said.

Simon struck a second match and they took a closer look at the mangled arm and shirt. The hand was laying palm up with the fingers splayed out like the hand was signaling stop.

"Turn the hand over Simon. Maybe there's a ring on the finger that we don't see."

"You turn it over. I ain't gonna touch that stinkin' thing," Simon said.

"We don't have to touch the damn thing," Willie said. "Go find us a stick."

Simon found a stick and handed it to Willie. Willie put the stick under the hand and flipped it over.

"Be careful ya idiot," Simon yelled. "You're flippin' rotten stuff to hell and gone and I don't want that thing's stink on me." Simon struck another match and put it closer to the hand.

He dropped the match, fell back, and sat in the mud. Willie gulped a sharp intake of breath but didn't move. He just stared at the dark shape on the ground.

"You saw the scars on the back of the hand too, didn't ya, Willie?"

"Yeh. They're just like the scars on Sam's hand from that bobcat he shot and thought was dead."

"Oh, God, Willie, if that's Sam's, that means Sam's dead. And what about Eddie?"

Willie cleared his throat "There were times I didn't get along with Sam, but I sure didn't want him dead."

"That hand may belong to Sam, but I can't bring myself to touch it. You'll have to do it," Simon said holding his nose.

"I can't do it alone," Willie groaned. "You gotta help. Get the sugar sack Mom packed your food in. It's water proof, and it'll seal out the smell.

"There's still stuff in that sack," Simon said.

"Damn it. Dump it out, idiot," Willie barked, his voice breaking with emotion. "Now hold it open while I push this thing in with the stick."

"Be careful. Don't get any on me," Simon said holding open the sack and turning his head away from the stink. "Okay, push it in."

Willie maneuvered the mangled piece of hand until he got it between the two sticks and lifted it up into the open sack. He took the sack from Simon and mounted his horse.

"How can you stand to hold that stinkin thing? It smells like a dead rat that's been in the sun for a couple of days," Simon complained.

"You better be careful what you say. If it really is Sam's and Pa doesn't think we're respectful enough, there'll be hell to pay."

"Damn, we couldn't have worse luck. We're on our way home to give Pa some important news about finding the Hessers, and we find this thing. It's gonna ruin everything. "

They crossed the ford without knowing they had passed within a hundred and fifty feet of where Sam and Eddie were buried. Willie rode with the hand, holding the sugar sack, extended out as far away from his body as he could. His stomach rolled whenever he got a sniff of the rotting flesh. Simon moved back and forth with each wind change to avoid the stench.

Tom Cooper was crossing from the barn to the house with a pail of fresh milk when the two boys came riding in. He set the pail of milk on the porch and turned to wait for them to reach him.

Willie got off his horse, approached his father, and set the sugar sack on the ground in front of him. Simon stayed on his horse and let Willie do all the talking.

"Well, don't just stand there like an idiot. What did you find out and why in the hell did you bring that stinking bag into the yard?" Tom demanded.

Jacob's Promise

"We have some news and we have something we want to show you," Willie said. "We think we know where the Hessers went, but first we have somethin in the bag for you to look at."

Gingerly, Willie took the sugar sack by the bottom corner and shook out the hand. It fell out palm down on the muddy ground, the scars showing white in the dim light.

"Just what in the hell am I supposed to see out here in the dark?" Tom asked.

Simon jumped off his horse and struck a match and held it above the hand, turning his head away to avoid the smell.

"Where did you get that?"

"Simon shot a coyote that was carryin it out on the other side of Riley's Ford."

Tom walked over and bent down to look. "What am I supposed to see?" he asked.

"Look at the back of the hand. See those scars?"

Tom let out a groan when he understood what Willie was pointing out to him. He stared at the hand even after the match had gone out.

"Hessers. It's those damn Hessers," Tom growled, as he slowly stood and faced his sons. His face was so twisted with grief and anger it frightened them. "It has to be the work of that Hesser kid. He must have shot them in the back. He had to.

"He could never have faced Sam and done this. He's going to pay for this. We should have taken care of him the minute we knew he was still alive."

"Pa," Willie said, "I know you've made up your mind that the Hesser boy did this, but don't forget the beatin' Sam gave that Thompson boy about a month ago. His daddy threatened to shoot Sam if he ever came near his place. Besides I don't think the Hesser kid would have had the guts to tangle with Sam."

Tom Cooper didn't give any indication he heard Willie. He was on his knees beside the sugar sack, great sobs racking his body. Finally, he looked up and said, "Get a shovel we'll bury Sam up by his baby sister's grave."

The boys dug a shallow hole next to their departed sister's grave before they bothered to unpack their bed rolls and tend their tired horses. The rest of the day everyone tip-toed around the Cooper farm avoiding Tom, who sat brooding on the front porch.

Bill Heyduck

At breakfast the next morning, Tom rose and rapped his knuckles on the table for their attention. "As soon as the livestock's fed we're going into town and get the law involved in this. We'll get up a search party and comb the area until we find Sam and Eddie. That Hesser kid did this and then left my boys to be savaged by the animals. I want to find my boys and then I want to find the Hessers."

CHAPTER 15

To Jacob's dismay, Beth Ann had shed her boy clothes before their guests arrived. She wore a singed dress she had managed to rescue from the cabin while Jacob was busy digging their parents' graves.

"I'm not going to face company dressed in that ratty looking shirt and baggy trousers," Beth Ann said, glaring at Jacob, daring him to argue.

Jacob knew it was useless to argue and besides it was too late. He heard the door to the shed close and knew their guests were on their way.

Joe Adams smiled when he saw a girl and not the boy he had expected to see. After introductions, Beth Ann handed out the tin plates of food. During the meal she watched Joe Adams and was surprised that he had such good manners.

It was difficult for her to believe he had an Indian wife and lived out in the wilderness most of the year. He seemed so cultured. Her early shyness slipped away as she and Joe talked. He had accepted her as an adult and a new feeling of confidence filled her. She didn't know what to think of Two Bears; he was so quiet he could have been a shadow.

"I'm not a nosey man by nature, but what are you two youngsters doing out on the prairie alone?" Joe asked. "You're too young to be headed west by yourselves."

Jacob told him the story of their parents' death and their search for their aunt and uncle. He left out the part about the Coopers burning the house or the shootout at Riley's Ford.

"You kids are pretty brave to have gotten this far. It shows a lot of character on both your parts."

"Like some more coffee Mr. Adams?" Beth Ann was filled with pride at his compliment.

"Please call me Joe. Mr. Adams sounds a little formal for people sitting around a camp fire together."

"All right, would you like to have some more coffee, Joe? You, Mr. Two Bears?"

Joe let out a belly laugh. "I don't think Two Bears has ever been called Mister in his life. Be careful or you'll have him so spoiled, I won't be able to live with him."

A small smile creased Two Bears face as he shook his head no to her offer for more coffee.

"I doubt he could get that spoiled," Beth Ann said returning the coffee pot to the fire.

"Well, this has been a fine meal with good company." Joe stood up. "But I have to go into town to do some banking business and I don't want to have to spend one more day than I have to. I'm anxious to get back to a slower pace with my wife and children."

"I didn't know you had children," Jacob said.

"Yes, and I don't want them to be orphans like you two, so I need to get away from the temptation of liquor and the wild women of this wicked city," he laughed. "It's also a good place to get a knife in the back if you happen to be in the wrong place."

"We need to go to town too. We want to see if we can find out anything about our aunt and uncle. We hope there's the possibility that we can catch them before they get too far away," Jacob said.

"What if you can't find them," asked Joe.

"We'll just have to keep going west and check with every wagon train we meet."

"You know you can't just join any wagon train you come across. There's a fee to become part of a train and you have to be accepted by the rest of the group," Joe said.

"We'll go it alone if we have to." Jacob said.

"You kids have more spunk than brains. Come by in the

morning when you're ready to go into town and we'll go in together."

After Joe and Two Bears left, Beth Ann turned to Jacob. "Don't think you're going into town without me. I'm not going to be stuck out in the country while you have all the fun of seeing the sights in town."

Jacob knew it was useless to argue. "Okay, bossy." He started helping her gather up the dirty dishes.

The next morning after breakfast he went to the pasture and saddled the horses. When they went to the shed Joe came out, but Two Bears wasn't with him.

"Two Bears decided to stay in camp and get our gear organized for our trip home," Joe said as he mounted his horse.

On the ride into town, Jacob asked Joe about the things they would need on their trip west. He was especially interested in the supplies they would need in case they failed to find their Aunt Ruth and Uncle Ralph.

"My first suggestion is that get rid of the wagon. Those horses of yours will never survive pulling the load over the ground you're to cover."

"How else can we get there when the wagon and horses are all we have?" Jacob asked.

"Sell the wagon and get some pack horses like I have, mules if you can afford them," Joe suggested. "On horseback, you can cover twice the ground in a day as you can with a wagon. A saddle horse can walk around places that would stop a wagon."

"I hadn't thought that far ahead I guess," Jacob said. "But what you say makes sense."

"Let me help with the horses. I know some reliable people here that'll give you a square deal on a good pack horse," Joe offered.

Beth Ann rode up on the other side of Joe and asked, "Do men only talk about horses when they get together?"

"I'm only trying to find out things we need to know, Beth Ann," Jacob said.

"I see you're still in a dress," Joe said.

"I talked to the lady we're renting our camp from, and she assured me I would be perfectly safe dressing like a girl in St.

Louis."

Joe smiled at her, "You're certainly a fine-looking young lady, and Jacob's going to have a hard time keeping the boys away from you once you reach town."

She felt the blush come to her cheeks and couldn't stop the smile that spread across her face on hearing Joe's words.

Reaching the center of town, Joe pulled away from them, "I'm going to leave you two now. I have business at Merchant's Exchange. I think you should go to the places that supply wagon trains to check on your folks. I'd start with Sublette and Campbell's Store and, if they can't help you, try Reddick's Store. You'll find it located between Clark and Elm Street."

Jacob and Beth Ann questioned clerks at the stores and stopped wagons in the street, but no one had heard of a man and a woman named Heinz on any of the wagon trains. Discouraged, the pair started their horses back through town at a slow walk.

Even the horses seemed to have caught their mood. They were headed north on Walnut Street when Jacob saw the Barnum's Hotel sign out of the corner of his eye. He got a whiff of the smell of coffee coming from the hotel and, on impulse, reined in his horse.

"Come on, Beth Ann, let's go drown our problems in a cup of good coffee and a sweet roll, not the chicory we've been drinking at camp."

"You told me we couldn't afford to spend money foolishly, Jacob. What's come over you? We aren't even dressed well enough to get in," Beth Ann said looking down at her scorched dress.

"Come on. This may be our last chance to be in a fancy place like this, so let's splurge this once," Jacob pleaded. "All they can do is kick us out."

Jacob tied the horses to the rail, left his hat on the saddle horn, and smoothed his hair down as best he could. He helped Beth Ann up onto the walk and held the door for her as they entered the hotel.

The hotel lobby was filled with men dressed in fine suits and women in fancy dresses. The coffee shop was off to the right and they self-consciously hurried out of the lobby and into it. They found a table near the door and nervously sat down. They ordered coffee and a sweet roll from the tall Negro waiter, refusing the menus he offered them.

"Jacob, I feel like everyone is looking at us," Beth Ann whispered. "I'm not sure we should have come in here.".

"Relax, Beth Ann. Try to act like you've been in a place like this before."

"That's easier so say than it is to do," Beth Ann answered.

Sipping the hot liquid, she began to relax and forget about the other people in the room. She suddenly set the sweet roll down and looked at Jacob. "What are we going to do? We didn't find out anything today."

"We just have to keep looking," Jacob answered.

Beth Ann's eyes had wandered around the room and came to rest on the couple seated next to them. "Don't stare, Jacob, but when you get a chance look at the fancy dress on the woman at the next table."

Out of the corner of his eye, Jacob saw Henry LaFarge and his wife in an animated conversation. "I see what you mean. They sure don't look like they're headed for a wagon train."

Henry Lafarge and his wife were well aware of Beth Ann's entrance. Their eyes had followed her as she walked through the door and sat at the table next to them. With a big smile on his face, Henry looked at his wife, tilted his head toward Beth Ann and whispered to his wife. "Look at that farm bred beauty."

She nodded her head in agreement. "Yes, she's a young beauty. I think she would be a winner in our new establishment.

"Watch how easy it is to move in on them." When he heard Beth Ann's lament about not finding anything out about their aunt, he had what he needed.

"Pardon me for eaves-dropping, but I couldn't help overhearing you," Lafarge said in his smoothest southern drawl. If you'll forgive my forwardness, I might be of some help."

"Oh, how wonderful," Beth Ann said surprised at being noticed by the well-dressed gentlemen.

"It's difficult to talk between tables this way. Why don't you bring your coffee and sweets over and join us?" Henry waved at empty chairs.

Jacob and Beth Ann were almost speechless by the offer to join such a distinguished looking couple. After getting settled at the table, Henry introduced himself, "I'm Henry Lafarge and this is my wife, Alice. You're a fine-looking couple. What are your names?"

"I'm Jacob Hesser, and this is my sister, Beth Ann. I'm very glad to meet you, Mr. Lafarge. Do you really think you can help us?

"I know I can, young man. Now why don't you two tell us something about yourselves and what your problem is," Lafarge said with as much sincerity as he could muster.

Jacob told their story but left out the Coopers. He just told them their parents had been killed in a fire, and they were trying to catch up with their aunt and uncle who were headed for Oregon.

"I'll check with the outfitters I know who organize the wagon trains. I am sure they'll have a list of names of the people traveling with each of them. Now where can I reach you if I should find anything out," Lafarge asked.

"You don't have to trouble yourself, Mr. Lafarge. I'll ride back tomorrow morning and wait around all day, if I need to."

"No, Jacob. It's no trouble at all. I have a man I can send to get you when I have some news. Where can he find you?"

Jacob gave the directions to where they were camped and a description of the house they were camped behind. He couldn't believe their good fortune in meeting Mr. Lafarge. He was doubly shocked when Mr. Lafarge insisted on paying for their coffee and sweet rolls. They were almost dancing with joy by the time they got back to their horses.

"Beth Ann, our luck has finally changed. That Mr. Lafarge is an angel sent from heaven. He makes me believe we're really going to find Aunt Ruth and Uncle Ralph."

CHAPTER 17

Henry Lafarge was pacing back and forth on the deck of the steamer, pounding his hat against his leg and cursing under his breath. He hated waiting. Where in the world was his wife with that girl, and where were the men he had sent for her? They should have been here half an hour ago. Surely two grown men could handle a sixteen-year-old girl.

His pacing was interrupted by the sound of the galloping hooves of his wife's buggy rushing toward the boat. He breathed a sigh of relief. At last he had the girl and they could get underway. He could see his wife, but where were the two men he'd sent with her?

Alice Lafarge sawed viscously on the reins, bringing the horses to a rearing stop.

"Help me down," she yelled. "Get someone to take the buggy to the stable and tell the captain to get us out of here."

"What are you talking about? Where's the girl, and where are the men I sent with you?"

"Something went terribly wrong. I waited like I was supposed to, but they never came back. I thought I heard the girl scream once and then there was only silence. I have a bad feeling about this. I think we better get out of here.

"If those two somehow got themselves caught trying to grab that girl, they might decide to tell who sent them. Do you want to deal with the law here in St. Louis?"

Lafarge helped her up the gangplank and paid a man double what he should have to take the buggy back to the stable. He hurried to the captain's cabin and found him half-dressed studying river charts.

"Get your tail out of that chair and get the crew feeding the fire. I want to be underway in thirty minutes."

The captain dressed quickly and as soon as the crew had raised a head of steam, the boat pulled away from the dock and headed down the Mississippi.

After leaving Lafarge, Jacob galloped his horse all the way back to camp. At their wagon he jumped off the horse and looked for his sister. "Beth Ann,"," he called. "Are you in bed already?"

"Oh, Jacob I'm glad to see you." She jumped down from the wagon and rushed into Jacob's arms. "The most awful thing happened. I was cleaning up things before going to bed and two men tried to kidnap me."

Jacob gripped her shoulders and pushed her back at arm's length. "Calm down and talk to me. Now who tried to kidnap you? We don't have any money to pay kidnappers."

"All I know is that a man grabbed me and tried to pull me behind the shed."

"He wasn't trying to kidnap you, he wanted to do something else," Jacob said overcome with anger.

"Joe said they were trying to kidnap me because there were two of them and they had ropes to tie me up."

"Joe was here? Is that how you got away?"

"Joe and Two Bears heard them ride their horses up behind the shed. They heard voices and slipped out to see what was going on. That was when they saw a man creeping up on me. While I was struggling with the man, Two Bears came up behind him and stabbed him in the back.

Joe caught the other one and after a struggle killed him, too. They told me to stay in the wagon while they got rid of their bodies. I've been hiding in the wagon ever since it happened."

Jacob paced angrily back and forth in front of the wagon, kicking himself for not being there when Beth Ann needed him.

"When did all this happen?" he asked.

Jacob's Promise

"A man grabbed me not fifteen minutes after you left for town." Beth Ann said. She stopped talking for a second and took a deep breath. "What did you find out from Mr. Lafarge."

"At least something good has happened tonight. Mr. Lafarge found out that Aunt Ruth and Uncle Ralph left St. Louis on a boat headed for Independence six days ago. If we get started in the next day or two, we might be able to catch up with them before they set out for Oregon."

Jacob and Beth Ann were still sitting by their campfire talking when they heard horses coming up from the back of the campsite and stop at the pasture gate.

"Get back in the wagon," Jacob whispered. He took the shotgun from where Beth Ann had leaned it against the wagon and started back toward the pasture. Reaching the edge of the pasture he stopped when he saw two shadowy shapes and four horses.

"Who's there," he called.

"Don't shoot," Joe cried. "It's just me and Two Bears."

Jacob lowered the shotgun and let out a puff of air. "I'm glad you're back. Maybe you can tell me what happened out here tonight. I'm not sure Beth Ann has it all straight because she's still so upset."

"There's not much to tell. Best we can figure someone wanted Beth Ann, and they sent these two yahoos to kidnap her."

"What's going on?" Jacob asked, his face in a worried frown.

"Jacob, things get bought and sold here, including people, black and white." Joe said. "She'd bring a good price at any number of bordellos along the river. You may be lucky you weren't here; they might have killed you to get at her."

"I don't think I'll ever be able to understand how people can be that way."

"There are a lot of evil people in the world, Jacob. Be careful who you trust, and only believe half of what people tell you." He put his hand on Jacob's shoulder. "Now get some sleep. Tomorrow we'll go in and sell your wagon.

"You won't need to buy packhorses," he smiled. "We kept the kidnapper's horses. It'll be days or weeks before anyone will miss them, if they're ever missed at all."

Neither Beth Ann nor Jacob got much sleep that night. Beth

Ann was still shaken by the kidnap attempt and Jacob excited about the news that Aunt Ruth were just days ahead of them. They both tossed and turned through the night. Anxious about what lay ahead he shook off his blanket before dawn and started building up the campfire.

Beth Ann heard dry branches break and knew Jacob was up. She climbed out of the wagon to join him. "I see you couldn't sleep either."

"I guess I'm upset about all that has happened to us in the last few weeks. I'm worried about catching Aunt Ruth and Uncle Ralph. I'm worried about our money holding out, and I'm worried about who we can trust."

"We have Joe and Two Bears."

"Thank God for them. They saved you, and they're going to be a big help in getting us to Independence."

"Go work out some of your nervousness by hitching up the team while I fix some breakfast. That way you'll be ready when Joe comes by to get you."

Jacob had driven the wagon up from the pasture and Beth Ann was putting the breakfast dishes away when Joe walked up leading his horse. "I see you're raring to go this morning."

"Yes, sir. I've emptied the wagon and put a saddle in the back so I can ride one of the horses home after I sell the wagon," Jacob answered. "I'm glad Two Bears is staying here. I didn't want to leave Beth Ann alone again."

In town the first stop they made was to sell the wagon. The wagon should have sold for more than he was offered, but Jacob knew he had to let it go, and so did the stable man.

Joe tried to help get him more money but gave up because he knew it was useless to bargain any longer. Joe tried to sooth Jacob's feelings by explaining that since he was getting two free horses, he was really coming out ahead.

He counseled Jacob to only buy enough for the trip to Independence. He could re-supply once they got there if he and Beth Ann didn't catch up with his relatives and decided to go on alone.

"There's one other thing that you'll need to buy and that's a rifle," Joe said. "That old shotgun of yours is fine for shooting a few birds or rabbits, but out on the plains, you'll need a rifle to bring down antelope or buffalo. You may even need it to protect yourself from any unfriendlies you might run across."

"Beth Ann isn't going to like having so many guns around, but maybe that struggle with the kidnapper has changed her mind a little," Jacob said.

When Jacob and Joe got back to camp Joe showed Jacob how to balance a load on a packhorse. Then he sat drinking coffee while he watched Jacob load and unload the pack animals until he was satisfied Jacob could do it right. Jacob was more than ready to stop, his arms felt like they were made of lead.

While Jacob was busy loading and unloading the packhorse, Two Bears helped Beth Ann sort through their gear to see what was necessary and what could be left behind. Beth Ann was heartbroken when Two Bears told her she couldn't take any of her mother's dishes. There were advantages to traveling with pack horses, but she was finding there were disadvantages too.

That night at supper Jacob and Beth Ann ate in silence, both weary from the day's activities. After a quick cleanup of the tin plates they stumbled to their bedrolls and fell asleep the minute they closed their eyes.

Jacob felt like he had just closed his eyes when Joe shook him awake. "Let's get a move on. We want to get out of here before the rest of the city's awake. We don't need anyone recognizing those horses. We can stop and eat later. Two Bears has your pack horses tied to the fence out back and ready to be loaded."

Jacob slipped on his shoes and went to get the horses while Beth Ann rolled up their bedrolls. Within the hour, they were packed and ready. They each took a lead-rope of a pack animal and tied it to their saddle horn. Following behind Joe and Two Bears they passed the last house and entered the open prairie. Jacob looked over and smiled at Beth Ann. They were finally on their way.

CHAPTER 18

They had been riding for three hours when Joe guided them off the trail and into the shade of some giant oak trees. "Time to rest the horses and get a bite to eat."

Jacob helped Beth Ann remove what she needed from one of the pack horses while Joe and Two Bears took the other horses to a grassy area to feed. Jacob got a small fire started for Beth Ann before he led the packhorse over to join Joe and Two Bears.

While the three stood talking Jacob noticed a man across the meadow repeatedly try to mount his horse but fail each time. "Did you see that," Jacob said nodding towards the struggling man.

"Drunk," Two Bears grunted.

"He sure looks like it," Joe said.

After a chuckle at his clumsiness Joe and Two Bears turned back to check the loads on the pack animals and Jacob wandered off to gather more wood for the fire.

The smell of frying side pork floating in the morning air reached them and like a magnet drew them back to the campsite.

"You're just in time,' Beth Ann said. "And here comes Jacob with more fire wood than I'll ever need."

Jacob laid down the fire wood and pointed to the man they had seen earlier. "He still hasn't gotten on that horse yet."

"If a man can't hold his liquor, he'd best stay away from the bottle," Joe said.

Jacob's Promise

Though they didn't mention the man again they all kept glancing in his direction. He pulled himself half way up then he fell back, prostrate on the ground.

Beth Ann, moved by the man's struggles, stood up watching him. "Joe there's something wrong with him. He needs help."

"He'll be all right once he sobers up," Joe answered.

Beth Ann faced Joe with her fists planted on her hips like a school teacher lecturing an unruly student." Joe, that man needs help and if you don't go help him, I will."

"If it'll make you happy, I'll go have a look." Joe got up and ambled over to the man.

They watched Joe lift the man to his feet and stand him next to the horse. With the man holding on to the saddle for support Joe led the animal over to their campsite.

The minute Beth Ann saw him she let out a gasp. The man's face was covered with black and green bruises. There were big scabs on his nose, eyebrow and chin.

"I guess I'm not a very pretty sight, Missy," the man said.

"I told him he looked like he had been throwed and stomped on," Joe chuckled.

"No horse did this. I was kicked and stomped on by a couple of ill-tempered fellows named Cooper back in Vandalia," the man answered. "I'm Ben Sutler." He extended his hand. "I could sure use a cup of that coffee to wet my throat."

Jacob's hand trembled when he gave the man a tin cup. Beth Ann glanced at Jacob with a worried look as she poured coffee.

Ben blew to cool the coffee. "It's my own fault I look this way. I talked back to a couple of mean fellas when I shoulda kept my mouth shut."

"Let this be a lesson to you, Jacob," Joe said. "Back away from trouble if you can. A man gets himself hurt out here, it's a long way to a doctor."

"Where you headed Mr. Sutler?" Jacob asked.

"There you go, Jacob, asking questions you shouldn't. If the man wants you to know he'll tell you in his own good time," Joe scolded.

Jacob got red in the face.

The man let out a hardy laugh, then groaned from the pain it caused. "That's okay, son. I don't have any dark secrets. I live just about six or seven miles from here. About a half a mile down this road you'll come to a bluff and I live six miles south of the bluff."

Joe and Two Bears sat quietly and listened to the man talk without joining in the conversation. Joe had sensed an uneasiness in Jacob when the man talked about Vandalia.

"I left my wife doing the chores back here while I when over into Illinois to visit my sick mother."

Sutler stopped to take a drink of coffee, "On my last night at the farm I went into town to have a beer. Two big drunk farm boys overheard me telling the bartender I was headed back home to Missouri. When I left the bar, they followed me out to the alley where my horse was tied and started asking all kinds of questions.

"Had I seen a boy and girl traveling alone? They asked questions so fast I couldn't have answered if I wanted to. I told them to go to hell and started to get on my horse." He eased down onto a log.

"One grabbed me by the shirt and pushed me against a wall and said that when any one of the Cooper boys asked someone a question he better, by God, have an answer for them."

"I can see they didn't take kindly to your back talk," Joe said.

Ben took another drink of coffee to wet his throat before he continued. "They left me lying there in the alley. It was past midnight before I came to my senses and was able to get on my horse. I don't know how I've made it this far. I seem to get stiffer every day."

Joe watched the color drain out of Jacob's face when the man mentioned the Cooper brothers again. He had felt from the beginning Jacob only told him part of the story about why they were headed west alone.

Jacob sat, barely able to breathe after hearing the Coopers were searching for them. He tried to think back at everything they had done in Vandalia. With a jolt he remembered he sold the two Coopers' horses there.

He also had the wagon fitted for travel west and had told the stable man where he was headed. He had used a different name, but that might not be enough to throw the Cooper's off their trail.

Ben Sutler finished his coffee and thanked them for their hospitality. He painfully got to his feet and let Joe help him get up onto his horse. After he was gone, Jacob got up and helped Beth

Jacob's Promise

Ann tie the cooking utensils onto the pack animals. They didn't see Joe watching them as they whispered to each other while they packed.

In the late afternoon they came to a small stream with clear running water and stopped for the night. After they unloaded the packhorses and removed the saddles from the others Joe took the horse to a grassy patch and put hobble ropes on their legs.

"I don't want to spend half of the day chasing after a horse that gets spooked and runs off. We might as well get used to keeping the horses close by. After Independence, we'll be in Pawnee country and they're the slickest horse thieves in the country."

While Joe and Jacob tended the horses, Two Bears started a fire and then sat and watched Beth Ann cook mush for their evening meal. As they ate, Joe turned to Jacob, once again becoming Jacob's teacher.

"This stream is running pretty clear we best fill our canteens and water bags. The next stream may be a muddy one."

Two Bears got up, grabbed the canteens, and headed for the stream without saying a word.

"Doesn't Two Bears ever talk?" Beth Ann asked.

Joe laughed. "You should hear him when he's with his Shoshone family and friends. But then he's speaking his own language. He isn't so sure of his English, so he doesn't say much around white people. He's learned there are some who don't like Indians, especially one they think is acting smart by speaking English. He's even been shot at a few times."

"That's terrible," Beth Ann said." He knows he's among friends with us, doesn't he? Especially after saving me in St. Louis."

"Since that fracas in St. Louis, he's acted like he's your Fairy Godmother," Joe laughed. "He thinks you and Jacob are both too green to be out on your own."

"What's a Fairy Godmother?" Two Bears returned with the full canteens.

"Someone who watches over another person to protect them from harm," Joe answered.

Two Bears grunted his understanding and left with the water

bags. When he was out of hearing range, Joe said, "It's funny, he's become fond of you two. He accepts me as part of the family since I'm married to his sister, but I can't recall him ever taking a great liking to any other white people."

"I know you told me not to ask people questions, but I need to know. Why did you and Two Bears decide to help us? I'm sure we messed up your plans to travel by boat."

"We decided you two were too young and green to be heading out alone. We were afraid you'd get yourselves killed before you got fifty miles out of St. Louis."

Jacob was embarrassed when he heard that Joe thought of him as too green to take care of himself but knew what he said was true. Beth Ann sat and hugged her knees, fighting back tears as she thought back to how close she came to being kidnapped.

The silence between them lasted for a number of minutes before Joe said, "Now Jacob it's time for you to do some explaining. What's the real reason you two are headed west? I saw how startled you were when Ben Sutler told about being beat up by those Coopers. Why did the name Cooper upset you?"

"Because I killed two of their brothers," Jacob blurted out.

Joe looked at Jacob in amazement. "Whoa! Start from the beginning," Joe said. "Two Bears, come over here. I want you to hear this story too."

Two Bears put down the filled water bags he was carrying and joined Beth Ann by the fire.

Jacob started with the day his father was beaten by the Coopers and ended with his killing of the brothers and their flight west. Beth Ann couldn't hold back the tears when Jacob told how their parents had burned to death in the cabin fire.

Moved by her tears, Two Bears shifted closer to Beth Ann, his shoulder touching hers to show his concern. This was the most emotion Joe had ever seen him show toward a white person.

"It looks like the Cooper brothers have figured out you're headed west," Joe said.

"They didn't figure it out. They're too dumb. Their old man does all the thinking in that family," Jacob said. "They can't be sure I killed their brothers unless they found the bodies. I doubt they found then because I buried them in deep woods. My big mistake was selling their horses in Vandalia."

Jacob's Promise

"There's only a 50/50 chance of them finding the horses," Joe said. "Horses are bought and sold every day in Vandalia. Hard telling where those horses are now."

"I was sure we had everyone thinking we were headed east. I never thought they'd come looking in this direction. I'm going to spend the rest of this trip looking over my shoulder."

"Don't worry too much. After we leave Independence it'll be easier to melt into the landscape," Joe assured him. "The west is a big place, and a lot of people get lost in it. The way Ben Sutler talked about those boys, they could get themselves killed if they start that rough stuff with the wrong people."

CHAPTER 19

Ruth and Ralph Heinz didn't know river travel could be so slow. They lost count of the number of times the boat ran onto hidden sand bars that had formed since its last trip up the river to Independence. Their progress was also interrupted when the men had to get off to chop wood to keep the fires burning and the steam engine chugging along.

They stopped every night because of the danger of the boat wandering out of the river channel or missing a twist in the river that would run them aground. Ralph kept reassuring Ruth every time they were stopped that boat travel beat trying to drive a wagon from St. Louis to Independence.

After helping push the boat off a sand bar, Ralph was changing into dry clothes when he felt the throbbing vibration of the steam engine slow and then stop.

"Good God, what now?" He groaned. Both he and Ruth left their cabin to go on deck to see what the problem was this time. On their way they met a crewmember near the front of the boat and asked him why they had stopped.

"Some fallen trees jammed across the channel are blocking our way. We're gonna have to break out the axes and see if we can't chop our way through. "

"Damn, I hope we can do it without getting in the water again," Ralph said. "The skin on my body is still wrinkled and puckered from the last sand bar we pushed off. That water's cold enough to freeze a man's manhood right off."

"Ralph! Please watch your language," Ruth said.

The captain pushed the boat tight against the bank of the river and the crew tied it securely to the trees, so men had easy access to the shore.

Ralph took an axe and scrambled off the boat to get a look at the problem. Soon ten men were swinging axes at the branches of what appeared to be trees tangled together forming the giant snag. Ralph climbed out to the end of the biggest tree and started chopping at the biggest branch. He thought it looked like the one holding everything together.

The branch was at least ten inches in diameter and partially submerged. It took Ralph a dozen swings before it snapped off and went careening off in the current. There was a sharp crack and a second limb broke away.

With a jolt the trunk suddenly rolled a quarter of a turn. Feeling his feet slip on the slick bark, Ralph dropped the axe and grabbed for one of the remaining branches. Suddenly the tree lurched and rolled over pulling Ralph under water. A few seconds later his head bobbed to the surface.

He frantically grabbed onto the tree trunk and struggled to work his way toward shore. As the swirling water twisted the tree a limb hit Ralph in the back and pushed him under again.

Another branch snagged his shirt and no matter how hard he struggled and fought he couldn't get free. The strong current dragged him through the muddy river bottom and swiftly moved him and the tree trunk down the river and out of sight.

Horror stricken, Ruth stared at the swirling water where Ralph disappeared. "Someone do something!"

Men ran along the bank trying to keep up with the tree, but thick brush and a tangle of low hanging tree limbs slowed them. After fighting the tangled shoreline for a little over a hundred yards they gave up and watched the tree round a bend in the river and disappear.

The boat stayed tied to the bank while men searched both banks for a mile down the river. It was dark before the last of the men returned, without finding a trace of Ralph.

Darkness came and Ruth was still standing on the deck staring down the river where Ralph had disappeared. The captain finally approached her, "Mrs. Heinz, I think you should return to your cabin and let us bring you a hot drink and some soup.

"You're not doing yourself any good standing out on this deck in this damp wind. Your husband was a good man and a ready hand to help when he was needed, but I'm afraid the river's claimed him. I hate to add to your misery but come morning light, we'll have to move on to Independence."

A small sob escaped Ruth before she could regain control of her emotions. She took a deep breath, turned, and allowed the captain to escort her to her cabin.

"I'll have some of the ladies bring you something to eat and sit with you for the rest of the trip if you want their company," the captain said.

Ruth heard the captain talking but didn't really absorb the words he spoke. Her mind was someplace else. One minute she and Ralph were excited about their trip west and the next she was standing alone staring out at the water where he had disappeared.

The captain took her arm and escorted her to her cabin. After he seated her inside, he sent two ladies to join her carrying hot rum laced coffee and hot soup.

Ruth drank the rum-laced coffee the ladies brought. The rum brought a little color back to her cheeks, but the soup sat on the table untouched. For hours she stared at the wall without saying a word to the ladies sitting with her.

Then, as if coming out of a trance, she announced that she wanted to be alone, and asked everyone to leave. The women told her to call them if she needed anything and quietly left the cabin.

Ruth was a strong woman and had faced grief before. A little over a year ago, she had lost her three-year-old daughter and had been broken hearted for months. Only the planning of this trip had brought her out of her lethargy.

She thought it might have been the reason Ralph sold the farm, just to get her away from the things that brought back unpleasant memories. Now she had to be stronger than ever, for she was alone. Crying wouldn't bring her baby or her husband back. They were gone and she had to think of her future.

She stayed in her cabin for the last two days of the trip and paid one of the women who had sat with her to bring food to her cabin. She didn't want company while she sorted out what she needed to do. Before the boat docked, she sent for the captain and explained that she planned to return with him to St. Louis, so she would be leaving most of her luggage in the cabin.

"That's fine, Mrs. Heinz," the captain said. "But you must realize that I intend to spend only one night in Independence. I need to load cargo this afternoon and depart the first thing tomorrow morning."

"That's fine, Captain. I just have a few things to take care of in town this afternoon," Ruth explained. "I promise to be here at dawn, so I won't hold you up."

At the Independence landing, Ruth hired a buggy to take her and one suitcase to the hotel. She secured a room and unpacked writing materials. She had only two letters she needed to write and have delivered.

The first letter was to a businessman Ralph knew out in Portland, Oregon. She told him about Ralph's death and requested that he make arrangements to meet the ship carrying the merchandise Ralph had shipped and have it stored until she arrived next year to claim it.

The second letter was to the wagon train master telling him why they would not be joining him on the westward trip. She requested he carry the letter she had written to the Portland businessman with him to Oregon.

For doing this service, she told him he could keep the payment they had made for their place in the wagon train. She found a boy with a horse, who the hotel clerk said was reliable, and sent him three miles out of town to the wagon train. She agreed to pay him only when he brought back a reply from the wagon master saying the letters had been received.

She spent a restless night and was up and dressed long before daylight. She sat in the hotel coffee shop drinking coffee until the ride she had hired the day before arrived to take her to the boat.

She fought back tears when they reached the spot in the river where Ralph drowned, gritting her teeth, she turned away from the water and marched back to her cabin. She had decided to go to Illinois, contact her sister, and try once again to convince then to come with her to Oregon.

She would offer Hans half interest in the store Ralph had planned to start in Portland. Surely, knowing she had lost Ralph, along with all the trouble he was having with his neighbor, he would jump at the chance for a new start.

He could keep all the profit from the sale of the farm. The only money he would need to spend would be for a wagon and team and supplies, and she would share in that. Surely the man wouldn't pass up an opportunity like that.

Mentally Ruth tried to push the boat over the water and back to St. Louis. She was anxious to be on her way to Illinois.

CHAPTER 20

"I think we should reach Independence in about two days," Joe said. "That's just a guess. I haven't traveled the road since the first time I came out west. It's a lot easier to make the trip by boat than on horseback."

"Why didn't we take the boat this time?" Jacob asked. "I thought you were the one who wanted to go overland."

"We left St. Louis with two horses that didn't exactly belong to us," Joe said. "I didn't want to take the chance that someone might recognize the horses."

"I see what you mean about the horses, and I can see that going by boat would have been a lot easier," Jacob said. "I don't see how people driving wagons could even make this trip with all the hills, muddy roads and swollen streams that we've had trouble crossing."

"They think they're saving money by going overland, but what they find out is that by the time they get to Independence, their oxen are worn to the point they can't make the rest of the trip. They'll have to buy new teams in Independence. You can see that being on horseback really has some advantages over wagons."

A mile farther down the road, they came on two wagons with people gathered around one of them. When they got closer, they saw a young boy about four or five years old lying on the ground with a weeping woman bent over him.

"Can we be of some help?" Jacob asked before anyone else had a chance to speak.

"No, there's no help for the boy," one of the men said. "He was trying to climb on the moving wagon and fell under one of the wheels."

"It's hard to lose young ones like that," Joe said. Then without saying another word, turned his horse and rode on with Two Bears right behind him.

Beth Ann kicked her horse in the side and caught up with Joe.

"Why didn't we stay and help bury that boy?" Beth Ann asked. "That seemed like the Christian thing to do."

"You can't stop to help and sympathize with every troubled group you meet. Everyone who starts out on the trip west will encounter problems and most of them should be prepared to handle them.

"If you start involving yourself with every group you meet, you'll never make it to Oregon. What if that boy or someone else in that wagon train had a sickness?" Joe asked. "What if you got sick because you stopped to help? I'm just saying that out here on the trail you have to think of yourself first or it could mean your death."

"I never thought of it in that way," Beth Ann said in a hushed voice. "I don't know if I can really adjust to that way of thinking."

"It's the way of life out here. I want you to realize that no one is going to stop and help you if you get in a fix, so you better save your strength for your own survival."

Joe turned to Jacob. "Jacob, I don't want to always seem to be chewing on you, but you have to learn that you don't offer your help with everyone you meet. You might get yourself involved in something you'll regret."

"I guess I'm still trying to learn my way, Joe," Jacob said, his face turning pink.

The big orange sun was beginning to cast long shadows hinting it was time to stop for the day. Joe pointed to line of trees strung out across the trail in front of them. "Must be a stream up ahead." As they got closer, they could see the water between the trees.

Joe pulled his horse to a stop at the edge of the water. "We best cross first and camp on the other side. If we're going to get wet, it's better to get wet today and dry off by the fire than to wait and get wet and cold in the morning."

Recent rains had made the stream bigger and running faster than Joe had expected. Studying the water, he figured it was about 150 feet from one bank to the other. "It's hard to tell how deep this is, but you can tell it's a ford by the tracks coming out on the other bank."

"I'll go first," Two Bears said and headed down the bank and into the water. He had traveled less than twenty feet when his horse's feet left the ground and started to swim. The swift water began to push the trailing packhorse downstream, but Two Bears quickly shortened the lead rope and pulled the animal closer to him.

"Beth Ann, I think you'd better go next," Joe said. "You saw how Two Bears did it, just do the same."

Beth Ann eased her horse into the water while Jacob called out encouragement "You sure she's going to be able to do this?" Jacob whispered to Joe.

"We all have to cross and we each have to do it on our own. Beth Ann's a strong girl. She's crossed other water and she can cross this stretch."

The words had just left Joe's mouth when Beth Ann's packhorse slipped at the edge of the rushing water and rolled on to its side. Her horse began swimming toward the other bank with all its might against the dead weight of the packhorse.

Beth Ann had tied the lead rope to her saddle horn and the pull on the saddle horn from the struggling packhorse was dragging them both downstream. The packhorse suddenly rolled onto its back with all four feet sticking up out of the water. Mid-stream Beth Ann's head was just breaking the surface and so was the head of her horse.

"Unwrap the lead rope," Joe yelled. "He's going to pull you under if you don't."

Beth Ann, too frightened to move, held on to the saddle horn with both hands, while both horses were swept down steam. Suddenly, without any help from her, the rope worked itself loose from the saddle horn and the packhorse drifted away.

Beth Ann felt her horse rise under her as soon as the rope was free. Her horse struggled up the far bank with Beth Ann still doggedly hanging on to the saddle horn with both hands.

Joe and Jacob watched the packhorse tumble down the swollen stream, turning over and over, probably dead before it had gone a hundred feet. The pack broke apart and everything in it either sank or floated away on the current.

Joe nudged Jacob, "Your turn boy. You see what happened to your sister, so you be careful, and be ready to react if you get into trouble."

Jacob made sure his packhorse stayed on his upstream side as he entered the water and started across. The water was cold and by the time he reached midstream it was up to his armpits. The packhorse turned out to be a strong swimmer and Jacob had no trouble crossing.

On the other side he was met by a frightened, shivering Beth Ann, through chattering teeth she sobbed, "All our extra clothes were in that pack. We don't have anything to wear except the clothes on our backs."

Two Bears rode up beside Beth Ann and touched her on the shoulder and said, "You no drown. Always get clothes."

"He's right. You're alive. We can always get new clothes in Independence," Jacob said.

"I'd settle for just some dry clothes. I'm going to die of chills in these wet things," Beth Ann complained.

"She's right. We have to get dry as fast as we can," Joe said. "Tie up your horses and everyone go pick up fire wood. When Beth Ann's far enough apart for modesty's sake, she can wring out her clothes and come back to the fire."

Beth Ann made sure no one could see her before she stripped and twisted the water out of her clothes. Her lips were blue, and her body was covered with goose bumps. She hated having to put her wet clothes back on, but she did. Running around to gather wood warmed her some.

Joe had a roaring fire going when she came in with her load of wood.

"I made a big fire so there'll be enough room for all of us to have a space around it to dry out," Joe said.

The four of them, turned like hogs on a spit, to get dry. Almost dry, they began to unpack the horses and started preparing for the evening meal. While Beth Ann cooked, Jacob hung the wet

Jacob's Promise

blankets near the fire to dry. Joe and Two Bears went off to find more firewood.

The food was soon cooked, and everyone sat down to eat. Beth Ann joined Jacob on a log next to the fire. In a quiet voice, low enough that the others couldn't hear, she said, "Jacob, are we really going to be able to make it all the way to Oregon if we don't find Aunt Ruth?

"Look what's happened to us. Mom and Dad are dead, the cabin was burned, we almost got killed in a tornado, I was almost kidnapped, I about drowned, and the Coopers are right behind us. Independence is only the beginning of our trip. The longest part is still in front of us. How many more disasters are we going to have to face?"

"We have to take one day at a time," Jacob answered. "We can make it if we stick together. You know Aunt Ruth and Uncle Ralph will welcome us as part of their family.

"I heard Mom and Aunt Ruth talking, and Mom really wanted to go with them. If they wanted the family then, they'll welcome us now." Jacob put his arm around Beth Ann's shoulders and gave her a little squeeze. "We'll make it. Maybe the worst part of the trip is behind us."

CHAPTER 21

Ruth endured the long boat ride back to St. Louis and when she arrived, she put her trunks in storage and kept out only what she felt were the bare necessities for the trip back to her sister's farm in Illinois. She had to wait two days before there was a stage going east to Vandalia and spent the delay familiarizing herself with the businesses of St. Louis.

She knew she would need to find work when she came back this way. If she convinced Hans to sell the farm, it would take time to pack and get back to St. Louis, much too late to start for Oregon. She would have to spend the winter in either St. Louis or Independence.

She always been an accomplished seamstress and decided finding a sewing job would be her best chance of finding work. After visiting most of the dress shops in town, she picked out the one she thought was making the most high-quality fashions and approached the owner with a sample of her work.

The owner of the shop, Mrs. Olive Terhune, inspected the needlework and said, "Can you start work tomorrow? The town is growing so fast that more and more ladies are coming to the shop with newspaper pictures of the latest fashions.

"They don't want to wait for orders to be sent from back east. They want their dresses made in less than a week. I have only one other seamstress and I can't keep up."

Jacob's Promise

"I'm sorry, but I have to go back to Illinois on some business before I can start," Ruth said. "It may take three weeks. Can you hold the job for that long?"

"I really need you now, but I'm sure I'll still need someone with your expert needle skills in three weeks," Olive said. "Come see me as soon as you get back."

Ruth thanked her and returned to her room much relieved. Knowing that work was available in St. Louis took a great weight off her shoulders. She wasn't sure her finances would hold out for another year without some sort of income.

The next day, she boarded the stagecoach with seven male passengers for its scheduled trip to Vandalia, Illinois. It was so crowded two of the male passengers rode on the top of the coach with the baggage. The journey took seven long days because the coach kept getting stuck in mud holes.

When this happened all the passengers crawled out. The male passengers were forced to help push and pry the coach out of the mud holes or they would have never gotten through.

The places they stayed overnight were often cold and damp. Sometimes the food was so bad Ruth refused to eat. At the end of the trip her legs were so numb she had to be lifted down from the coach. She held on to the side coach for balance as she took her first few wobbly steps.

She paid in advance for two days at the rooming house in Vandalia, hoping she could finish her business in that time. She needed to find some sort of transportation that was going as far east as her sister's farm. She shut the door to her room, undressed and tried to wash off the dirt from the trip with the small amount of water in the pitcher and basin on her dresser.

Ruth put on her nightclothes, crawled into bed, and fell into a dreamless sleep. She awoke to the smell of bacon and discovered she had slept fourteen hours. The clock on the dresser read seven o'clock and she was starving. She dressed quickly. She knew most rooming houses had strict dining times and if you missed it, you were out of luck.

Entering the dining room, she saw a large table with five people sitting around it eating breakfast, four men and a woman. A chubby little woman came bustling out of the kitchen carrying a large platter of biscuits, her face red from the heat of the stove.

Smudges of flour dotted her nose and cheek.

"We missed you at supper last night, Missy, but guessed you were just to worn by the trip," the little woman said in a cheery voice. "You must be hungry enough to eat a horse by now. Sit yourself down and I'll bring you some coffee," She sat the platter down and hustled back to the kitchen to get the coffee pot.

Two of the gentlemen stood up, the other two remained seated. One, a skinny dark-haired lad seemed glued to the side of a pretty, rather bashful, young lady. The couple seemed to only have eyes for each other and hadn't even noticed Ruth come into the room. The other rather rough looking man shoveled eggs into his mouth while he observed her out of the corner of his eye.

"You must be the Mrs. Heinz that missed supper last night," one of the standing men said. "I'm Hamilton Jones and standing beside me is Thomas Akers. Mr. and Mrs. Wilson, newlyweds as you have probably guessed, are seated next to you. The gentleman at the far end of the table is Mr. Frank. He runs the stable just down the street. What brings you to our fair city, Mrs. Heinz?"

"I'm headed to my sister's place, sixty miles east of here, and looking for a way to get there, since no stage coach goes in that direction."

"Thomas might know of something. He travels all over the country east of here. Any suggestions, Thomas," Hamilton asked.

"Going east is harder to do than going west. It seems almost all the traffic is headed west these days. Your best bet is to find a freight wagon headed in that direction. What town are you trying to reach," Thomas asked.

"I'm headed to my sister's place on Goose Prairie."

"I know that area well," Thomas said. "I sell pots and pans and such and I sharpen knives and saws, so I know most of the farmers out there."

"Oh, good. Then you probably know my sister and her husband. Katherine and Hans Hesser."

Thomas sat very quiet for a few moments trying to think of a way to tell Ruth the unhappy thing he had heard when he had last passed through Goose Prairie.

"Mrs. Heinz, I don't know how long it has been since you last saw or heard from your sister's family," he said carefully. "But my guess is that you haven't heard about the tragedy. It seems there was a terrible fire at the Hessers' place, and the cabin was destroyed."

The color drained out of Ruth's face. "Are the Hessers okay? Where are they now?"

"From what I understand, the two kids got out, but their parents were not that lucky. A man at the general store said that the kids packed up and headed out to Virginia,"

"You must have heard wrong. The kids don't have anyone back east to go to. I'm the nearest relative they have."

"There's more to the story," he continued. "Old Tom Cooper was in town the day I was there, and he was having a fit. He claimed the Hesser boy killed his two sons and he wanted the law after them. He buried a piece of an arm and a hand that he said his boys took away from a coyote. He swore it was the hand of one of his boys. The store owner said Cooper sent his other two boys west to hunt the Hessers down."

"Jacob and Beth Ann are headed west," Ruth gasped. "They'll be looking for me and Ralph. Oh, my goodness. I must have passed them when I left Independence and headed east."

The man at the end of the table looked down the table at Ruth. "I may have saw them two kids, a boy about seventeen or eighteen and an auburn-haired girl a little younger."

He took another bite of food, chewed then said. "They asked me to sell a couple of horses they were pulling behind their wagon. I sold the two horses and fixed up a cover for their wagon before they set out. Not more than two weeks after they left, two big boys named Cooper showed up asking about them.

"They wanted to see the horses I sold, but the man who bought the horses was long gone. I think they still may be in town." He turned his face back to his plate ignoring others at the table and started shoveling food in his mouth again.

Ruth's mind was in turmoil. Her sister was dead. Jacob and Beth Ann were headed west, probably looking for her and Ralph, and two toughs were looking for Jacob. She jumped up from the table. "Mr. Hamilton, When does the next stage coach leave for St. Louis? I need to be on it."

"The one you came in on is due for its return trip this morning," Hamilton said. "You go pack and I'll run down and have them hold it for you. Of course, it may be full, and you might have to wait a week," he warned.

"Oh, please try. I'll hurry as fast as I can."

Both she and Hamilton bolted out of the room. She went upstairs to pack and be ready for the stagecoach station. Ruth stuffed her few belongings into her suitcase, grabbed her purse and rushed out of the boarding house. The landlady came into the dining room with Ruth's breakfast only to find her gone. "Where's Mrs. Heinz?" she asked.

"Gone back to St. Louis if she can get on the stage," Adam Frank said between bites. "Don't throw them eggs out, I'll eat 'em."

"But she's paid for two day stay. I just don't understand all this rush of people to go out west."

At the stage office Ruth could tell by Hamilton's face that he had bad news. "The coach is full and there isn't any more room."

Ruth was not to be denied. She ran up to the coach and approached the passengers. "I'll give three dollars to the man who'll give me his seat and ride up on top with the baggage," she said.

A woman on the coach jammed her elbow into her son's side and made him get out of the coach. "He'll ride on the top," she said. "I'll take the three dollars to hold for him."

Ruth smiled at the little drama and, with relief, boarded the coach for St. Louis to start her search for Jacob and Beth Ann.

CHAPTER 22

Jacob pointed to the smoke rising on the horizon and turned to Joe. "What do you figure is causing all that smoke? Is it a prairie fire?"

"Too early in the year for a prairie fire," answered Joe. "That smoke is coming from all the campfires around Independence. We should be seeing the outskirts of town by noon time."

"It'd be nice to have a hot bath in a tub and some new clothes to wear," Beth Ann said.

"My hope is we've gotten here in time to find Aunt Ruth and Uncle Ralph," Jacob said.

"Don't get your hopes too high," Joe warned him. "There's a mess of people passing through here and I think you'll be mighty lucky if any of them remember seeing your folks. If your aunt and uncle's train has left, no one in Independence is likely to remember them."

"They had to buy supplies so they had to deal with the trade people in town and some of them might remember Aunt Ruth's red hair," Jacob said.

"Those shopkeepers have dealt with hundreds of people this spring. If you had a picture of them, you might have a chance. I hate to crush your hopes, but without a picture, I think you may be out of luck."

"That could be true, but I won't be satisfied until I have tried everything I can to find them."

"You know if you don't find them, you two are welcome to travel with me and Two Bears until we reach Laramie. At Laramie we turn north and head for Two Bears' summer tribal grounds. You and Beth Ann will be on your own from there."

"You and Two Bears know how much we've depended on you in the tough going. We wouldn't think of leaving Independence without you."

Near the middle of the day they began passing pastures filled with oxen and mules. There were long sheds at the end of each pasture holding hay, corn, and oats for the herds of animals. The air was heavy with the overpowering stench of animal waste.

Beth Ann covered her mouth and nose with her neckerchief and kicked her horse into a fast trot to get past the smell as fast as she could. She hurried ahead and waited by a shed where wagons were being put together until the others caught up with her.

She could hear the ringing sound of the blacksmith shaping the metal rims for the wagon wheels, and carpenters pounding wagons together. It was so different from the weeks of quiet on the prairie. The choking black smoke from the blacksmith had replaced the stench of manure.

Reaching the first commercial buildings, Beth Ann stopped the first person she met to ask where she could get a bath. The stranger pointed to a building at the end of the street that offered twenty-five-cent hot baths and for another twenty-five-cents, a laundress would wash, and iron dry her clothes while she bathed.

"After riding through the stink of the feed lots and the blacksmith's smoke my clothes and hair smell like a cow that was caught in a barn fire. I can even taste it," Beth Ann said.

"Let's go out to the other side of town to find a campsite," Joe said. "Then Beth Ann can come back and get her bath."

After the animals were unpacked and staked out to graze, Jacob and Beth Ann mounted up to go back into town.

"You two might as well eat some decent food while you're in town. Me and Two Bears will go after you get back," Joe shouted after them.

"After we eat, I'm going to go down to the boat dock while you bathe," Jacob said. "Then we'll go shopping for some new clothes."

Jacob's Promise

"Aren't you going to take a bath too? You stink as badly as I do."

"I have too much running around to do. I'll wait and come back in with Joe and Two Bears. Remember when you're taking your bath to keep that money belt in sight. You're carrying half of all the money we have."

Beth Ann jerked her horse to a dead stop and through gritted teeth said, "Jacob Hesser, that's the one hundredth time you have warned me about the money. If you don't trust me with it, then you can just keep it all yourself."

"Now don't get huffy. I'm just trying to be careful. It has nothing to do with trust."

"You take care of your half and I'll take care of mine. You're the one that'll be running around down at the river with all the riff raff that hangs around at the docks. Where are the boat docks anyway?"

"Joe said they're about three miles from town. They were smart enough to build the town up here above the flood plain."

They tied their horses in a side street and walked to the café. At the café entrance Beth Ann stopped and looked down at her soiled clothes. "We should have bathed first," she whispered to Jacob. "I'll bet everyone can smell us."

"All I smell is food and I'm not about to leave until I'm full," Jacob answered. "Come on."

Later, his appetite satisfied, Jacob pushed back from the table. "Time to get moving. You go get your bath while I head for the docks." Outside he mounted his horse and left for the boat docks.

"You take care of yourself, and don't be gone too long," Beth Ann called after him. "I don't like sitting out on the street by myself."

At the docks, Jacob walked over to a row of buildings that looked like they contained offices. He talked to every ticket agent in every steamboat company, questioning them about passenger lists. The agents all told him the same thing: they didn't keep lists, just the number of passengers. Any lists they made they gave to the captain of the boat so he would know who was on board for that trip.

Jacob trudged back to where he started and sat on a coil of rope next to an old man smoking a pipe.

"Do you work on the dock?" Jacob asked.

"No, son. You see that buggy and team parked over there by the fence? That's mine, I come down to meet the boats and ferry folks into town that need a ride. You need a ride into town? It only costs fifteen cents."

"No. I'm down here looking for information about my aunt and uncle. Ruth and Ralph Heinz. You didn't happen to hear of them, did you?" Jacob asked.

The old gentleman listened while Jacob did his best to describe what they looked like.

"I'm sorry, son, but I can't recall seeing anyone that fit your description. I did hear a crewmember talking about a man named Ralph that fell off a boat and drowned about a week or two ago," the old man said.

"Was his name Ralph Heinz?" Jacob asked.

"I didn't hear no last name, and they didn't mention any woman so it could be the man you're looking for or any of the river rats that come up and down the river."

Uncle Ralph was a pretty cautious man and wasn't likely to get himself in any position to fall off a boat, but the thought lingered in Jacob's mind.

"Sorry I can't be more help, son," the old man said.

"That's okay. You're not the first one I've talked to that hasn't heard of them."

"Don't waste your time, boy. People in the wagon trains forming out west of town now won't know anything about those that have already gone. They're all anxious to get going so they can get over the mountains before the snows start."

Later Jacob picked Beth Ann up at the bathhouse and took her to buy their new clothes, then accompanied her back to the campsite where Joe and Two Bears were waiting. When they arrived at camp a dejected Jacob told Joe about his failure in getting any information on his trip to the boat docks.

"I think we're wasting our time looking. I have a gut feeling they've already left for Oregon."

"If that's the case we might as well get the rest of our supplies and leave first thing in the morning," Joe said. "But first I 'm hungry enough to eat a horse. Come on, Two Bears, let's head for town."

Jacob's Promise

"Aren't you two going to bathe?" Beth Ann asked.

Joe laughed. "After you left, we found a woman doing laundry and paid her to use her tub. And at half the price you paid."

"I'm going back with you," Jacob said. "I didn't get a chance to get a bath. That is, if Beth Ann thinks she'll be all right here alone."

"Go on and get your bath, you need it worse than I need company. I'll be fine. There are enough people around us that if I need help, I'm sure someone would hear me. If all else fails I still have the old shot gun we carried from home."

"I think I'll leave my money belt with you and just take enough for my bath. That way I won't have to worry about it while I soak away all the stink."

It was dark by the time they reached town. They tied their horses at the end of an alley and agreed to meet back at the horses in a couple of hours. Jacob left for his bath, while Joe and Two Bears headed for the café.

"Don't wash off too much skin trying to get all that dirt off," Joe called after Jacob.

Jacob laughed at Joe's comment and headed for the bathhouse. The bath had been full earlier in the day, but Jacob had it to himself now. He soaked until the water cooled and when he had dried off, he found his clean clothes waiting for him. Dressed in clean clothes, he left the bathhouse with time to kill before he was to meet Joe and Two Bears. He found a bench and entertained himself by watching the parade of people and wagons pass by. It looked like the whole country was heading west.

The day had been busy one, and Jacob, wearier than he thought, dozed off. He woke with a start, wondering how long he had been asleep. He jumped up and headed for the horses.

Joe and Two Bears shopped for some extra ammunition, before making their way to the café. At the café they lingered over their meal, which included two pieces of pie and numerous cups of hot coffee. Filled to the brim with good food, they got up, paid their bill, and started back to the horses to wait for Jacob.

They were standing by the horses quietly talking when they were interrupted by two rough looking drunks stumbling down the alley toward them. The drunks stopped when the saw Joe and Two Bears.

The larger of the two was a big rawboned man with an ugly scar that ran down across one eye and the side of his face. With a grin that grotesquely twisted his face into an ugly sneer he said, "Well, looky here. We got a squaw man and his little pet Injun."

A third drunk staggered down the alley from the opposite direction and was headed their way.

"Hey, Zeke, look what we found hiding down here in the alley," the scar-face said as he blocked the path of Joe and Two Bears. "A stinking Injun and a squaw man who stinks just like an Injun. What do you think we ought to do with a white man that loves Injuns?"

Zeke, the last drunk to come down the alley, bent down and picked up a piece of wood lying next to one of the buildings. Joe and Two Bears stepped away from the horses to have room for the attack they were sure was coming.

"My partner was killed by a stinking Indian and now it's my turn to get even," scar-face said as he lunged for Two Bears. Two Bears drew his knife and turned toward his attacker. When he turned, Zeke swung the piece of wood and struck Two Bears a solid blow to the ribs.

When Two Bears doubled over, Zeke swung the club again delivering a crushing blow to the back of Two Bears' head. Scarface pushed the falling body of Two Bears aside and lunged at Joe.

The knife in Joe's hand slashed out and struck the big man, a glancing cut just below his rib cage. The man screamed and stumbled back against the side of a building holding his side.

As Two Bears lay sprawled on the ground the man swinging the wooden club hit him in the head again and again. The third man lowered his head and charged at Joe, but Joe nimbly stepped aside and cracked the heel of his knife into his skull.

Before the man could get up Joe gave him a swift kick in the groin. The man folded into a ball groaning. The scar-faced man with the knife wound screamed, "Kill that Injun-loving bastard, Zeke!"

The club swinging drunk took two steps toward Joe but stopped when he saw the knife Joe was holding.

Jacob's Promise

"If you want to live, you'll take your two friends and get out of here," Joe snarled.

The man just grinned at Joe as he drew a gun out of the back of his belt. "You ain't cuttin' nobody, mister," he said, smiling.

Jacob, coming around the corner of the building and into the alley froze when he saw Two Bears lying lifeless on the ground and a man pointing a gun at Joe. He flattened himself against the building and crept down the alley, trying to get to a place where he could help.

The man Joe had kicked had crawled over to the one with the stab wound and pulled himself to his feet.

"You can kill him any time you like, Zeke, but make him die slow," the wounded man said.

The gun roared in the man's hand. Joe screamed, grabbed his knee and toppled over, face first into the ground. The shot jolted Jacob into action. He charged the last few feet down the alley and crashed into the back of the shooter.

The gun flew out of the shooter's hand and landed in the dirt near Jacob's head. Jacob grabbed the gun, rolled over and shot as the man lunged at him. The man died while reaching out just inches from Jacob's face. Jacob turned the gun on the two men standing by the building. His hands were trembling so violently it was hard for him to hold the gun steady.

"I don't know who you are, but if you aren't out of my sight in the next minute, I'm going to kill both of you," Jacob screamed.

Their hands in the air the two men backed out of the alley and around the corner of the building.

When Jacob was sure they were gone, he ran to Joe and Two Bears. The shots had drawn people to the end of the alley. The braver ones eased down the alley to see what had happened.

Shaking so hard he could hardly talk, Jacob managed to ask some of the men to help him. "Help me get them to a doctor. Hurry!"

He followed those carrying the two friends not realizing he was still had the gun dangling from his hand. At the doctor's Jacob had to explain that he wasn't the one who shot Joe. The doctor seemed doubtful until Joe, through gritted teeth, explained what happened.

The doctor did a quick examination of Two Bears and shook

his head. "I can't do anything for this one. The back of his head is crushed, and he's gone to meet his maker."

He turned to Joe and started cutting away his pant leg above the knee. One look at the mangled knee was enough for him to know that the leg could not be saved.

"The thigh bone is okay, but the knee cap and the bone below the knee is shattered." The doctor said in a quiet voice to Jacob. "There's no way I can put them together again. The leg below the knee has to come off."

Jacob nodded that he understood.

"I don't think you'll want to be here when I take the leg off. It's bad enough for a boy to see as much as you've seen. Go back to your camp. You can come back and see him in the morning."

"Jacob," Joe called, his voice weak. "Come closer. I need to talk to you before you go." Sweat beaded on Joe's brow from his effort to talk through the pain. "Bend down so you can hear me. Take Two Bears' and my horses to the stable and board them for me."

"Joe don't worry about anything now. Just get yourself fixed," Jacob pleaded.

"Damn it boy, shut up and listen. Those two men you let get away are not going to rest until they get a chance to get you for shooting their buddy. You take our two pack horses and the supplies along with yours. You should have enough to get to Oregon."

"Joe, we're not leaving without you."

"You pig headed tenderfoot, listen to me. Take the horses and get out of here at first light. It'll be a month or more before I'll be in any shape to go anywhere." Joe stopped, grimacing in pain. "By that time, it'll be too late for you to make it over the mountains before the snows start. If you don't go, you're going to have to face those other two men you saw in the alley. You might even have to face a court for shooting that man. If enough lies are told you could end up on the end of a rope. Now do what I say and get out of here."

Exhausted, Joe fell back on the bed and closed his eyes. Jacob wasn't sure if Joe was asleep or if he had passed out.

The doctor pushed past Jacob and pulled a knife and saw out of a cabinet beside the bed. "He's out cold. Let's get that leg off before he wakes."

He turned to Jacob. "Get out of here, young man. You don't need to see this. Go back to camp like he told you."

Trying to hold back tears, Jacob stumbled back to the alley to get the horses and started back to camp.

CHAPTER 23

Willie Cooper woke up with a start and looked around trying to figure out where he was. Three walls were bars and the brick wall beside him had a barred window. His head pounded as if rocks were bouncing around in it. He tried to sit up, but fell back on the hard cot, his head swirling.

He closed the one good eye that worked and slowly brought his hand up to his cheek and felt the lump on his jaw. He tried again to open his eyes, but only the left one moved. The right one was swollen shut. He closed his left eye, hoping the darkness would make the pounding in his head stop.

Willie vaguely remembered jumping in to a fight to help his brother, but his hangover blocked out the rest of his memory. Loud banging on the bars of his cell sent an electric shock through Willie's head.

"Hey in there. Wake up. You ready to pay your fine and get out of here, or are you staying for breakfast?"

Willie opened his good eye and saw the jailer standing outside the bars. "What's for breakfast?"

"Beans."

Willie's stomach rolled over at the very thought of beans for breakfast. "I'll skip breakfast. Where's my brother?"

"He's out front waiting for you. He says you have to pay the fine with your own money cause he paid with his."

Jacob's Promise

Willie, moving with the speed of chilled mush, used the bars of his cell to pull himself up. He rested there until his head stopped spinning before pulling himself to a standing position. Several minutes passed before he was steady enough to take his first tentative steps.

The jailer unlocked the cell door and marched Willie down the hall to the sheriff's office. The sheriff looked up from the papers he was studying and squinted at Willie.

"Drunk and disorderly," the sheriff said. "That'll cost you five dollars."

Willie dug the money out of his pocket and dropped it on the desk.

"I told your brother and I'll tell you. If I catch you two drunks again, I'm going to keep you locked up for a week." When Willie nodded his head, indicating he understood, a bolt of pain bounced around inside his skull.

The two brothers left the jail and stood on the walkway in front of it, squinting into the morning sunshine through blood-shot eyes.

"You sure got us into a hell of a fix, Simon," Willie said.

"That guy hit me first," Simon barked back.

"Only because you took a swing at him, you idiot." Willie winced as the memory of the fight came back to him. "We better stay out of saloons for a while or we're going to be broke. We've stayed in Vandalia too long anyway. We should've left the minute the stable man told us the Hessers were headed west."

"We still aren't sure it's them since we didn't find Sam's and Eddie's horses."

"Pa said he was sure the Hesser kid shot Sam and Eddie in the back. You want to be the one that goes back and tells him we gave up looking because we couldn't find the damn horses? He sent us out to even the score, and we had better do it. Besides," Willie continued. "Those Hesser kids know too much about their cabin burning for our own good."

"How's your money holdin' up?" Simon asked, changing the subject.

"If we stop drinkin' so much and stay out of jail, we should be okay. If Pa found out we spent our money on beer he'd beat us half to death."

"Well, you tell me how Pa's going to do all the chores and the spring plowin' if we're runnin' around out west lookin for the Hesser kids?" Simon asked.

"You wanna be home plowin'? If you do, just turn around and go home and face Pa. I'm gonna buy a few more supplies, pack up and head for St. Louis." With that, Willie turned and started down the street with Simon following meekly behind him.

By noontime the brothers had managed to get some food to stay down without being sick. They loaded their pack horses and wearily headed west out of town. The May sun had come out and the combination of humid heat and the bouncing of the horses made the brothers ride a miserable one.

"If I ever get drunk again, I hope someone shoots me," Simon moaned. "My head feels five times its normal size and this horse must have one leg shorter than the other to jar me the way it is."

"Think of how bad it woulda hurt after Pa got through bangin' on it if he'd knowed you'd got drunk and been throwed in jail," Willie said.

The third day out of Vandalia, the brothers came upon the stagecoach to St. Louis. One of its wheels was off, and two men were trying to lift one corner of the stage while the third man held the wheel ready to slip it on the axle.

The two men struggled but couldn't get the coach's axle high enough to fit onto the hub. The brothers sat on their horses and watched the struggle without offering any help. The man holding the wheel looked up at the brothers in disgust.

"You going to sit watching all day or are you going to make a little effort and climb down off your horses and give us a hand?"

"People wantin' favors should watch their mouth," Simon sneered.

"So, are you gonna ask nice like or should we ride on?" Willie added.

Ruth Heinz was sitting under the shade of a scraggly tree a little off to the side of the road and heard the conversation begin to get nasty. Fearing that it would escalate and leave them stranded until some other help came along, she got up to see if she could stop a fight.

She walked up behind the Cooper boys' horses and said, in what she hoped was her sweetest voice, "Oh, it's so good to see two strong gentlemen who have come along just in time to rescue us."

Willie and Simon were shocked by her sudden appearance and from ingrained habit jerked their hats off their heads in unison.

"We didn't know there were ladies present, ma'am," Willie said. His cheeks reddened a little in embarrassment, because he couldn't remember if he had used cuss words when he was talking to the struggling men.

"You can see we women and that little boy are no help at all," Ruth said in a plaintive voice.

The brothers looked over at the tree where the passengers were sitting and saw a crippled old man, and the woman with her ten-year-old son. Without another word, the brothers climbed down off their horses and in minutes had the wheel firmly on the axle.

Those resting in the shade got up and started boarding the stage the minute the wheel was firmly in place. Willie turned to Ruth and asked, "Where you all headed?"

"This stage is headed for St. Louis, but some of the people are headed for Independence to join wagon trains," Ruth answered.

"This Independence, is it the only place wagon trains start?" Willie asked.

"It's the only one I know of," Ruth said. "Is that where you are headed?"

"If that's where all the wagon trains head west, I guess that's where we may be goin too," Willie said.

"How are the roads the other side of St. Louis?" Simon shouted up to the driver.

"Ain't no roads. Most folks take the riverboat up the Missouri. Takes less time and you don't wear out your horses before you start west," the driver called back as he slapped the reins and the coach jerked to a start.

"Thank you for helping out," Ruth called from the moving stage. "You've been real gentlemen."

The brothers sat and watched the stage pull out and head down the road. "Come on, Willie. Don't just sit there. Let's get a move on," Simon said.

"Let them get out ahead. I don't want to get roped into helping them again if they get stuck in some mud hole. Let's get off the road and make our own trail until we know we're ahead of them," Willie said.

"That pretty red headed lady called us gentlemen. Think we'll ever see her again?" Simon asked.

"Not if I can help it," Willie said as he punched his horse with his heels and headed off and angled away from the road.

CHAPTER 24

The crackling of the campfire was the only sound to be heard when Jacob finished telling Beth Ann about Joe's injury and Two Bears death. She sat stunned, tears forming in her eyes.

"There's more to this that I haven't told you yet," Jacob said, breaking the silence. "I shot and killed the man who shot Joe."

"You were in the fight too? You could have been killed. You said there were three men what happened to the other two?"

"I was so shaken by the fight I let them go. After I found out they killed Two Bears, I wished I had shot them all."

"Two Bears killed. Joe shot. The Coopers burned our cabin. How can people be so evil," Beth Ann asked, one question piling onto another.

Jacob didn't seem to hear Beth Ann's questions. "Joe said we should get away from here as fast as we can. Those men I let get away may come looking for me."

"We can't leave Joe after all he has done for us."

"This is one time we have to think of our own safety."

"Can't you go to the law and have those men arrested," Beth Ann asked.

"No. The law may even be looking for me because of the shooting. If the law held me for trial, we'd never have a chance to catch Aunt Ruth. I could be killed by the men I let go if I stayed. And don't forget the Coopers are getting closer every day."

"Isn't there some other way to get out of this?"

"No. We can't take the chance."

Beth Ann listened with her face buried in her hands. "I can't believe Two Bears is dead."

They sat in silence for over an hour before they moved to their beds and crawled under the blankets, but neither of them got any sleep. In the early, still dark, morning hours Jacob heard Beth Ann tossing and turning, "Are you awake?" He called out softly.

"Yes, I can't stop thinking about Two Bears and Joe. "

"Why don't we get up, get packed and get out of here," Jacob said

They struggled in the dark to load the pack animals and saddle their horses. Jacob felt he was fortunate that his sister was at home around animals and could saddle her own horse. She was always willing and able to take on her share of work.

Not too long after sun up, they reached the first stream they would have to ford that day.

"Joe said the first creek we came to would be Blue Creek and then in about fifteen or sixteen miles, we'd hit Indian Creek. He said Blue Creek had an easy ford, but we'd have to deal with steep banks on the other side of Indian Creek."

At Indian Creek Jacob saw what Joe meant by the creek having steep banks.

"You cross first," he told Beth Ann. "I'll put a rope on your pack horse to make sure it doesn't get pulled down stream. I'll follow after I see you safe on the other side."

He watched Beth Ann get to the other bank and was ready to cross himself when he looked up and saw two Indians on their ponies standing on a bluff above the creek.

Jacob kicked his horse in the ribs and eased down the bank while trying to keep the Indians in sight. The riverbank was slick with mud, and the second of his two packhorses lost its footing and fell. It skidded past the lead packhorse and landed in the water on its side. In its struggle to get up, the pack slipped, unbalancing the horse so it couldn't regain its feet.

Jacob jumped off his horse and into waist-deep water. He held the horse's head above the water and calmed the frightened animal. Once he had the animal under control, he pushed the pack back in place and helped the horse to stand. He tightened the cinches holding the pack in place before he remounted to cross the stream.

"All we need is to lose our supplies again out here in the middle of nowhere," Jacob said when he finally reached Beth Ann. "Did you see the Indians? I lost track of them when the horse fell."

"What Indians?" Beth Ann asked, twisting her head one direction and then the other.

"Before I started across, I saw two Indians on the bluff on this side of the creek. Joe said we might run into Pawnee between here and Laramie."

"How dangerous are they?" Beth Ann asked staring at the top of the bluff.

"They can be dangerous, but usually all they want to do is steal horses. They would have to show up just when we're about to make camp. Now I'm going to have to stay up all night and guard the horses."

"We can take turns. You watch half the night, and I'll watch the other half," Beth Ann volunteered.

"What would you do if you saw Indians stealing the horses? I don't think you've ever fired a gun in your life."

"I can learn," she said stubbornly.

"I wish we had enough ammunition so I could teach you, but we don't so forget about being a guard."

Jacob stood night watch the first night, but by the second night he was so exhausted he had to relent and let Beth Ann take her turn at guard duty.

"Sit right beside me and if you hear the slightest noise wake me," Jacob instructed. They hadn't seen any sign of the Indians for two days, but Beth Ann insisted on keeping their guard rotation just to be safe.

They had been pushing the horses hard and when they reached the Kansas River. Jacob took one look at the wide expanse of water and said. "I think we'd better camp on this side of the river for a couple of days. We need to let the animals rest before we ask them to swim across."

"Animals aren't the only ones who need rest." Beth Ann slumped forward in the saddle.

"Joe said to get into Oregon we have to reach a gap in the mountains called South Pass by the middle of August, before the snows come. We're still pretty early and if we keep up this pace, we'll be faster than any wagon train. We can wait on South Pass for Aunt Ruth's wagon train to come through."

They slipped off the horses and stretched their stiff legs. "You sit and rest a spell while I tend the horses," Jacob said. "Then I'll fetch some firewood while you unpack your cooking things."

Darkness had fallen by the time they had cleaned the plates from the evening meal. Without another word they slipped beneath their blankets and were soon fast asleep, both too exhausted to think about standing guard.

After breakfast the next day, Jacob took some extra time tending to the horses. He rubbed them down with a currycomb and pulled off burrs stuck to their fetlocks.

He checked for abrasions on the horses' flanks and legs and medicated those he found.

"While you work with the horses, I'm going down to the river and wash some clothes. When it gets a little warmer, I'm going to take a bath, if the river isn't too cold. You could use one too," Beth Ann laughed.

That afternoon Beth Ann braved the cold river water and stood knee-deep soaping her body and her hair. She held her breath and fell backward into the water to rinse off. She bounced up gasping from the shock. Shivering she rushed to the bush where her towel was hanging and started to dry herself off.

On a bluff a little way down the river, unknown to Beth Ann, two men watched.

"Am I dreamin' or is that a naked white woman down there in the river?" one man asked the other.

"You're not dreamin'," the other man replied. "How about we pay her a visit tonight and introduce ourselves?"

"I thought we were gonna avoid people until we got to Laramie," the first man said.

"Where's yer head? Didn't ya see the packhorses they had with them? We left Independence so fast we didn't bring enough to last the two of us more than a week. Besides I didn't know there was a woman travelin with those packhorses."

"I thought it was two men. After seeing that sweet young thing down there in the water makes me realize how long it has been since I've been with a woman," the second man said with a smile.

"I take it ya ain't counting that Indian gal a couple of months back."

"Indians don't count. Besides she weren't a woman, she weren't over twelve years old," the second man growled. "I want someone that looks more like a woman than she did."

"Well, that Indian gal's pappy was out lookin for you."

"Where'd ya hear that? He don't have any idea who got to her. She was in the woods a half mile from her camp when I caught her."

"Well, I tell you he's lookin for you. A passel of Indians come up on a group of us outside of Independence a few weeks back and the girl's daddy was leadin' the bunch.

"He was madder than hell and we thought we were all going to get scalped. He spoke a little English and even knew your name was Jewel Peters. To save our hides one of the men said he knew ya and that ya was headed fer Independence the last time he saw ya."

"Knowin' my name ain't gonna to help any Indian find me," he laughed. "You worry too much, Jack."

"He may not be following you, but it's one more worry along with the killin' of that Indian back in Independence. Zeke shooting that squaw man didn't help either. We were lucky to get out of town before the law started lookin fer us," Jack said.

"The law ain't gonna bother about a dead Indian."

"What about the squaw man? You were the one yelling for Zeke to shoot him," Jack said.

"Just forget about Independence and think of all the fun we're gonna have tonight with the sweet little lady we saw in the river," Jewel said.

CHAPTER 25

Jacob was leaning against the trunk of a tree watching the horses graze when he saw Beth Ann come up from the river wearing a change of clothes with a towel wrapped around her hair. She hung the wet towel over a bush to dry and sat down beside Jacob.

"I know this sounds silly, but while I was taking my bath, I had the feeling someone was watching me. Do you think the Indians are back?"

"The Indians really have you worried, don't they?"

"I guess that's it, but it gives me the willies to think I'm being watched."

"Would it make you feel better if I saddled up one of the horses and scouted around a little to see if I can find some tracks?"

"No. It's just me, I guess. Even so, I'll be glad to get across the river and on our way again. The hills around here could hide a whole tribe of Indians, and we'd never know it."

"Just sit here and take it easy for a while. I need to move the horses. You better rest while you can. It may be a week before we stop to rest again."

Four eyes followed Jacob as he staked the horses out on a new patch of grass.

"Did ya see what fine lookin' animals they had?" Jack asked.

"I weren't lookin' at the animals, I was lookin at who was

stakin' them out. It's just a boy, and I thought we were gonna have a man to deal with. This is gonna be easier than I thought."

"Did ya see where the gal went?" Jack asked.

"She went over by that tree on the other side of the horses."

"Let's go do 'em now," Jack said.

"Don't be in a rush, the boy's too far away. Later when they're asleep we'll sneak into their camp. Let's go back and get somethin' to eat."

"A good hot mess of bacon sounds good to me," Jack said.

"No fires and no bacon cookin'. The smell and smoke might give us away. But I don't think we have to watch them. They ain't gonna go anywhere today."

When they were far enough away to stand, Jack saw Jewel grab his side as he straightened up. "Still hurt where that squaw man cut ya?" Jack asked.

"I tore it a little with all that crawlin' around we been doin'," Jewel answered.

"You're lucky ya had enough fat on yer belly that the knife didn't cut deep enough to hit somethin to bleed ya bad."

"Yeah, but it still hurts like hell if I move too sudden."

They secured the horses when they reached camp and broke out some beef jerky. With nothing to do they stretched out in the warm afternoon sun and dozed. Jewel was the first to awaken when he heard the horses pawing the ground.

Groaning with the effort, he reached over and shook Jack awake. "Jack. Get up and go move the horses. They've chewed the grass down to the roots around their stakes and are eatin' dirt. Their gittin' antsy and I don't want 'em to start squalin' and give us away," Jewel ordered.

"Why do I always have to do all the work? Why don't ya git off yer ass once in a while?"

"If yer side hurt like mine, ya'd not have to ask. It'd kill me to pull up those stakes. Now go on and do what I say. While yer workin', keep thinkin' of the good food we'll have when we get over to those tenderfoots' camp. Ya can think of the food while I think of the fun we're gonna have with that pretty lady we saw down at the river."

When Jack returned from moving the horses, he sat down by Jewel and watched the afternoon sun disappear below the horizon.

A full moon rose to light the night sky. Though darkness had settled in Jewel made no move to get up.

"Come on, Jewel, my guts are chewin' on my gizzard. Hear my stomach growlin'? Let's git goin'."

"Chew on some more jerky or whatever ya need to do to stop that noise. If yer stomach gives us way, I'll shoot ya," Jewel snapped

"They're not gonna hear my stomach. Why are we waitin? It's dark and my bet is they're already asleep. Let's get the horses and go," Jack said.

"Okay, okay. Stop yer naggin'. Just keep the noise down. We'll walk the horses down to the trees behind their camp and tie them there. I don't want to git too close and have the horses start callin' to each other."

They rode as close as they dared and left the horses. Dismounting, they walked until they were about fifty yards from Jacob and Beth Ann's camp. They crept forward, crawling the last ten yards. Jewel tapped Jack on the shoulder and pointed at Jacob, asleep by the trunk of a tree. Beth Ann sat beside him with the rifle across her knees.

"She looks like she's half asleep, "Jewel whispered.

They laid there another fifteen minutes watching Beth Ann's head tilt forward and then snap back up with a start.

Jewel motioned for Jack to go to one side of the tree and take care of Jacob, while he went to the other side to grab Beth Ann. Reaching the back of the tree Jewel rose to his knees. He stretched out his arm and clamped his hand over Beth Ann's mouth, pinning her to the tree trunk. She kicked out in surprise and bumped Jacob's leg. He sat up with a start and found a gun pressed against the side of his neck.

"Tie him to the tree, Jack." Jewel pulled Beth Ann away from Jacob's side and took his hand off her mouth. Beth Ann let out a scream the minute his hand was gone.

Jewel threw back his head and laughed. "Scream all you want, honey, ain't nobody gonna to hear you out here but the bats and the owls."

He took Beth Ann roughly by the arm and pulled her over near the fire and threw her down. He added wood until the flames leaped two feet in the air. "I want a lot of light so I can get a good look at ya, girl."

"Ya want me to shoot the kid or leave him tied to the tree?"

Jewel turned and looked at Jacob for the first time. "Well, I'll be damned. Jack do you know who you have tied up over there? That's the little bastard that come into the alley and shot Zeke."

"Want me to kill him?" Jack asked, cocking his pistol.

"Not yet. Let him see the fun we are going to have with his girlfriend first. Then I'll figger how he's going to die."

"Shoot me, but leave my sister alone," Jacob yelled.

"So, she's yer sister? Well, don't worry. We ain't gonna kill yer sister if she's nice to us. She's no good to us dead. We plan to keep her as long as she does what she's told," Jewel snarled.

Jacob strained at the ropes binding him, but they were too tight, and all his struggling did was tear the flesh on his wrists.

"Let her go. Take anything you want, but just don't harm her," Jacob begged.

"Shut up, boy. She's what we want, along with your horses and supplies. Now keep yer mouth shut and watch and see how nice I'm gonna be to yer sister." He turned to Jack. "If he keeps yapping, kick him in the head until he shuts up."

Jack nodded that he understood, but he never took his eyes off Beth Ann.

Jewel turned to Beth Ann, "Git up and git over on the other side of the fire, girl, where I can see ya better."

Beth Ann struggled slowly to her feet and stood, too paralyzed with fear to move.

"Every time ya don't do what I tell ya that there brother of your'n is gonna pay for it. Jack give the kid a kick in the side so she gits what I mean."

Jack put down the food he had been eating and viciously kicked Jacob in the ribs.

"Now ya see how things are gonna be. Ya git the idea or do ya wanna see Jack give him another kick?"

The sound of the breath rushing out of Jacob from the kick shook Beth Ann. Trembling violently she could hardly stand, Beth Ann, her arm in Jewel's vice like grip, shuffled closer to the fire.

"Ya have a choice, honey, take off your clothes or I can rip them off and leave you out here on the plains naked," Jewel sneered. He dropped Beth Ann's arm and stepped back to watch her undress.

Beth Ann had trouble undoing the buttons on her trousers because of her shaking hands. She turned her back as she undressed and finally stood nude with her back to the two men and Jacob

"Don't turn bashful now, gal. Yer among friends." Jewel laughed. "Turn yerself around and let us get a good look."

Beth Ann gritted her teeth and slowly turned to confront the scarred face staring at her. A flush of shame reddened her face and fear shown in her eyes. The two men were not looking at her eyes.

"Jack, ain't that the best lookin thing ya've seen since we left Independence? Gal, go get yer bedroll an put it next to the fire." Jewel began lowering his pants as Beth Ann pulled the bedroll next to the fire.

"Jack, ya go back to eatin while I entertain our lady friend. I won't take long. Ya can have yer turn when I'm done."

Jack's face twisted into an angry mask, but he knew better than to argue with Jewel when there was a woman involved. He found a cold biscuit and a piece of bacon and sat on a log and watched the big man force Beth Ann down onto the blanket and crawl over her. She brought her hands up against his chest and tried to twist away, but Jewel only laughed and held her in his powerful grip.

Jacob screamed at the top of his lungs and strained at the ropes in his attempt to get free. His eyes were so clouded with tears, he heard rather than saw something swish by his head.

The swishing sound was followed by a soft thud. When his vision cleared, he saw an arrow buried in the middle of Jack's chest. Jack made a small grunting sound and fell forward with his face mashed into his tin plate of food.

An Indian appeared out of the darkness as if by magic and stepped into the light behind Jewel. He grabbed Jewel by the hair and with a knife pressed against his throat pulled him off Beth Ann and turned him toward Jacob.

Beth Ann rolled up in the blanket and curled into a ball to hide her nakedness. Sobs racked her body.

"What the hell?" Jewel yelled in surprise but stopped when the point of the knife dug into his throat, a trickle of warm blood ran down his neck and chest.

Jacob's Promise

Jacob felt a surge of triumph when he saw the half-naked man kneeling on the ground with a knife at his throat. There was a flash of fear on the man's face when three more Indians materialized out of the darkness.

Suddenly a fourth Indian stepped out from behind the tree where Jacob was tied and barked orders. The Indians dragged Jewel over between two trees and tied him spread eagle between them. A knife flashed and Jewel's shirt slashed from collar to tail.

Jacob felt a surge of joy when he saw the fear that blazed in Jewel's eyes. A trembling Jewel was stretched between the trees. His shirt ripped open and his pants around his knees.

"I have followed you for many weeks, you named Jewel. Now I have found you." The Indian spoke in perfect English.

"No, ya made a mistake. Ya have the wrong man," Jewel whined.

"You rape little Indian girls and even women of your own tribe. How do white people let you live with them?"

"I'm tellin' ya, ya have the wrong man," Jewel wailed.

"My daughter said the man who took her had a scar over his eye and down the side of his face. You have a scar over your eye and down the side of your face. She said the man had part of his right ear missing. You have part of your ear missing. I described you to other white men and they say that is Jewel Peters."

Overwhelmed by fear Jewel's body began to shudder and his bladder emptied. The Indians roared with laughter.

"You say you are not the one who took my daughter." He pointed at Jacob. "Will you also tell this man that you didn't take his woman?"

Jacob watched all of this, so filled with hate he failed to think what the Indians might have in store for him. The Indian in command said something else that Jacob didn't understand.

One of the Indians stepped over next to Jacob and cut the ropes binding him to the tree. Jacob pulled himself up and started rubbing the circulation back into his hands. He wanted to go to Beth Ann but feared what the Indians might do if he moved.

The Indian facing Jewel motioned for Jacob to come. "Come and share in the punishment of this man who takes little girls. For you it was even worse, you had to watch."

With the knife clutched in his hand, the Indian stepped over in front of Jewel and looked into his twisted face. "An animal like you doesn't deserve to live but dying is too easy. First you must suffer as my daughter suffered."

The knife flash and a bleeding cut appeared across the big man's chest. Jewel's scream of surprise and pain sliced through the night air. Using the point of the knife the Indian lifted a corner of the wound and began peeling a three-inch-wide piece of skin down across Jewel's chest and into his groin.

"That is for my daughter's sleepless nights."

Jewel's screams turned into a whimper as he tried desperately to pull away.

"You are caught like a rabbit in a trap, Jewel Peters," the Indian said. The knife slashed again, and another strip of skin was peeled down Jewel's chest and over his stomach. Jewel trembled and moaned in pain. "That is for the shame my daughter must carry when she seeks a husband."

The Indian turned to Jacob and offered him the knife. "Your woman has suffered as my daughter did. Take the knife and make him feel her pain."

Jewel strained to push away when he saw the hot hate in Jacob's eyes. Jacob hated this man enough to kill him, but he couldn't bring himself to join in the torture.

The Indian seemed surprised at Jacob's reluctance to take the knife, but when Jacob backed away, he returned to Jewel. "You will have a long time to think about the evil things you have done before you die, Jewel Peters."

With a swift slash of the knife, the Indian cut open Jewel's stomach and pulled his intestines out until they hung to his knees. Jewel passed out, but the Indian knew it would only be for a short time before he awoke and felt the pain again. He stepped behind Jewel and cut out a piece of his scalp.

"I will take this to my daughter to show her what happened to the ugly man who took her." Looking at Jacob, he said. "We have both suffered this man's evil, and I have no reason to punish you. We will only take the horses of the evil ones. You and your horses are safe, but I have one last warning for you. I will know if you do not heed it.

"Do not bury these two white men. Let the crows and the coyotes scatter their bones over the prairie so their souls will

Jacob's Promise

wander forever with no peace."

The Indians slipped back into the darkness as silently as they had come. Jacob stood stunned, trying to absorb all that had happened. His attention was pulled away from Jewel's mangled body by Beth Ann's soft sobbing.

He rushed over, picked her up, and moved her away from the two men. He held her in his lap, telling her everything was going to be okay. Beth Ann finally fell asleep, but sleep would not come to Jacob until much later. He was haunted by his failure to protect her when she needed him most.

Beth Ann awoke in Jacob's lap and found him bent at an awkward angle over her and still asleep. Feeling her move, he opened his eyes and in a raspy voice said, "How you doin, Sis?" Then groaned as he tried to straighten his back.

"I don't know how I feel," she said, tears forming in her eyes. "It's just...just. Oh, Jacob, why are all these bad things happening to us?" She clasped her hands over her face and let the tears flow.

"I guess we're still too green to see danger when it's staring us in the face. Joe warned us about keeping vigilant out here. We're on our own now, and we have to be tough and keep going." Jacob was near tears himself.

He felt the muscles in Beth Ann's body tighten, and she sat, up pulling out of Jacob's arms wiping away her tears, "I don't know if I have the courage to face the rest of this trip, but I'm going to try."

Beth Ann's back straightened and she pulled the blanket tightly around her. A new defiance entered her voice. "We can't depend on anyone to help us anymore."

Tears ran down her face and over her clamped jaw. "I hate what happened to me, but I can't change any of it." She struggled to stand and still keep herself covered with the blanket. "I'm going to the river and wash away the filth of that horrible man."

She walked past the stinking body of her attacker and picked up her clothes. Turning her face away from the sight and smell of Jewel, she headed for the river.

Jacob couldn't believe what he was seeing. The trembling, crying girl he had held all last night had turned into an iron-willed woman. He rose stiffly to his feet on numb legs and struggled over to Jewel. He wanted to get rid of the bodies of both men before

Beth Ann returned.

He found a knife in a sheath folded under Jewel's pants and cut him down from the trees. The knife had been hidden in the folds of Jewel's pants, and the Indians hadn't seen it. He took the knife scabbard off the man's belt and threaded it onto his own.

Keeping his head turned away and doing his best to block out Jewel's sight and smell, he pulled him down wind of camp and out of sight. He pulled the second body over to join the first. He added wood to the fire and had hot mush waiting when Beth Ann returned from the river.

"Are you hungry?" Jacob asked.

"Believe it or not, I am. I want to eat and then get as far away from here as fast as we can."

Jacob was concerned about the change in his sister. Was she okay or was it a fragile shell she had built around herself that could crack at any time? If she suddenly went to pieces out here on the prairie, what would he do?

Back in Illinois he had seen a woman become unstable from the pressure of pioneer life. The possibility that it could happen to Beth Ann was frightening. He decided to play along with the new mood. He didn't want to upset her, but he couldn't help asking.

"Are you really well enough to travel today?"

"I have to get away from this place. Please don't fight with me, Jacob."

Jacob started packing while Beth Ann ate. The minute she finished she saddled her horse and climbed aboard.

"Let's go to Oregon," she said as she rode off.

CHAPTER 26

Ruth climbed down off the mud splattered stage in St. Louis, grimy and sore from the ride. She picked up her bag and hailed a buggy to take her to the hotel. She wanted to clean up and rest before she went to the dress shop to talk to Olive Terhune. She had intended to take a short nap but fell into a deep sleep and didn't awaken until the sun was breaking over the horizon the next day.

She hurriedly dressed and went down to the hotel restaurant for breakfast before heading out to Mrs. Terhune's dress shop. While she was waiting for her order to be served, she saw the two men who had helped put the wheel back on the stage coach enter the restaurant. They didn't notice her, but as they passed her table, she spoke up, "Well, we meet once again."

The brothers stopped at the sound of her voice and took a second look at her. "Well, if it ain't the little red-headed lady from the stage coach wreck," Willie said.

"I thought you boys were headed for Independence."

"That's where we plan to go as soon as we can catch a boat going that direction," Simon answered.

"You boys be careful on that boat. They can be dangerous. I want to thank you again for helping us out of a tight spot when that wheel came off," Ruth said.

"The Cooper boys are always ready to help ma'am."

Ruth was jolted when she heard the name Cooper. That was

the name of the family the Hessers had had all the trouble with. She hoped she didn't show her shock. Trying to control her voice she asked, "Where are you boys from?"

"Goose Prairie in Illinois," they answered in unison.

"Our Pa owns a farm there," Willie added.

Hearing the name Goose Prairie confirmed what Ruth feared. "That's a long way from here. Don't you boys live on the farm anymore?"

"Our pa sent us on a mission to find a boy who shot two of our brothers," Willie said. "We know he and his sister are headed west, and we intend to catch up with them."

Ruth was so shocked by this bit of news she couldn't speak. The boys took her silence as a signal for them to move on. They took a table on the other side of the room and ordered breakfast. Ruth was in more turmoil than she had been before.

Receiving the bad news about the Hesser family had shaken her. How could she help Jacob and Beth Ann if they were wandering around out on the prairie while she was stuck in St. Louis. She took some comfort in the fact that the brothers were probably going to be stuck in Independence until next spring too.

The brothers wolfed down their breakfast and were out of the restaurant while Ruth still sat nibbling at her food. They headed for the river to catch the first boat bound for Independence they could find. They had no intention of waiting until spring. They felt they were hot on Jacob's trail, and they didn't want him to get any farther away.

Ruth was torn with worry. The children were headed for Oregon looking for her while she sat in St. Louis. She wondered if they knew two wild-eyed brothers were following them. Was it possible that Jacob had killed two men? If he killed someone, he must have been driven to it.

She let out a long sigh. There was nothing she could do to help them. Her own survival had to be considered before she could run off looking for Jacob and Beth Ann. All she could do was get to Oregon and hope they did, too. With a new resolve she rose from the chair and headed for Mrs. Terhune's dress shop.

Olive Terhune welcomed her with a big smile and a hug. "I'm so glad to see you back so soon. I was afraid you'd end up staying in Illinois, and I really do need help. Would it be possible for you to start today?"

"I need to find a room first. I can't afford to stay in the hotel much longer."

"I might be able to help you with that," Olive said, pulling out a chair and offering Ruth a seat. "I have a spare room in my home I could rent you. It would be cheaper than the hotel. "

"That's very generous of you, Olive."

My husband died two years ago, and I've been rattling around in that big house alone ever since. It would be good to have company."

"I accept, if you're really serious about the offer," Ruth replied.

"Now with that settled, I can put you to work today. After work, I'll help you move your belongings over to my house."

At noontime Olive invited Ruth to come to the back of the store and share the lunch she had packed for herself that morning. "I know you had no way to pack a lunch for yourself, and I have plenty to share."

In the middle of the lunch, the tiny bell attached to the front door of the shop jingled, announcing the arrival of a customer.

"Oh shucks, I forgot to lock the front door before we came back here. Sit still, Ruth, I'll get it."

"No, you sit still. I'm the employee. I'll do my duty and take care of the customer," Ruth laughed.

Ruth entered the front of the shop and saw a tall man standing by the door holding the hand of a small girl.

"How may I help you, sir?" Ruth asked.

The man cleared his throat, "I've never been in a woman's shop before and I feel a bit out of my element. I need to order some dresses for my little girl. She'll be starting school in the fall and she doesn't have any suitable school clothes."

Ruth knelt in front of the little girl, "What's your name, young lady?"

"Mary Ann," the girl answered in a whispery voice.

"Mary Ann. That's a pretty name. Well, Mary Ann, I think we can fix you up with three pretty dresses long before school starts in the fall."

The gentleman sat in a chair and watched Ruth measure his daughter. As Ruth worked, she carried on an animated conversation with Mary Ann. With the measurements done, the smiling girl led Ruth over to where her father was sitting.

"It seems you have charmed my daughter. This is one of the few times I have seen her smile since her mother died," the man said.

"I am glad a dress was brought some sunshine into her life," Ruth said.

"Forgive me, I don't think I have even introduced myself. My name is William Copple, and you must be Mrs. Terhune."

"No, I'm not Mrs. Terhune. She owns the dress shop. I only work here. My name is Ruth Heinz."

"Well, Miss Heinz, I am very glad to meet you, and I know Mary Ann will be very happy with the dresses you plan to make."

"Mary Ann is a sweet little girl. I can imagine how much she misses her mother. It must be hard for you to be left with the responsibility of raising a small child. I can understand how you feel. I lost my husband almost a month ago."

They stood quietly for a moment before William asked when the dresses might be finished. After a day was set for him to pick them up, William and Mary Ann left the shop and Ruth returned to her lunch with Olive. She told her about the three dresses the man ordered and about the sweet little girl who had lost her mother.

Two weeks later, William and Mary Ann returned to the store to pick up the dresses. Mary Ann was overjoyed when she tried them on. Ruth had added some extra frills, at her own expense, to help put a little happiness back into the girl's life.

"These are the prettiest dresses I have ever seen," exclaimed MaryAnn. She ran over to Ruth and gave her a mighty hug.

A week after buying the dresses, William returned to the store to buy ribbons for Mary Ann's hair. Then a few days later, he stopped by to order a small vest to go with the dresses.

On his fourth visit, he faced Ruth and blurted out, "I'm going to go broke if I keep coming in here to buy things just to get better acquainted with you. Will you do me the honor of having supper with me and my daughter Friday evening?"

Ruth was a little taken back by the sudden invitation to supper, but he seemed like a nice gentleman. He almost had to be to have such a sweet, well-mannered little girl. She smiled back at him. "I would be delighted to have supper with the two of you.'

Jacob's Promise

The dinners became a weekly event with the three of them. Ruth learned during their many suppers that he, too, was headed for Oregon with the intention of opening a dry goods store there. He, his wife and daughter had arrived in St. Louis from Ohio on a riverboat.

His wife had gotten sick on the boat and had died with a raging fever three weeks after they landed in St. Louis. Her lingering illness held them in St. Louis until it was too late to join the wagon train.

"I think Mary Ann has suffered by not having a woman in her life and she has become as fond of you as I have. What I'm trying to say in my stumbling way is, will you marry me?"

Ruth was a practical woman and knew she would have a difficult time making the trip to Oregon alone. She had become fond of both William and Mary and there was a benefit in joining the resources of the two families.

They were married Christmas Eve.

CHAPTER 27

Willie and Simon Cooper arrived at the St. Louis dock to find that the first boat leaving for Independence would not depart for two days. With time to kill, they wandered around town talking to merchants about what they would need in the way of supplies for the trip past Independence.

As they asked questions, they always inserted a description of Jacob. It finally paid off. At the gun shop, while inspecting a new rifle, Willie gave his well-practiced description of Jacob and was surprised when the man said he recollected such a boy.

"A young tenderfoot that sort of fit that description came in here a few weeks ago with Joe Adams. Joe is an old customer of mine, and he was helping the young man pick out a rifle for the trip west."

"Where might we find this fellow Joe?" asked Willie.

"Oh, I'm sure he's long gone by now. He was headed for an Indian village out north- west of Laramie. You might ask old lady Greenfield about him. He always rents a shed at her place whenever he comes to town."

"How do we find this old lady Greenfield?" Willie asked.

"Go out west on Fourth Street. She lives in one of the last houses on the left side of the road at the edge of town. There'll be a sign out front advertising a shed for rent."

"Thank ya sir," Willie said as he laid down the gun he was

looking at and headed for the door.

"Where we headed now," Simon asked.

"To the stable to git our horses and find an old lady named Greenfield."

The Greenfield house was as easy to find as the gun merchant said it would be. Willie tied his horse to the fence in front of the house, went to the front door, and knocked.

Mrs. Greenfield cracked the door open about six inches and peered out. "If you're here to rent the shed, you're too late. It's already rented, I just haven't had time to take the sign down yet."

"No ma'am." Willie tried to sound as mannerly as he could. "I'm here lookin for Joe Adams."

"You won't find him here. He left about three weeks ago. He took off early one morning with his Indian friend and that boy and girl who were camped out back. Woke me up real early that morning making a racket with all their packing and banging around."

"Thank ya ma'am,' Willie said and headed back to his horse.

"Well, what did you find out," Simon asked.

"It's them all right. They left about three weeks ago. They're ahead of us, but a man at the hotel said the boat was faster than travelin by horseback."

The morning the boat for Independence was due to leave, Willie and Simon arrived at the landing early. Once underway they discovered the boat traveled at a much slower pace than they had expected.

Willie spent each day pacing the deck, "I swear we git hung up on every sand bar and snag in the river.

"And why in the hell do payin' passengers have to help clear snags and cut wood to keep the damn boat runnin'. I thought they said the boat was faster. I didn't know they tied the damn thing to a tree ever night."

"Quit yer belly achin," Simon said. "The captain said we'd likely git there sometime tomorrow."

When the boat docked in Independence they rushed into town, stopping at each store to describe Jacob and ask if they had seen him. They had been at it over an hour before they found a merchant who remembered a boy who might fit the description.

"That sounds like the boy involved in the shooting that killed a man not too long ago."

"Is he in jail," Simon asked.

"No, he skipped out the night it happened, and no one has seen him since. The man who could tell you the whole tale is Joe Adams."

"Where can we find this Joe Adams?" Willie asked.

"You're in luck. See that man sitting on the bench there across the street sunning himself? That's Joe. Got his leg shot off in the fight I was telling you about."

Willie almost knocked Simon down getting out of the store. He ran across the street, dodging horses and wagons, not stopping until he was face-to-face with Joe.

"You Joe Adams?" Willie was breathing hard from his short run.

"Who wants to know," Joe asked.

"I'm Willie Cooper, and this is my brother Simon. We understand ya know a friend of ours."

As soon as Joe heard the name Cooper, he knew who they were and what they wanted. He sat quietly and waited to see what else Willie had to say.

"We heard you might be travelin with Jacob Hesser and his sister. Do you know where they are? We're from Goose Prairie same as they are and we'd like to say hello to them," Willie said.

"I travel with a lot of people, but I can't recall if any of them were named Jacob," Joe replied.

Willie wasn't about to let some old one-legged man get smart with him. He grabbed Joe by the neck of his shirt and pulled him up until they were nose-to-nose.

"Listen, you old cripple, I'm tired of messin' with ya. I want some straight answers and I want them now. Where can we find Jacob?"

"You plan to kill me right here on Main Street, boy?" Joe offered a crooked smile.

"I don't have to kill ya, I can just kick ya in that stump of your'n a few times and cause ya enough pain that ya'll be happy to tell me anythin' I want to know."

Before Willie had finished his threat, Joe grabbed Willie by his belt and had a knife firmly pushed against his ribs.

Jacob's Promise

"You best take your hands off my throat and step away before I lose my temper and slice you open," Joe growled.

Fear replaced anger in Willie's eyes. He released his grip on Joe's shirt and eased back. Once he was away from Joe's knife and standing by his brother, his bravado returned.

"I'll be around and see ya again, old man. And when I come back, I'll be ready for ya. Ya'll be sorry ya didn't tell me the first time I asked," Willie said with more confidence than he felt.

"The next time you come near me, you'll end up a dead man," Joe said through clinched teeth.

"Come on, Simon," Willie sneered. "Let's go get a beer. There are other people in town who can tell us what we want to know. We'll take care of the old crippled fart some other time."

Joe watched them walk away and mumbled, "So that's the Cooper boys Jacob talked about."

He could see why Jacob was worried. He wasn't sure Jacob would be able to handle those boys if they caught up with him.

CHAPTER 28

Jacob and Beth Ann reached a slow running river at mid-afternoon. Near the shore they saw some low ramshackle buildings made of sod.

"I wonder what this place is called?" Beth Ann asked.

"Whatever it's called, it's not someplace we're going to stop," Jacob answered.

They moved to an open field past the buildings before Jacob made camp for the night. Several cold mounds of campfire ashes gave evidence that wagons camped in this area before. There was a wagon parked up ahead by some trees on the river bank.

Jacob, still leery of other people, pulled fifty yards past it before he stopped. He relieved their horses of their burdens and staked them out to graze before he set off to gather wood for their evening fire.

Beth Ann, her hat off to cool her head, was busy sorting out what she needed for the evening meal when she saw the small figure of a woman walking toward her from the other wagon. As the woman got closer, Beth Ann noticed how frail she looked. A broad smile appeared in the woman's gaunt face when she saw Beth Ann.

"Hello there, young missy. Do you have a minute to visit?"

The woman had seen her long hair. "Hello," Beth Ann answered, wondering why the woman had walked so far to speak to her.

"My, I need a minute to catch my breath. Mind if I sit a spell? That walk plum tuckered me out."

"I don't have much to offer for a place to sit, but you can sit on that blanket I've spread out under the tree," Beth Ann said.

The woman eased herself on to the blanket and let out a long sigh of relief. "I'm not as spry as I was when we started. It's been a long trip from Ohio, and I can feel stiff from all the ruts that wagon bounced over today."

"We've come a way, too." Beth Ann did not want to disclose much to this stranger. "I know how hard the wooden bench on a wagon can be."

"I'm Anna Whipple, and I came over here to see if you and your husband would like to come eat with us tonight. I've only had my husband and two boys to talk to, and it's not often I get a chance for some woman talk.

"I'm Beth Ann and I'm traveling with my brother, Jacob." Beth Ann didn't bother giving her last name. They had given up using their mother's maiden name many miles back and had started just using only their first names with strangers. "I'm sure Jacob would like to have an evening with someone to talk to besides me. Can I bring anything to add to the meal?"

"Lordy no, girl, we have plenty. Just having your company will supply all I need."

With a great deal of effort and Beth Ann's help, the woman got to her feet.

"I best get back and start getting things together." With that, she started her slow shuffling journey back the way she had come.

"As soon as we're settled, I'll be over to help with the meal," Beth Ann called after her.

Jacob saw the woman leaving their camp as he returned carrying an armload of firewood. "Who was that?" He set the wood down.

"A very nice lady from the wagon over there has invited us to eat with them this evening. As soon as we get straightened away, we can go over. The least I can do is give her a hand with the meal."

"Good. Maybe I'll get a decent meal for a change." Jacob smiled.

"Anytime you want to take over the cooking, you're welcome to it," Beth Ann replied. "And another thing, she spotted me with my hat off and knows I'm not a boy."

After they unloaded the pack horses they set off across the expanse between the camps. Entering the other camp, they saw the woman stirring a large iron pot hanging over the fire. A young man of about fifteen or sixteen was chopping wood, and a stout man with a gray streaked beard sat on a box reading the Bible. His ample belly hung over his belt, testing the strength of the buttons of his shirt.

On seeing them, the potbellied man exerted some effort to stand. "You must be the young people my wife invited to eat with us." He extended his hand to Jacob.

"I'm Eli Whipple, and that's my son Mathew over there chopping wood. I think your sister and my wife Anna have already introduced themselves."

"Glad to meet you, Mr. Whipple. This is my sister Beth Ann and I'm Jacob."

"Jacob, that's a good biblical name and Beth Ann is a pretty name for a girl. Welcome to both of you to our humble offerings," Eli Whipple said.

Beth Ann acknowledged Eli's greeting and then turned to Anna, "What can I do to help?" Leaving the men, she joined Anna by the fire.

"Mathew, come over here and meet Jacob," Eli ordered.

Mathew was tall and lanky with a rather dour looking face for one so young. He was wearing a crumpled felt hat, pulled down over a mass of yellow hair and clothes that showed the wear of travel. He gave Jacob a feeble handshake but didn't utter a word. He stood a moment looking Jacob up and down before he moved off to sit on the tongue of the wagon.

Eli pulled a box from under the wagon, "Come sit a spell, Jacob, while the women cook. Tell me how you young people ended up out here on this lonely prairie."

"Not much to tell, Mr. Whipple. We're headed for Oregon just like everybody else. We're trying to catch up with our relatives who left a few weeks before we got started."

"God's made a big country out here, Jacob, and trying to find someone in it could be a real trial. I'll pray for you, for you'll need

Jacob's Promise

God's help for the task in front of you," Eli said.

Their conversation was interrupted by the arrival of a rider coming into camp with an antelope hanging across his horse in front of the saddle. He stopped at the end of the wagon, pulled the antelope off the horse and let it fall the ground.

"Take that animal off away from camp to clean it and then come over here and meet our neighbor," Eli called.

The new arrival looked to be in his early twenties, a picture of what Eli Whipple must have looked like at that age. He picked the dead animal up and carried it some distance from the wagon. He laid it down, sauntered back, and stood by Jacob. There was an arrogance to his manner, that coupled with the scowl etched in his sunburned face caused Jacob to immediately dislike him.

"Jacob, this is my oldest son, Mark."

Mark looked Jacob up and down with eyes that said he couldn't care less. Jacob offered his hand, but Mark acted like he didn't see it. Without a word he turned away and went back to butcher the antelope.

"Looks like God has supplied us with some fresh meat for supper tonight," Eli said.

"Fresh meat will be a welcome change from the salt pork we've been living on," Jacob said. "I killed a couple of rabbits between Independence and here, but that's the only fresh meat we've had."

While Jacob and Eli talked Mark skinned the antelope, cut some steaks and took them to his mother. Then silently returned to finish the butchering.

The sizzling antelope steak's aroma sent hunger pangs lacing through Jacob's stomach. It seemed to take hours before Anna called everyone to the fire to eat. After they had gathered Eli commanded everyone to silence while he gave the blessing.

Jacob was afraid that his growling stomach would drown out the prayer. He thought the old man would never stop praying and let them eat. After what seemed an eternity the prayer ended. Meat, mush, and a slice of fresh baked bread were placed on every plate. The minute his plate was filled, Jacob started shoveling it in. This was the best meal he had eaten since the café in Independence.

With everyone's appetite satisfied, the women began gathering up the cups and plates. Eli filled his pipe and after several puffs to get it started, settled back against the side of the wagon and stared silently at Jacob. After a while he said, "Are you and your sister planning to go on alone from here to Laramie?"

"Yes, sir. The ones we plan to travel with are still up ahead of us."

"I don't think you realize how dangerous it can be for a lone traveler out there on the prairie. The Indians will find you, sooner or later, and those Sioux are not a friendly bunch. If you run into the Pawnee, they'll steal your horses with you sitting on them. Now I'm not just saying this to scare you. God knows I'm just giving you the facts."

Jacob nodded that he understood, but kept his mouth shut.

"The two of us are really in the same boat," Eli continued as if Jacob and Beth Ann were his only concern. "Our wagon broke down and the group we were with moved on without us. The wagon's fixed now, but we'll never be able to catch up with our bunch.

"Now if we joined forces, our two groups would be strong enough that we wouldn't be bothered by Indians between here and Laramie." Eli settled back and let his message soak in. "The Lord looks after those who look after themselves, Jacob."

Even with all the threats, Jacob wasn't too keen on joining up with anyone. He'd been worried about them traveling alone after what had happened to Beth Ann, but not worried enough to want to join this outfit. Beth Ann would welcome the company of another woman, but the thought of having to travel with the Bible thumper and his unfriendly sons for weeks was enough to turn his stomach.

He knew he and Beth Ann would be hard pressed to keep up the night watches for the weeks of travel that laid ahead of them, but he hated to be slowed down by having to travel with a wagon. Maybe he should think more about Beth Ann's safety and less about how uncomfortable he would be.

"I'll talk it over with Beth Ann and let you know what we decide," Jacob said, avoiding the answer Eli wanted.

"I don't want to rush you, son, but we plan to leave tomorrow morning."

"If we're going with you, we'll be ready to go when you are," Jacob answered.

After Jacob and Beth Ann left, Mark faced his father, "Why

do we need those two with us? We have enough guns with the three of us to take care of ourselves. We don't need any outsiders tagging along."

"Are you volunteering to be the cook on this trip?" Eli asked his son. "Look at how poorly your mother has been getting lately. I saw God's goodness in that girl's eyes, and if we handle it right, she'll be more than obliged to help out if your mother gets down.

"The Lord sent that girl to us, so you be quiet and act nice around the both of them."

"We may need the girl, but we don't need the boy. He'll be just another mouth to feed," Mark growled.

"Shush now, Mark. You leave him be. If you do anything to cause them to leave, I'll make you mama's little helper for the rest of the trip."

Mark heard what his father said but had made up his mind right then that the girl could stay, but Jacob's time with them would be short if he had his way.

Mathew saw Mark and his father talking but didn't hear what was being said. He stopped Mark when he came around the end of the wagon and asked, "Are those two going to tag along with us?"

"Yeah. They'll be with us. The girl's all right, I kind of like her looks, but if I have my way the boy will get lost somewhere between here and Laramie."

CHAPTER 30

"I don't really want to be slowed down by a wagon," Jacob said when they returned to their camp. Jacob didn't say that his real reason was that Eli and his boys weren't exactly the people he'd choose to travel with. But still, he was worried about the two of them being out on the prairie alone.

"I think Mrs. Whipple is a pleasant woman and it would be nice to have a woman for company, but I'll leave it up to you."

"I guess we don't have a lot of choices. Hopefully we can find better people to travel with when we get to Laramie. We may even catch up to Aunt Ruth by then," Jacob said trying to raise Beth Ann's spirits.

"Try to look on the bright side." Beth Ann crawled into her bedroll. "I'll have a woman to visit with and I'll be out of your hair all the way to Laramie. Now go to sleep. Things will look brighter in the morning."

The next morning when the Whipple mules pulled their wagon onto the trail, Jacob and Beth Ann rode out to meet them.

"Good morning," Eli called. "Glad to see you've decided to join us. I'm sure Anna will be pleased."

Jacob waved his good morning but didn't answer Eli's greeting. Jacob and Beth Ann rode off to the side of the Whipple wagon to avoid their dust. The going was slow because every steep bank and stream presented a challenge for the wagon.

Jacob's Promise

Jacob cussed himself for joining them every time he had to slow down and wait while something was cleared from the trails so the wagon could pass. His unhappiness showed plainly on his face and Mark saw it.

"Anytime you want to leave us, you go right ahead," Mark said with a crooked smile. "Don't let me stop you. We'll get along just fine without you. I think Pa's doing you a big favor letting you tag along with us."

Jacob knew Mark was right but resented his attitude. He was determined to keep as much distance between the families as he could. He insisted that he and Beth Ann have their own fire and cook their own food.

He didn't want to be beholden to the Whipple's for anything. Traveling with them was enough togetherness. Mark and Mathew were an unfriendly duo and there was something about Eli's over friendliness that got under Jacob's skin.

Eating supper that night Jacob asked, "What's your impression of the Whipples', Beth Ann?"

"Mrs. Whipple is a sweet lady, but she's so frail. I'm beginning to doubt she's going to make it all the way to Oregon. Mr. Whipple has been nice to me, but I think he should do a little less Bible quoting and be a little more help to her. He sits around reading his Bible while she loads and unloads all the food, cooks the meal, and does all the cleanup."

Their conversation was interrupted by the sound of Eli calling to them as he came hurrying cross the field that separated their wagons.

"I wonder what new suggestion he has for us this time?" Jacob groaned.

"I hope I didn't disturb your meal," he said, panting from his trip. "But Anna has taken on a sick spell that needs a woman. I wonder if Beth Ann would come over and give me a hand?"

"I'll be glad to come, Mr. Whipple, but I'm not sure how much good I'll be," Beth Ann said as she got up to follow Eli. "My mama took care of all the sickness and hurts in our family. I'm not sure I remember all she tried to teach me."

At the Whipple campsite, Beth Ann crawled into the musty smelling wagon holding a kerosene lantern. She was shocked by Mrs. Whipple's appearance. Two frightened owl-like eyes stared out at her from a chalk white face. The sheet covering Anna was stained with bright red blood from her waist to her knees.

"How long have you been bleeding like this?" A frightened Beth Ann asked.

"I first noticed some spotting just before we got to Independence. I thought it was my monthly, but it didn't stop. Then two days ago it started getting worse."

"Why didn't you go to a doctor in Independence?"

"I wanted to, but Eli said it would be a waste of money. He said prayer was better than any quack doctor I'd find in Independence."

"I don't remember ever seeing mother work with this kind of bleeding, but I know she said pressure on bleeding wounds could do the job," Beth Ann said and squeezed Anna's hand, trying to reassure both. "Get me some warm water and clean towels," Beth Ann called out to Eli.

Eli didn't like being ordered around by a woman and rather than obey, called for Mark to bring some towels and for Mathew to bring the heated water.

Beth Ann used a wet towel to clean as much blood off Anna as she could, but it was hard to see in the dark, cramped space of the wagon. After she dried Anna's body and legs, she rolled up a towel and pressed it up between Anna's legs. "Press your legs together and hold the towel as tight against you as you can. The pressure should help stop the bleeding."

Beth Ann didn't want to let on that she had no idea of what was causing the bleeding. It wouldn't make Anna feel any better to know that, but it was the only thing Beth Ann could think to do.

Anna gave her a weak smile, "Thank you, Beth Ann. I don't know what I would have done if you hadn't come."

Beth Ann held Anna's hand and listened to her shallow breathing as she drifted off to sleep. Sometime in the early morning hours Beth Ann dozed off. When she woke, she found she was still holding Anna's now ice-cold hand. Beth Ann rolled up onto her elbow and looked down into Anna' open, unseeing eyes. She gently pulled the sheet over Anna's face with trembling fingers and climbed out of the wagon on cramped legs to tell Eli his wife was dead.

Eli took the news without showing a twinge of emotion as he

ordered Mark to get a shovel and for Mathew to get out the old brown blanket out of the storage box to wrap his mother's body in for burial.

Beth Ann was shocked at how fast Eli rushed to get his wife buried and out of sight. In less than an hour Eli had Anna underground and was searching for his Bible to read some scripture over her.

Beth Ann and Jacob waited until Anna was buried and Eli had finished his Bible reading before they approached the grave. They stayed just long enough to hear Eli say a quick prayer then hurriedly returned to their campsite and started packing,

Eli and his sons lingered at the grave until Jacob and Beth Ann had gone. Once they were alone, Eli said, "We've lost mother, the cook and mender of our clothes. I'll approach Beth Ann and see if I can persuade her to cook at least one meal a day for us. I think she has a good heart and may be agreeable, but if she refuses, it will fall on one of you to take on that chore."

"I'll not do a woman's job," Mark growled. "Mathew is the youngest, let him do it."

"Don't try to push it off on me," Mathew said. "I'll share the chore, but I'll not do it alone. Being older doesn't make you special, Mark."

The boys stalked off, leaving Eli standing at the grave.

"There's only one way to get what we want," Mark said when they were out of Eli's hearing. "We have to get rid of Jacob. With him out of the way, his sister will be easy to handle."

"What are you going to do, shoot him?" Mathew asked.

"No, she'd tell the law the first thing we got to Laramie. It has to look like an accident and the best place for an accident to happen would be while we're out hunting."

"How soon is this accident going to happen?" Mathew was a little nervous at what Mark was planning.

"I'll have Pa convinced we need fresh meat, before the day is over. Then we'll take Jacob on a little hunting trip. Just keep your mouth shut and let me do the talking."

Later that afternoon, as Beth Ann rode by the Whipple wagon, Eli called to her.

"Everyone is so quiet and in such a sad mood since we buried Anna that Mark thinks we need something to give our lives a bit of a change. He says a meal of fresh meat might lift our spirits. We'll stop for the day over where that stream bends by those trees. It looks like a good place to camp while the boys go find some fresh meat. I'll tell my boys; you get Jacob and send him over."

Mark smiled as he heard Eli tell Beth Ann to fetch Jacob. He couldn't believe how easily his father had been sucked into his plan. With a laugh he spun around and punched Mathew on the shoulder, "Let's get the horses, brother, we're going hunting."

Beth Ann slowed down and waited for Jacob to come up beside her. "Mr. Whipple said he's going to stop early today so you and his boys can go out hunting. He thinks we'll all feel better if we have a meal with fresh meat in it for a change."

"Eli is always deciding things without asking what we think. It's just one more thing to slow us down," Jacob snapped.

When they reached the trees, Jacob left Beth Ann to unpack and stake out the horses while he went to joined Eli and his boys.

Seeing Jacob approach, the two brothers started riding out of camp away from the river. Jacob, none too happy about their stopping to hunt, reluctantly followed them. He couldn't understand why they were headed away from the river. Wouldn't they be more likely to find game near the water?

After riding four or five miles without seeing any game, they stopped on the top of a ridge overlooking a dry gully to scout out the area. Jacob shaded his eyes with his hand and searched the prairie for movement.

With Jacob distracted Mark eased his horse up behind him and punched him in the back with the mussel of his rifle. "Get off your horse," Mark ordered.

Jacob jerked around in the saddle and angrily brushed the rifle away. "No need to get off, I can see fine from where I am."

Mark swung the barrel of the rifle hitting Jacob in the ribs." I want you off the horse, and I want you off the horse now," Mark repeated in a more demanding voice.

Jacob slowly dismounted not liking the menace he heard in Mark's voice. He got even more apprehensive when Mathew stepped forward and led Jacob's horse away. He was now stranded between Mark's horse and the open space at the edge of the ridge. It was then he realized they intended to push him over the edge. He lunged at Mark, but Mark anticipated the move and smashed him in the side of his head with the barrel of the rifle.

Staggered by the blow, Jacob's knees buckled, and he toppled over the edge of the embankment.

Mark watched with a wide grin on his face as Jacob's body bounced down the steep incline, smashing into rocks on the way to the dry streambed below.

"Why did you do that," Mathew yelled, "We'll never be able to get his body out of there without riding ten miles to get to the end of the gully."

"We'll just have to make up a good story." Mark turned his horse away.

"What kind of a story is his sister going to believe," Mathew whined.

"We'll say the Indians got him. We'll say we were separated from each other, and we saw a bunch Indians chasing Jacob. We'll say there was no way we could help because there were too many of them, and that after they caught Jacob, they saw us, and we had to ride for our lives."

"How are you going to explain us having his horse?"

"For God's sake, don't be so stupid, Mathew. Take the saddle off the horse and drive it off to the south away from our camp." We'll throw his rifle and saddle in the first hole we come to."

All the way back to the camp, Mark and Mathew rode their horses hard so they would be lathered and winded when they rode in to tell their Indian story.

After hearing their story Beth Ann wept and begged them to go back and look for Jacob, but Mark refused. "Damn it, Pa those Indians could be forming up a party to come after us while we stand here jawin."

Eli was shaken by Mark's trembling hands and flushed face. Eli was a coward but tried to hide it by shouting at Beth Ann and the boys to start packing. "We need to put as much distance between us and the Indians as we can before it gets dark." Eli didn't know Mark's nervousness came from what he had done.

Beth Ann kept begging them to look for some other travelers to help them search, but Mark refused, and Eli stood by him. Eli left them to start packing the wagon. When he was gone Beth Ann confronted Mark.

"You're a coward Mark. You're afraid to go back."

Mark lashed out in a fury and slapped Beth Ann so hard it knocked her to the ground.

"Get up and get your gear packed," he ordered. "The only place we're going is Oregon, and you're going to cook and mend for us until we get there. Don't you say a word to Pa about that little love tap. It'll be our little secret. Understand?" Mark grabbed her by the front of her shirt and pulled her to her feet.

"When we get to Laramie, I might even find a preacher and take you on as a wife. You can start practicing the obedient part on the trip between here and Laramie"

Beth Ann had never felt such rage. She held it in, turned her back on Mark, and headed for her campsite to pack. "You just think you're taking me to Oregon," Beth Ann muttered. "I'd starve myself to death before I'd marry the likes of you, Mark Whipple."

Jacob's Promise

CHAPTER 31

It was the middle of the night before Jacob returned to consciousness. He lay blinking at the star-filled sky wondering where he was. He tried to sit up and a jolt of pain tore at his ribs. He fell back and rested for a minute before making another effort to move.

Carefully, he moved his right hand up to the side of his throbbing head and felt dried blood caked down the side of his face. Painfully he rolled on to his stomach and tried to push up, his right arm worked, but his left arm refused to move. Using his good arm, he levered himself onto his knees.

The world began spinning around him, and he wilted back onto the ground and rolled over. Once again flat on his back. The thought that this was going to be the place where he might die swirled through his head. Then the world went black.

The sun was high in the sky before consciousness returned. He blinked at the bright sunlit sky trying to remember where he was. After his head cleared, he eased himself onto his stomach and using his good arm, pushed until he was on his hand and knees.

He rested a few moments, fighting the dizziness. Crawling across the stony ground, he reached a boulder. He waited until his head cleared, then inch-by-inch, he pulled himself up until he was standing. When the world quit tilting, he opened his eyes and looked around.

Bill Heyduck

He saw he had landed in a dry streambed at the bottom of a ravine that ran from the southwest to the northeast. To get back to Beth Ann he needed to travel straight north, but the sides of the ravine were too steep for him to climb in his condition. The only way out was to follow the rocky streambed of the ravine northeast until he found an escape route.

Jacob tried a tentative step and then another. Slashing pain shot through his battered knees with every step. The bad knees and the streambed's uneven surface kept causing him to stumble. He waited after each fall to regain enough strength to doggedly rise and staggered forward.

By mid-afternoon he had covered less than five hundred yards. His lips were cracked, and his throat parched dry from thirst. He knew he had to find water if he was going to survive. He struggled out to the lowest part of the streambed and knelt.

He began pulling up rocks searching for moisture. He was ready to give up when he suddenly felt moisture on the bottom of a large rock he pulled up, his hand touched damp sand. He eagerly dug into the sand until he felt a trickle of water begin to seep into the hole. First an inch of water gathered, then three inches.

He plunged his head down and eagerly sucked up every drop of the gritty water. He pulled back and watched the agonizingly slow seepage of water once again fill the hole.

The sun was low in the sky before his thirst was finally satisfied. Too weary and filled with pain to go any farther he crawled over to the shade of the ravine wall and collapsed. Worry lines creased his forehead. What if he never found a place to get out of the ravine? What was going to happen to Beth Ann if he didn't make it back? These were his last thoughts before he blacked out.

Hunger twinges joined the agonizing pain in his ribs waking Jacob on the morning of third day. He had found enough water to survive, but no food. Only the thought of Beth Ann in the hands of the Whipples' gave him the strength to struggle to his feet.

He had only taken a few steps when he thought he heard horses on the northwest rim of the ravine. He shook his head. Was he so far gone that he was beginning to hear things? He stumbled out to the center of the streambed and started yelling as loud as his fractured ribs would allow him.

Jacob's Promise

He prayed it wasn't Indians, but being an Indian captive had to be better than dying of thirst or starvation in the bottom of a ravine. He heard a horse stop at the edge of the cliff. To Jacob's relief, the head that appeared over the edge of the ravine wasn't wearing feathers.

"What in the bloody hell are you doing down there," the man called.

The fact the man spoke English raised Jacob' spirits, even if the stranger did speak with a funny accent.

"God are you a welcome sight," Jacob groaned.

"I'll throw you a rope, and we'll pull you up."

A rope came snaking down the side of the ravine and stopped fifteen feet in front of Jacob. Using the last of his strength he stumbled to the rope and tied it around his chest and under his arms.

"Take it easy pulling me up, I think I have some cracked ribs and maybe a broken arm."

The rope that tightened around Jacob's chest caused a pain so severe, he couldn't breathe. Half conscious, he could make only feeble attempts to keep from bumping the side of the ravine on his way up. By the time he reached the top, the pain had overwhelmed him, and he once again lost consciousness.

He came to lying on a cot in a tent. Painfully turning his head, he saw a man sitting at a portable desk on the other side of the tent. Jacob tried to sit up, but an excruciating stab made him fall back with a groan. The man turned at the sound.

"I see our mystery guest has once again joined the living. Are you ready for some nourishment?"

"Yes, please," Jacob answered, through cracked lips "And some water please"

"Beaman," the man called.

"Yes sir." A man appeared at the open flap of the tent, as if he had been waiting to be summoned.

"Bring the boy some food and a cup of water. It seems he is going to live, even in his beat-up condition."

Jacob rolled over on his side, dropped his legs over the edge of the cot and slowly sat up. After he had steadied himself, he said, "Thank you for pulling me out of that ravine. If you hadn't come along, I don't know how much longer I would have lasted."

"I say, how in the world did you get yourself in a fix like that?"

"Two of my hunting companions hit me in the head and pushed me over the edge. That's the last thing I remember before you came along."

"I'm sorry, I'm not being very mannerly, my name is Winston Bellington. I'm touring your western county with my manservant, Beaman. The other horsemen are guides and security. I've come all the way from England to see your magnificent west and to study your wild Indians."

Jacob wasn't sure what a manservant was, but he wasn't going to show his ignorance by asking. "I'm Jacob Hesser from Illinois and on my way to Oregon with my sister, Beth Ann."

Beaman entered the tent carrying a tin plate of beans and some kind of meat, a tin cup of water, and a steaming cup of coffee. He sat the food and coffee on a stool by the cot, handed Jacob the water, and left the tent.

Jacob drained the cup of water and reached for the plate of food. It was then he noticed how clean his hand was. He touched his face and found the dried blood was gone.

Winston saw Jacob touch his face, "Beaman cleaned you up a bit while you were unconscious. He bound your ribs and put your arm in a sling while you were out and couldn't feel the pain. He's really quite good at caring for cuts and bruises."

"I guess I was pretty much of a mess when you found me."

"You were that," Winston said. "Now finish eating and when you're done Beaman and I will help you out to the fire. We're anxious to hear your story."

Twenty minutes later with Beaman on one side and Billingham of the other Jacob half walked and was half carried out to the fire where they eased him down onto a canvas camp stool.

He started his story at the point where he and Beth Ann left Independence and stopped with them finding him at the bottom of the ravine.

"You've certainly had an adventure young man. What do you plan to do now?" Winston asked.

"I have to get up to the Oregon Trail and catch up with the Whipples' so I can find my sister."

"We're headed north for Indian country and should come near

the Oregon Trail in less than half a day," Winston said. "But I can see you're in no shape to ride. I'm not rushed and don't have a fixed schedule so a few days rest will do you and the horses some good."

"Just get me to a place where I can find the trail to Oregon, I'll make my way from there somehow," Jacob said, his pain racked body filling him with doubt. "I'm worried about what's happening to my sister."

CHAPTER 32

Beth Ann grudgingly prepared the evening meal for the three Whipples', then withdrew to the shadow of the wagon to eat. As she ate, she began planning her revenge. A smile ticked at the corners of her mouth when she suddenly remembered something her mother had taught her about the herbs and weeds growing in their woods. She had a way to make Mark pay and with luck get her back to Independence.

The next morning, she got up early and slipped out to walk the edge of the woods. She wished she had paid more attention when she went with her mother to gather medicinal plants.

Right now, she needed a plant that would make Mark sick, but not kill him, though his death wouldn't make her unhappy. She wanted him sick enough to convince Eli to turn back to Independence for a doctor.

She found the plant she hoped was Water Hemlock. She remembered her mother saying the weed made horses and cows sick. If it made them sick it should do the same to people. She would have to experiment with the amount to use.

Back at camp she hid the weeds in an empty sugar sack. She took a few leaves, crushed them, and smeared the juice on the bottom of the red handled tin cup Mark always used. She brewed extra strong coffee that morning to cover any taste of the weed.

She busied herself with breakfast chores and was frying bacon when the others crawled out of their beds. She took the cup containing the Water Hemlock, poured the strong coffee into it and handed it to Mark. She watched him take his first sip and held her breath. When he took his second sip with no reaction, she turned away to hide her smile.

Eli sat on his camp stool like a king on a throne and started issuing orders. "Beth Ann, get the cooking things packed, Mathew get the livestock rounded up, and Mark, you hitch up the mules to the wagon while Mathew rounds up the stock."

"Why don't we use Jacob's horses on the wagon? That way we can save the mules for the trip on the other side of Laramie," Mark said. "We can sell the horses when we get to Laramie."

Beth Ann charged over and waved a fork at Eli's nose, "You can't use Jacob's horses for pulling that heavy wagon. And Mark can't sell what doesn't belong to him."

Mark's face went red with anger. He pointed a finger at Beth Ann and said, "Get it through your thick head, girl, Jacob's gone. Those Indians killed him, and he ain't coming back. I'll damn well do anything I please with the horses."

Eli stared at the ground, avoiding Beth Ann's wrath.

Beth Ann turned away, gritting her teeth. Under her breath she muttered, "That's what you think, Mark."

At the noon stop to eat and rest the horses, Mark wasn't feeling well and refused the bowl of mush Beth Ann offered him. He had crawled down off his horse and was stretched out in the shade of the wagon.

"What you need is a good hot cup of coffee to settle your stomach, Mark," Beth Ann said as she poured some from the heated pot into Mark's tainted breakfast cup.

By nightfall Mark was doubled over with cramps and nausea. Eli couldn't understand his son's sudden illness and nervously tried to comfort him.

Hiding her smile, Beth Ann brought him more hot coffee to sooth his nausea. Mark drank the coffee but refused to eat anything. He lay in the wagon moaning while the others ate.

During the evening meal, Beth Ann moved over by Eli and said in a low voice, "Mark is really sick, Mr. Whipple. I saw a case like this back in Illinois, and it turned out to be a bad appendix. I think you'd better get him to a doctor. If his appendix pops out here, he'll suffer a lot of terrible pain and more than likely die a slow death."

Eli had seen a case of ruptured appendix once and his face twisted in anguish as he considered what Beth Ann said.

Beth Ann, feeling more confident by the minute, pushed on, "Mark's in no shape to go on, Mr. Whipple. If we turn around right now, we can get him back to a doctor in Independence in a few days."

"Maybe you're right," Eli said. "First Ma died, and now Mark is too sick to know where he is. We can afford to lose Mark. I believe the Lord is telling us to head back."

Beth Ann turned away and had to control herself to keep from dancing. Now she had to make sure Mark stayed sick, until they got to Independence. Once there, she would figure out how to get away.

Early the next morning, they turned the wagon east and headed back to Independence. Beth Ann made sure Mark downed a cup of hot coffee before they broke camp. Mathew and Beth Ann herded the livestock while Eli drove the wagon.

Mark was really beginning to look bad, so Beth Ann decided to stop feeding him the tainted coffee for a day. When he seemed to be feeling better, she returned to adding the juice to his cup. Her only worry was that she would run out of the hemlock before they reached Independence. She pushed Eli to start each day's trip before sunrise and prodded him not stop until well after dark.

It took four days of hard travel before they reached Independence and made their camp. It had become too painful for Mark to ride horseback and he had spent the last day stretched out in the back of the wagon.

Before the horses were unhitched Eli had Mathew help him carry Mark out of the wagon and lift him onto a horse. Mathew held him while Eli mounted and reached out to balance Mark as they headed toward town to find a doctor. Beth Ann begged to come along, but Eli told her to stay with Mathew to get camp set up.

After an examination the doctor told Eli that Mark had probably eaten some tainted meat, and a few days of eating mush would straighten out his stomach. He just needed some time for his system to right itself.

Jacob's Promise

Eli was furious with Mark for being such a weakling and mad at himself for letting that Hesser girl talk him into coming back to Independence. His anger cooled some when Mark was able to finish a bowl of mush at breakfast and announced that the stomach cramps were gone.

The lack of cramps didn't make Beth Ann happy, but she was afraid to try using the hemlock again. She had to figure out a way to get to town. She slammed cooking pans around in frustration. She had gotten back to Independence and was still a captive.

The morning of their second day in Independence, Eli announced that Mark was fit enough to travel and that they would be leaving the next day.

Beth Ann was panic-stricken. She had been trying feverously to figure out a way to get into town, but Eli had kept her in camp and far out on the edge of the city.

The afternoon before they were to leave, Beth Ann knew she had to do something fast or she was going to be stuck with the Whipples'. The answer came as she was washing the coffee pot. She dried the pot and cautiously slipped around to the back of the wagon, out of Eli's sight.

She found a sturdy, sharp pointed knife, and slowly worked a hole in a rusted spot on the bottom of pot. Satisfied the hole looked like natural wear, she carried the pot over to Eli, who was sitting on his stool reading his bible in the shade of the wagon.

"If you want any more coffee on this trip, I'm going to need a new pot. This one has a hole rusted in it and is leaking like a sieve."

"The boys are off watering the stock, when they come back, I'll send Mark to get a new one," Eli answered and went back to reading his Bible.

Beth Ann's face went white. She had to think fast.

"No," she said a little louder than she intended. Getting control of her emotions she said in as calm a voice as she could muster. "Those boys don't know what I need in a coffee pot. They'll come back with some cheap piece of junk that'll rust out in about three days. If I'm the cook, I want to pick out my own coffee pot."

"All right," Eli growled. "You can go, but I'll send the boys in with you just to see that you get back safe."

"Safe," Beth Ann muttered as she turned away. "They just want to keep me under their thumb." She hurried out to find the boys and tell them they were going to town.

Beth Ann's mind was in a whirl on the ride into town. How was she going to get away? As they rode down the street Beth Ann searched every bench and doorway looking for a sign of Joe. She tried to delay their return to camp by refusing every coffee pot she was offered. After this happened for the third time Mark exploded.

"You'll take the next pot you're offered, or I'll pick one." He grabbed her by the arm and pulled her into the next store. "Now pick a damn pot and let's get out of here."

Beth Ann was determined to make one last desperate try to escape. When they left the store, she decided she would run to the middle of the street and start screaming for help. She was ready to make a run for freedom when someone yelled, "Hey, there girl. Yeh, you. Just hold on a minute."

Beth Ann and the two Whipple boys turned to see who had yelled. Two unshaven men came running down the street toward them. The blood drained from Beth Ann's face when she recognized it was the Cooper brothers. She turned her back and stood facing Mark.

Willie stopped behind Beth Ann, grabbed her by the arm, and jerked her around to face him. "Where's yer no-good brother?"

Mark angrily stepped between them and gave Willie a rough shove. "Let her go. If you have questions to ask, you ask me."

Willie's fist flew out like a lightning bolt and smashed Mark square on the nose. Seeing Mark fall to his knees, Mathew charged forward and clamped his arm around Willie's neck. Simon stepped around Willie and grasping Mathew's hair in one hand he began punching him with the other. The punches caused Mathew to let Willie slip from his grip.

Mark jumped to his feet and drove his shoulder into Willie's gut, wrestling him to the ground. Mathew stomped on Simon's foot, jerked free and turned to deliver a punch to Simon's midsection. Trading punches the men stood toe-to-toe slugging each other, while Mark and Willie thrashed around on the ground under their feet

Beth Ann saw her chance and slowly backed away from the fighters and ran. She was searching for a place to hide when she saw the thin frame of Joe Adams sitting on a wooden bench.

"What are you doing back here?" He asked when she came to a stop in front of him. "Where's Jacob?"

"Oh, Joe. I can't believe I've found you."

"Come over here, sit down, and tell me what's going on. I saw you come out of the store with those boys but didn't see the other two until that scruffy looking one grabbed you."

"Help me Joe. I need to hide. Those are the Cooper brothers."

"Yes, I've met the Cooper boys," Joe said with a chuckle. "I think you can stop worrying, Take a look."

Beth Ann looked where Joe pointed and saw two lawmen collar all four of the boys. She let out a sigh of relief as she watched them being marched off. She became aware that she was still clutching the coffee pot. With disgust, she dropped it and kicked it out into the street.

Suddenly she realized how alone she was. "Joe, I need help. It's not just the Cooper brothers, it's the Whipple brothers too. They're holding me captive."

Joe put his arm around Beth Ann. "Lean back, take a deep breath, and tell me why Jacob's not with you."

Beth Ann relaxed a little and let the story tumble out. Joe kept stopping her to get her to slow down. By the time she was finished, she was crying.

"Help me get some men so I can go look for Jacob," Beth Ann said as she wiped her eyes.

"Beth Ann, if Jacob was caught by Indians, I'm afraid he's probably dead. Someone must have done something to those Indians to make them want to run Jacob down the way they did."

"I just can't believe he's dead," she sobbed.

Joe gave he a squeeze and tried to console her. "I'm sorry to hear about Jacob. He was a fine boy. It won't make you feel any better, but at least the Coopers can now go home and leave you alone. As for the Whipple's, I'll talk to the sheriff and see that they won't trouble you anymore.'

That evening, Joe took Beth Ann down to the jail to see the Coopers. His new crutches slowed him some, but he managed to keep up with Beth Ann. At the jail, Joe went to the cells of the Cooper boys. "I don't like you, so it doesn't give me any pleasure to tell you, Jacob Hessers dead. You have no call to be bothering

Beth Ann. If you bother her in any way, I'll see that you're put back in jail. Now you can go home and tell your daddy what happened."

He stepped over to the Whipples' cell. "I understand you both saw the Indians catch Jacob. Tell me about it."

"Yeah, we saw the Indians catch him, but we were too far away to help," Mark said.

Mathew let out a giggle. "We sure did see them grab him. I bet he was dead before the day was out."

Joe's face turned as hard as stone. "This is the way it's going to be, boys. If I see any of you within fifty feet of Beth Ann after you get out of jail, I'm going to file kidnapping charges against you and demand that you be held for trial. The judge makes his circuit here every six weeks. He was here last week so it will be five weeks before he comes back. Which one of you wants to take his chances with a trial five weeks from now?"

"Just let us pay our fine and get out of here," Mark said.

"I'm sure that'll please Beth Ann." Joe turned back to the Coopers. "Okay, what have you boys decided you are going to do?"

"We'll leave town too," Willie said, "but I want Beth Ann to answer one question. Did Jacob gun down our brothers?"

Beth Ann looked straight into Willie's eyes and asked, "Did you and your brothers set our cabin on fire and burn my parents to death? I've figured out the answer to my question, you have to figure out the answer to yours."

Turning to the Whipples, Joe said," I understand you have Jacob's horses and supplies. What you don't know is that some of those supplies belong to me. I'm going to make a list of everything that belongs to the two of us and ask the sheriff to see that it's returned."

Beth Ann gave the sheriff a list of the supplies the pack horses were carrying. Two deputies took the list and left with the Whipples.

The next morning Joe rented a buggy and took Beth Ann down to the docks to watch Willie and Simon get on the boat, but Willie and Simon never showed up to board.

CHAPTER 33

Winston entertained Jacob with stories about his travels down the Ohio River and across the wilderness of Missouri and Kansas, while Jacob slowly recovered most of his strength and Winston's animals were rested enough to travel. At the end of four days Winston apologized, but said he had to be moving on. He knew Jacob was not completely healed, but four days were as long as he could delay his travel.

"You're welcome to ride with us. I don't have a saddle to offer you, you'll have to ride bareback," Winston said.

"I'll ride standing on my head if it will get me back up to the trail," Jacob answered.

The next morning Jacob had to be lifted onto his horse to start the trip. Winston purposely kept the pace slow, knowing how painful the ride was for Jacob. In late afternoon Jacob told Winston they had reached the point where he needed to get off.

"Sorry we couldn't get you closer to your goal, but this is the best we can do. I had Beaman pack you enough dry food to last a week. I hope that will sustain you. Good luck in your search for your sister."

Jacob watched them ride away then pulled the pack they had made for him onto his back and started west. He still had some miles to go before he reached the trail. He hadn't traveled far before the pull of the pack caused an aching pain in his rib cage.

He took the pack off and sat by the road disgusted at his weakness.

It took him a day and a half day of slow painful travel to reach a part of the rutted Oregon trail he recognized. Too weary to go any farther he sat down to wait for the first sign that wagons used this part of the mile-wide trail. His biggest fear was that his food would run out before any wagons appeared.

He had camped by the trail for four days without seeing a soul. He had kept himself on half rations for the last four days and felt his strength slipping. At about noon on the fifth day of his vigil, he saw dust on the horizon.

Two hours later three freight wagons pulled by oxen emerged from the dust and headed straight for him. The wagons were bigger and more heavily constructed than any Jacob had seen before. He slipped his pack on his shoulders and waited for the first wagon. Pushing himself to the limit he matched the oxen's speed and walked along side

"Have you got room to give a ride to a man stuck out here without a horse?"

"I'm not going to stop. You'll have to throw your pack in the back and climb up with the wagon moving."

Jacob's ribs rebelled when he tried to lift the pack up into the wagon. He gritted his teeth and using all the strength he could muster heaved the pack up over the tailgate. His climb up the side of the moving wagon was another struggle that left his side burning with pain.

"Mister, you just saved my life. I thought I was going to be stuck out here for the rest of the summer. My name's Jacob Hesser."

Jacob offered his hand. The driver took it with a callused hand so big it engulfed Jacob's. The man was wearing a dark felt hat, and a dark jacket covered with dust. Coal black hair peeked out from under the hat and black eyes shined from under his bushy eyebrows. A deep voice came from the moist opening between a thick mustache and beard.

"Dulucky Sanders." He shook Jacob's hand. "How in the world did you end up out here in the middle of nowhere without a horse?"

"It's a long story. I'm sure I'll have plenty of time to tell it if you let me ride along. Are you headed to Oregon by any chance?"

Jacob's Promise

"No, we're hauling supplies out to Jim Bridger's trading post," Dulucky answered.

"Is this Bridger place near Oregon?" Jacob asked.

"Right now, we're headed in that direction, but to get to Bridger's place, we turn off from the trail that leads to Oregon territory and head southwest."

"If you'll let me, I'd like to ride with you until you turn off. I'm willing to work to pay for my keep."

"We might be able to put you to work. One of the boys helping herd the animals had his horse fall on him and broke his leg. We sent him back to Independence on a freight wagon headed east. You know how to ride?"

"Yes sir, I can ride and herd. I appreciate the chance to show you."

"I'll see what the other drivers say when we stop to rest the animals. But I don't see any problem with them agreeing with your hire. Now tell me that long story you promised."

Jacob told about how he started out in Illinois but skipped over everything that happened between Illinois and leaving Independence. He told about joining the Whipples and how the Whipple brothers pushed him off the cliff.

"So, the Whipples got rid of you and kidnapped your sister? I take it you're trying to catch up with the Whipple's before they get to Oregon?"

"I know they're a week or so ahead of me, but they have my sister and I'll do anything I have to do to catch them."

They rode in silence until the noon rest stop. There Jacob met the other two drivers, Pink Hays and Luke Hinson. Billy and Tommy Flanagan, the two young boys riding herd on the animals, rode in and were introduced. The boys didn't look like they could be more than fourteen or fifteen years old. The two drivers readily agreed they could use another hand.

"It's one more set of eyes for night watch," Billy said.

"And one more gun to chase off horse thieves," Tommy added.

Jacob took an immediate liking to Pink. He had an open face and a merry twinkle in his blue eyes. He had a beard stained from tobacco juice and long blond hair that reached down his back and over his shoulders.

Bill Heyduck

Luke Hinson was a dark quiet man who seldom spoke unless asked a direct question. He had the look of a man who had lived a hard life. His lined face made him look older than his true age.

"The saddle, from the boy that was hurt, is in the back of the wagon. Tommy can roust it out while Billy cuts out a horse for you to ride."

Billy delivered the horse, but Jacob found he needed help to lift the saddle onto the horse and cinch it. He refused help to get on the horse, determined to ride the day without complaint.

At sundown, when the wagons stopped for the night, Jacob slid from the saddle and almost collapsed. He had to lean against the horse and hold onto the saddle horn until the pain subsided enough that he felt he could stand erect. Through gritted teeth he unsaddled his horse without asking for help.

He grew stronger and more pain free with each passing day. By the end of the second week he was almost back to his old self.

The days along the trail passed with numbing similarity. The slow pace of the animals kept the horses at a walk giving Jacob's ribs a chance to heal. He was lucky that his arm was only sprained and not broken.

The Flanagan brothers were glad to have Jacob as part of the crew. It meant they had one more person to put in the night watch rotation. The three wagons parked each night in a triangle formation with all the animals driven up between them and ropes tied between the wagons to keep them penned in.

One afternoon in the second week Jacob was riding in a cloud of dust behind the herd when he saw the lead wagon stop. As he watched, the other two wagons pulled up beside the first.

"What are we are stopping for?" Jacob asked Billy, who was riding beside him.

"I think they've spotted some Indians on the trail up ahead," Billy answered.

Jacob looked up through the dust and saw that a group of Indians were blocking the trail. Both Billy and Jacob pulled their rifles from their saddle scabbards and nervously watched.

"What do ya think they want?" Tommy asked as he rode up beside them.

"Think we should ride up there in case there's trouble?" Jacob asked.

Jacob's Promise

"No," Billy answered. "Dulucky's dealt with the Indians before. He'll let us know if they need us."

They watched Dulucky climb down off the wagon and walk out to meet the Indians. They couldn't hear what was being said, but there seemed to be a lot of hand movement and gestures. The longer they talked, the more agitated the Indians became. Suddenly, the Indians broke away yelling and rode off waving their weapons.

"Go find out what's going on, Jacob, and come back and tell us," Tommy said.

Jacob got to the wagons just as Dulucky returned.

"What was all the ruckus about?" Jacob asked.

"They want rifles and ammunition as payment for us crossing their territory. I'm not about to give them rifles. Said we'd give them an ox. They refused and rode off."

"Think they're finished with us?" Jacob asked.

"Those Sioux are tough customers and don't run off that easy. They'll be back either to fight or to see what they can steal. So, keep on your toes. Go tell the Flanagan's to keep their eyes open," Dulucky said.

That night there were two men on each tour of guard duty, and everyone slept with the rifles by his side. Three hours before sunrise, Billy was walking his post about half asleep when he came around a wagon and almost stepped on an Indian. The Indian was half way to his feet when Billy swung his rifle around and pulled the trigger.

A second Indian charged out of the darkness before Billy could reload. The Indian was only a step away when a shot rang, dropping the Indian. Pink stepped up beside Billy reloading his rifle.

At the sound of the first shot, everyone was up with rifles ready. Dulucky and Luke checked the area around the outside of the wagons and came back to report the Indians had pulled back.

"I think it best if we all stay up. It'll be dawn in a couple of hours," Dulucky said.

At dawn they ate a quick, cold breakfast while Dulucky reviewed what had happened, "It's too bad you had to shoot two of them," he said. "They'll want revenge for sure. They'll be back."

That morning they had traveled less than a mile when the Indians appeared on the trail ahead of them. Pink was driving the lead wagon and yelled a warning. Jacob and the Flannigan's' hurriedly drove the herd between the circled wagons and jumped off their horses to get ropes to secure the animals. They had finished tying the last rope into place when the Indians let out a wild yell and charged.

"Take turns firing. One person fire while the next one reloads," Dulucky called out.

Jacob had often shot running rabbis, but a wild Indian charging straight at him had his adrenalin charged heart racing at full gallop. He couldn't stop his hands from shaking as he aimed, and he hit the horse and not the rider. The front legs of the horse folded and sent it plunging head first to the ground. The Indian twisted through the air, smashing to earth a few feet in front of the horse, his neck broken. The fall had done the job Jacob had intended his bullet to do.

Arrows filled the air, one missing Jacob by inches as it thudded into the side of the wagon. The blue sulfurous smoke from burned gunpowder filled the air, burning Jacob's eyes. He frantically reloaded and searched for a second target, his heart pounding from fear and excitement.

As suddenly as they had appeared the Indians withdrew and galloped over a hill and out of sight. Jacob saw three Indian bodies lying in the dust in front of the wagons. If he had counted right the Indians had lost a third of their war party.

"Let's get out of here and let the Indians pick up their dead," Pink said.

Everyone ran to untie the ropes holding in the stock and then stopped when they heard Tommy yell, "Over here. Luke's hurt."

They rushed to Luke stretched out beside a wagon wheel with an arrow in his throat.

"Quick, get him in the wagon before the Indians see him. Seeing one of us down might give then just enough courage to come at us again," Dulucky said. "Jacob, you're a farm boy you should know how to drive a wagon. Get up there and drive Luke's wagon."

Jacob jumped on the wagon and pulled it in behind Pink. The minute they started to move, Jacob started to shake. The fight was

Jacob's Promise

over, and the adrenalin had drained away leaving him so weak he could hardly hold the reins.

CHAPTER 34

They traveled the rest of the day without sighting any more Indians. After they stopped for the night, they waited until dark to dig a grave to bury Luke. They ran the oxen back and forth over the grave to trample it down so the Indians wouldn't be aware that they had lost a member of their crew.

After eating the evening meal, Pink said he would take the first four hours of night guard with Dulucky taking the second four hours. The boys worked a rotating two-hour shift through the night. Those not on guard duty lay with their rifles in their hands expecting to hear an Indian war whoop at any minute.

They were a sleepy bunch the next morning as they sat around the fire eating their breakfast of mush and bacon. After eating Dulucky stood before the group and waited for everyone's attention.

"With Luke gone, me and Pink have decided we need Jacob to drive Luke's wagon the rest of the trip. He's had the most experience driving a team." He paused then said, "There's one other thing we need to clear up.

"Luke doesn't have any kinfolk that Pink and me know of, so we decided that since Billy and Tommy make the least amount of money they should get one-fourth of Luke's pay, and Jacob will be entitled to three-fourths." He waited a minute to give anyone who wanted to disagree. "Since no one has anything to say let's get hitched and get on our way."

It took what seemed like endless weeks before they reached the flat, meandering Platte River and began following it west along its south bank. Dulucky swore every time they had to cross the many shallow muddy flats of the South Platte River. The crossing of each branching tributary was a struggle with floundering animals and axle-deep mud.

At the end of the third day, everyone was worn out and mud caked. Pink told the boys to make camp and expect to spend a few days. The animals needed to rest and graze to recover their strength. The men and boys were as weary as the animals. They spent the rest of the day washing their muddy clothes and lying in the shade telling stories.

The third day out from the Platte Jacob was driving the lead wagon. He enjoyed being able to breathe clean air for a change and not eat the dust of a wagon traveling in front of him. The reverie of the morning suddenly stopped when one of his wagon wheels dropped in a deep hole.

The wagon's axle split with a crack like a rifle shot followed by a nerve tingling screech. The wagon pitched violently to the right, throwing Jacob off his seat and onto the hard-packed ground. Flat on his back he watched helplessly as the leaning wagon leaned over him.

It teetered menacingly for a few seconds before it settled back upright. His heart in his throat, Jacob scrambled out of the shadow of the menacing wagon. He had managed to escape uninjured, but one of the oxen, twisted grotesquely in its yoke, was screaming in pain.

Jacob had climbed to his feet by the time Dulucky and Pink reached him.

"Are you alright, boy?" Pink asked as he studied Jacob's pale face.

"I'm okay," Jacob said trying to catch his breath." It all happened so fast."

"Somebody shoot that damn animal before it panics all the others," Pink yelled.

Dulucky ran to his wagon for his rifle and returned to shoot the ox. Pink and Jacob worked frantically to free the others before they panicked. When the last animal had been freed, Dulucky crawled under the wagon to inspect the damage.

"The axle's broke and needs to be replaced. One wheel's bent, but I think it's salvageable," Dulucky grunted. "We won't know until we get the wagon lifted. It's going to take a while to get it fixed."

Pink, Dulucky, and Jacob started unloading the wagon, while Billy and Tommy moved the animals over to the river to drink. It took all five of them to lever the wagon up so boxes of freight could be put under the frame to hold it up for the axle to be removed. Dulucky worked the rest of the afternoon to free the axle, but darkness stopped him from finishing the job.

The next morning Dulucky freed the axle from the wagon frame and showed Pink the twisted metal frame that held it in place. "We're going to have to unload the blacksmith tools to straighten this out. The axle's a total loss, we'll need to use the spare."

"Billy and Tommy can help Pink get the new axle out of the wagon. Jacob can help me unload the forge," Dulucky said.

Soon the sturdy legged fire pan was set up and coke fire burning. Sweat poured from Jacob as he pumped the billows to bring the fire to white heat. After heating the metal rim and a lot of pounding, Dulucky forced it back on the wheel. When the wheel was finished, Jacob brought the twisted axle bracket to the forge to be straightened.

He was busy pumping on the bellows when Billy and Tommy came driving the animals in between the wagons.

"Indians down by the river," Billy yelled as he rode in.

Everyone stopped what they were doing, secured the animals, then grabbed their rifles, and faced the river. Three Indians sat on horses watching. An hour later they were joined by ten more and started riding slowly toward the freight wagons. Before they came within rifle range they turned and rode in a wide circle around the wagons. They would stop and sit for a while, then circle again.

"Damn, I wish they'd make some kind of move or go away so we could get back to work," Dulucky growled.

"You and Jacob get back to straightening that bracket. Me and the boys will watch the Indians," Pink said.

The fire to heat the metal bracket had died down to embers so

Jacob's Promise

Jacob had to pump furiously to get the metal hot again. They worked until dark getting the bracket straightened and fitted to the axle. Overcome by weariness and the fading light they gave up trying to secure the axle to the wagon bed. Tired as they were, they had to spend another nervous night guarding the horses.

At daybreak, the Indians were back. This time they made small threatening charges, but again pulled up out of rifle range. With each charge, everyone dropped what they were doing and grabbed a rifle, only to see the Indians retreat.

Each time this happened, Dulucky got more frustrated. "To hell with those savages," he said. "Billy, you and Tommy watch them and let us know if they come any closer. The rest of us will get the axle on. I want to be on the road before noon tomorrow."

Jacob, Dulucky, and Pink went to work fitting the axle back on the wagon but were never more than a step away from their rifles. By dusk, all that remained to be done was to slip the wheel back on the hub and pull the blocks out from under the wagon bed. They ate a cold supper and grudgingly took their turn at guard duty.

The next morning the Indians had disappeared. The travelers were all a little bleary eyed from lack of sleep as they stumbled to the fire and ate cold breakfast of hard biscuits and jerky. The axle had been strapped back in place before dark and they only had the wheel to wrestle with. When the wagon was resting on its four wheels again, they were ready to hitch the oxen and start on the trail to Laramie.

The wagons were moving before the sun was midway in the sky. The rest of the day was uneventful. Each day started the same. Feed the campfire, cook and eat, hitch the oxen, and head west. The numbing sameness of each day's routine turned into weeks.

The sudden appearance of smoke on the horizon caused a tingle of excitement to run down Jacob's spine. Laramie.

Jacob was disappointed in what he saw when they reached the settlement. Fort Laramie was nothing but a two-story log building surrounded by a wall. He had expected to see a town, not a trading post and a few shabby buildings.

Dulucky, driving the lead wagon, didn't stop to camp until he was a quarter of a mile west of the Indians camped around the fort.

Bill Heyduck

The Indian camps were filled with women, children, and a lot of barking dogs. This was the first time Jacob had seen any Indian women. Pink said they were mostly Cheyenne, Arapaho and a few Sioux, here to trade furs for calico cloth, trinkets, and guns, if they were available.

"I thought the different tribes didn't get along," Jacob said. "They seem peaceful enough here."

"There's a truce when they come to trade, but if they met each other out on the prairie there'd shore enough be a squabble," Pink said.

"Don't leave anything loose laying around or some Indian will be running off with it," Dulucky cautioned.

"I want to go into the fort and see if I can get any news about the Whipples or my aunt and uncle," Jacob said.

"Take Pink with you," Dulucky said. "He knows the man who runs the trading post, and he'll know if your sister or other of your kin folks came through."

Jacob and Pink rode through the gate of the post and tied their horses to the rail in front of the building. They ducked through a low door, framed in rough cut logs and into a dark room piled high with animal hides. The room stunk of tobacco smoke and half cured hides. The stink of hides turned Jacob's stomach and the smoke burned his eyes.

"How can anyone spend a whole day in this place and still breathe?" Jacob whispered to Pink.

"It's like any job, you get used to it," Pink answered.

The interior of the post was dark, the only light came from two small windows and the open doorway. The proprietor, standing at the end of the room, finished settling with an Indian for his furs. He looked up and saw Pink.

"Pink Hays! I do declare you've survived another trip to St. Louis and back. I thought you'd be tired of hauling freight and have stayed in St. Louis to settle down," he said.

"Hi, Cleo. I see you're still here cheatin' the Indians." Pink chuckled.

"Don't say that too loud, someone might believe you. You wanna get me scalped?"

"Sorry, I didn't mean to cause a ruckus. I've got a boy here that's looking for some people you might have seen."

Jacob's Promise

Jacob stepped forward and extended his hand. "I'm looking for some people by the name of Whipple or Heinz who might have passed through here on their way to Oregon. The Whipples would be a father, two boys, and a young girl. The Heinz would be a man and his red headed wife."

"I remember the Whipples. They was through here 'bout a week ago, and they'd be hard to ferget, but there weren't no girl with 'em. I don't recollect anyone named Heinz, but then again I don't get all the names of those that passes through."

"Are you sure a girl wasn't with the Whipples?"

"Oh, Lordy, yes I'm shore," Cleo said. "Them folks caused a real hullabaloo. The older Whipple boy tried to grab on ta a little half-wit Indian girl to cook for 'em. He filled her head with promises of finery oncet they got to Oregon. Gave her some sparkly beads to get her in their wagon afore they took off.

"They was five miles out of town for her daddy heard about it. He and some kin chased 'em down and got the girl back. The Whipples was damn lucky to get away with their scalps."

Jacob was dumbstruck by the news that Beth Ann wasn't with the Whipples. He finally accepted the fact that Beth Ann wasn't with them and numbly followed Pink back to camp.

They were still in the saddle when Dulucky called out to them, "Any news?"

"Cleo says the people Jacob was looking for passed through, but his sister wasn't with them," Pink answered.

Dulucky studied Jacob's drawn face "You have to face it, boy. If your sister wasn't with the Whipples it means she's probably someplace behind us or then again, I hate to say it, but you have to realize something may have happened to her."

"If the Whipples did anything to her, I'll track them down and kill the whole bunch." Jacob yanked off his hat and beat it against his leg. Then his face twisted in anguish as he added, "I'm sure in a fix. I don't know which way to go."

Dulucky walked over to the side of Jacob's horse and put his hand on Jacob's knee. "Why don't you stay with us? In a week or two it'll be too late for anyone to get through South Pass before the snow closes it. There's no way your sister's going to get ahead of you."

"Come winter with us at Bridger's," Pink added. "With the

money you'll earn driving and a job in Bridger's you'll have enough to outfit yourself for the trip west next summer."

Jacob didn't answer. He was too lost in troubled thoughts about Beth Ann.

CHAPTER 35

That night at supper Jacob mechanically shoveled beans and biscuits into his mouth. His head filled with such a jumble of dire thoughts he didn't taste the food or hear the conversation. He was thinking about Beth Ann.

Was she hurt? Was she ahead of him, or as Pink suggested, was she behind him? If she somehow got back to Independence, there was still the chance he could catch her at South Pass late next summer.

Pink was right. He was going to have to wait until next summer to find out. With that settled in his mind, he spoke to the others sitting around the fire.

"I've decided to go with you to Bridger's fort. I'll wait and try to catch Beth Ann at South Pass next summer."

"I didn't think you had any other choice," Dulucky said. "I knew you wouldn't want to sit here in Fort Laramie all winter."

After coming out of his mental fog, Jacob half-heartedly joined in the story telling and lies around the evening campfire. The weight of worry was still there, but like Dulucky said, he wouldn't be happy sitting out the winter in Laramie.

They left Fort Laramie the next morning and ventured out onto the flat, dry prairie to the west. It was slow, monotonous travel, broken up by troublesome hills and gullies. Relief came when they reached Independence Rock and the Sweetwater River.

They found grass for the animals and clear water to drink. They spent two days resting the animals for the final push into Bridger's fort.

"Rest up because it doesn't get any easier from here on out," Pink said. "The area up around Devil's Gate really gets rough."

Jacob lost count of how many times they had to ford the Sweetwater as it wandered across the landscape like a snake. The trip past Devil's Gate was everything Pink said it would be. On this stretch it was Dulucky who suffered a wreck. The left rear wheel cracked when it slipped off a boulder and took a half a day to repair.

At South Pass, the only known pass over the mountains, Dulucky pointed out to Jacob that they would be turning south off the trail that led to Oregon and heading to Bridger's fort.

"The Oregon trail runs straight on west of here," Dulucky said. "This is where you'll have to come to meet the wagon trains next summer. The first ones from Independence should start getting here around the first part of August.

The trail south to Bridger's fort was a rough, dangerous one for the freight wagons. More than once they came close to toppling a wagon over into a steep sided ravine. The welcome sight of Bridger's fort came into view a little after noon on the sixth day.

The wagons rolled to a stop in front the largest of a group of low, squat log buildings clustered together on the valley floor. The three weary drivers climbed down and stretched their stiff muscles. Billy and Tommy corralled the spare oxen and horses before joining the others. The long trip was over, and they could look forward to a good meal and a night's sleep under a roof. Maybe even a bath.

Jim Bridger came to meet them with a big smile and a loud whoop for a greeting.

"Glad to see you got here and that you came loaded with supplies. I was getting a little worried that the snow might get here before you did."

"We made it, and we'll make it back with your furs," Pink said.

"Where's Luke?" Bridger said as he led them through the front of the trading post and into a small room behind shelves filled with an assortment of trade goods. The room was sparsely furnished with little to no decoration.

The walls were bare logs and the lone window had no curtain. There was a small stove in the corner, a bed against one wall, and a round table in the middle of the room surrounded by stools and a few roughly made chairs.

A man in buckskin with long flowing blond hair and a beard to match was sitting at the table. He had a cup in his right hand and a sling made of calico cloth holding his left arm against his chest. Between his beard and mustache, he had a broad smile that showed shining white teeth.

"Hello, Snow," Pink and Dulucky said in unison.

"I see you boys survived another trip to civilization and were able to escape," Snow said.

"You know St. Louis has no hold on us, Snow," Pink joked. "Hey, I got some people I want you to meet. These two are our herders, the Flanagan boys, Billy and Tommy. And this here's Jacob Hesser, our spare wagon driver. Boys meet Snow, a mountain man you've probably heard tales about." Pink winked at them.

"I'm sorry sir, I didn't get your last name," Jacob said.

"I left my last name back in Independence, and I don't need it anymore." Snow leaned back in his chair. "Out here a man needs a new name to go with his new life."

Jacob was surprised at how articulate Snow sounded, not like he expected from a mountain man.

"Everyone have a seat," Bridger said, "There's coffee for the three boys over on the stove, and I have something a little stronger for the rest of you."

"Where's your partner, Vasquez?" Dulucky asked.

"Louis is out making a visit to one of the Shoshone villages to show off some of our trade goods. He should be back by the end of next week."

"How was the trip out?" Snow asked as soon as everyone was seated.

Pink and Dulucky took turns telling about the trip and how Jacob had happened to join them. The Flanagan boys joined in when they got to the Indian attack and Luke's death. They told how Jacob filled in driving Luke's wagon and what a good, dependable driver he turned out to be.

Jacob sat without saying a word, hoping Pink and Dulucky would remember to ask about work for him at the fort. He relaxed when Pink spoke up for him.

"Jacob is going to need a job to carry him over 'til later next summer. He needs to make enough for his keep and for horses and supplies to get to Oregon," Pink said.

"He wants to be up at South Pass next August when the first wagon trains start getting there. He has a sister that he expects will be on one of them," Dulucky added.

"I'm sure we can find some work for him," Bridger said. But I'm not sure it's going to make him enough to outfit him for a trip all the way to Oregon."

"He'll have his pay for driving the wagon so that should be enough if he doesn't get in too many card games," Pink laughed.

"Thank you, sir, I really appreciate it," Jacob said to Bridger.

"I need to change the subject, and I'm not sure Pink and Dulucky are going to like what I am going to say," Bridger said. "I know you two were planning to winter over here at the fort, but I really need you to turn the wagons around and head back to St. Louis.

"I'm up to my ears in pelts, and I'm going to need trade goods as soon as I can get them. I figure if you leave as soon as you rest a day or two, you can be back in Independence by October and get down the river to St. Louis before it freezes. Wouldn't you rather spend the winter in St. Louis?"

"We'll need fresh animals and a driver to take Jacob's place," Pink said.

"I'll have the wagons as good as new, fresh animals, and a driver in a couple of days. Will you be able to roll by then?" Bridger asked.

"We'll be ready. We'll miss Jacob. He did a fine job for us," Dulucky said.

Snow sat quietly and listened to them haggle over fees and loads for the trip back to St. Louis. When they had it all settled, he turned to Jacob.

"Pink and Dulucky seem to have high praise for you, boy. I wouldn't make this offer to just anyone, but since those two are so high on you, I'll make it."

Jacob wondered what kind of an offer Snow was talking

about. He knew that if it took him away from South Pass, he would turn it down.

"You can see I only have one good wing and it's going to be a month before I can use the other one. If I'm going to haul my supplies and get to a trapping camp, I'm going to need some help.

"If you'll agree to come with me and help me trap this winter, I'll furnish all the supplies and give you one-fourth of all the pelts we get. It'll be hard work, but you'll be able to make more than you can working here at the post."

Jacob looked over at Pink and Dulucky, hoping they'd give him some sign as to whether he should take up Snow's offer. Bridger gave him his answer before they could.

"What he says is true," Bridger said. "Going with Snow will be a free ride as far as food and lodging is concerned. If you have a good catch, you could make a lot more than you could working here."

Pink and Dulucky nodded their agreement.

"If I can be back to South Pass by the first week of August, I'll take you up on your offer, sir," Jacob said.

"We'll be done trapping come spring and get you back in plenty of time to get to South Pass. There's one other thing we need to get straight son. Don't call me sir. I'm Snow, and that's what I want you to call me."

"I guess that settles where Jacob is headed, but I didn't think to ask the Flanagan boys what they wanted to do. Are you boys going to stay here or go back with the wagons? I have work for you if you want to stay," Bridger said.

"Spending the winter in St. Louis sounds better than staying out here," Billy said.

Tommy nodded his head yes and it was settled.

"Since you'll be here for a few days before you start back, we need to find a place for all of you to bed down," Bridger said.

"Jacob can come with me to my shack," Snow said. "We'll start getting our supplies together. I want to get to our winter camp before the snow flies."

CHAPTER 36

Pink and Dulucky left the fort two days later while Snow and Jacob were packing to leave. Jacob worked steadily loading the packhorses under the watchful eye of Snow. The training Joe gave him back in St. Louis helped him demonstrate to Snow he wasn't a complete idiot when it came to pack animals.

With the last horse loaded, Jacob turned and faced Snow, "I know I'm a greenhorn at this trapping business, but aren't we starting out a little early in the season to be trapping beaver? I thought their pelts weren't much good until it got cold and they took on their winter coat."

"We need an early start because we have to go up north to a Shoshone village and pick up my woman. I drop her off each summer so she can visit with her kinfolks. We'll have to spend some time with her family, or we'll hurt their feelings."

Jacob's face showed his surprise. "You didn't say anything about a woman going with us."

"I've been with her for five years now. She doesn't speak too much English, but she can get across to you what she wants. I got a four-year-old boy that'll be coming along, too."

Jacob wondered what other surprises Snow had in store for him.

Snow led the way out of the fort and started down the trail that would take them to the Shoshone village. The day was warm when they started out, but the nights in the mountains were beginning to get chilly. Each night they sat around the fire with blankets draped over their shoulders while Snow educated Jacob on how to trap and skin a beaver.

"Before we do any trapping, we have to build ourselves a shelter. Some trappers live in a lean-to all winter, but I like something a little more comfortable, especially since there'll be my woman and boy with us," Snow said. "When I come in wet and cold from running a trap line, I want a warm, dry place to come to."

"Can we get that fancy a shelter built before the snow flies?" Jacob asked. "It sounds like a lot of work."

"You're going to be the only one able to do the heavy lifting, and that's another reason we left early. I wanted to make sure we had enough time to get it done. My woman, Blue Flower, will be a big help. "

Smoke from the Shoshone village came into view near the end of their tenth day of travel. Shoshone outriders had warned the village of their coming and Snow's arrival was greeted with barking dogs and shouting children. Jacob was a little jittery. He'd never been surrounded by so many Indians. Hearing all the babbling voices in a strange language was a little upsetting.

Snow smiled at his confusion. "You'll begin to catch on to what people are asking after a while. Just don't fight it or you'll never understand. You're my friend, and I'm thought of as a member of the tribe, so that makes you their friend."

Blue Flower came toward Snow holding a boy. Seeing Snow, the boy let out a scream of joy, wiggled away from his mother and ran to his father. He hung on to Snow's foot until Snow dismounted and took him into his arms.

Blue Flower pulled Snow and Jacob over to her sister's lodge and handed them a gourd filled with a steaming hot stew. She kept filling Jacob's cup until he couldn't take another drop and had to hold her off from refilling it again.

As Jacob ate, he watched the boy sitting in Snow's lap. His skin was lighter than the other Indian boys and his light brown hair had sunburned streaks of blond running through it. It was obvious he had a lot of Snow's blood in him.

That night there was more food and dancing to welcome Snow back. It was the small hours of the morning before the festivities ended, and Jacob was able to stumble off to his bed roll.

The next morning, while Snow and Jacob were sitting with Blue Flower's brother-in-law, Wounded Bull, a rider raced into camp shouting. Everyone jumped up and ran to their lodges for bows and arrows, then jumped on their horses and rode off.

"What's going on, Snow?" Jacob asked.

"They've spotted a herd of buffalo and everyone's going on the hunt. Get your rifle and horse this is an experience you'll never forget."

Snow and Jacob saddled their horses and followed the men out of the camp. The women rushed around settled children with the elders, searched for skinning knives and sent young boys out to bring in horses for them to transport the meat.

The buffalo herd was grazing in a low grassy valley three miles north of the Shoshone's camp. The Indians stopped below the crest of a hill overlooking the grazing herd. Snow tapped Jacob on the shoulder and pointed to the leader of the hunt. Jacob watched as the leader divided the braves into two groups.

With words and gestures, he instructed them on how he wanted them to approach the herd. Hidden behind the low hills one group rode around to the other side of the herd while the other group waited. With the groups in position on each side of the herd, they started riding slowly toward the valley.

Buffalo on the outer fringe of the herd saw them approaching and started to move. Their movement was picked up by the main part of the herd, and as if of one mind the herd surged away from the approaching riders.

With their horses at a full gallop, the braves charged down into the valley and alongside the thundering animals. They each picked one of the charging animals, matched its speed, and fired an arrow into its side.

Jacob had never seen such skillful horsemanship. His eyes swept over the two groups until he found Wounded Bull racing along beside a huge shaggy monster.

Wounded Bull raised his bow and let an arrow fly. The buffalo took a few steps and collapsed. Wounded Bull rode past the fallen animal, notched another arrow and pulled alongside another buffalo for the next shot.

The fever of the hunt overcame Jacob and like the Indians he was soon riding at breakneck speed alongside the charging herd. He had not realized what monsters they were until he was riding next to them. He matched one stride for stride but was having difficulty keeping his rifle pointed at the side of a big cow he had picked out. Holding the reins in his mouth he pointed the rifle at the beast's side and pulled the trigger.

The rifle cracked and the bullet pierced the cow's side, but instead of crumpling to the ground the cow swerved into the legs of Jacob's horse. The horse and Jacob went tumbling end over end. Some instinct made Jacob hang on to his rifle as he rolled away from the struggling horse to avoid being crushed.

The terrified horse jumped up and limped away before Jacob could catch it. Buffalo ran by on both sides of Jacob, one even brushing him with its hairy hide. Dust, noise, and the stink of their hot breath churned in the air around him. Any moment Jacob expected one of the huge horned heads to smash into him.

He was ready to make a wild dash between two huge buffalo when a young Indian raced through the swirling dust and pulled him up on the mount behind him. With Jacob clutching his rescuer's back they rode away from the stampeding herd. Out of danger the Indian unceremoniously shoved Jacob off the horse and returned to the hunt.

The herd passed and the dust had settled before Jacob found his horse grazing on the side of the hill. He led the horse back to the cow he shot and found a young girl skinning the animal.

She looked up at Jacob and smiled, then turned to her task. Jacob didn't know if he should claim his kill or if the buffalo now belonged to the tribe. Not knowing what he should do, he did nothing. He sat and watched the girl skin and butcher the buffalo. While he was watching the girl work, Snow rode up, his horse blowing hard from the run.

"I see you've learned the Indian way of letting the women take care of skinning and butchering. That's Blue Flower's youngest sister, Willow. When she's done you should offer the meat to Wounded Bull's family as a goodwill gesture, that way you'll become a big man in the eyes of the family."

"I hope I at least get to taste some of the meat before we

leave," Jacob said.

"Tonight, there'll be a feast and dancing that'll last all night. You've never seen a white man who appreciates his food the way these people do," Snow said as he rode away.

The dancing and feasting lasted two days. Jacob managed to stay up the first night, but by noon the next day he had found a shady spot and gone to sleep.

Later the dancing stopped, but the activities of the young people didn't. Jacob was pleased when the young men of the tribe included him in their foot races and other contests of speed and strength.

He held his own in most of the activities but became the butt of teasing when one of his wild shots with the bow and arrow put a hole in Wounded Bull's tepee. He became proficient at throwing a hatchet and, after some bumps and scrapes, he gave up trying to hang out of sight on the side of a running horse.

The time with the Shoshones allowed Jacob to relax and accept the fact that he had to take it one day at a time He knew he would find Beth Ann he just needed to be patient.

Jacob's Promise

CHAPTER 37

After eleven days with the tribe, Snow told Jacob they would be leaving in the morning. That night Snow gathered up their supplies and staked the horses near the lodge so they wouldn't have to sort them out of the main herd before they left.

By sunrise Jacob had loaded the packhorses and saddled his and Snow's horses. Blue Flower sat astride her horse bareback, using only a blanket for a saddle. Snow's young son sat in front of her, his small hands holding tight to the horse's mane.

"Blue Flower has another horse behind the lodge you need to get, Jacob. We have another rider going with us," Snow said.

"Who's the other rider?"

"Willow, Blue Flower's sister, the one who skinned your buffalo. Wounded Bull says he has supported her long enough. She has seventeen winters and is not yet married, so he's kicking her out. Blue Flower won't let me leave her, so she's coming along." Snow hid a smile.

Jacob didn't mean to feel selfish, but the girl coming along would mean another horse to care for and another mouth to feed. He found the horse Wounded Bull was giving Willow tied behind the teepee. The horse looked old, but capable of carrying Willow's slight frame.

Jacob threw the blanket Wounded Bull offered him, over its back and turned to find Willow standing at his elbow. He blushed when he realized she wanted him to lift her onto the horse.

He tentatively placed his hands around Willow's slender waist and lifted her onto the horse's back. Hoping the blush had left his face he turned and mounted his horse. With the whole camp gathered to wave goodbye, barking dogs included, they headed west toward the mountains.

After two weeks of travel Snow stopped them at a spot where they would build their winter quarters. The site was a flat area on the south side of a sloping incline. The camp would have sun most of the day and be protected from the chill of the northwest wind. There was a nearby stream for water, an abundance of trees for the cabin's construction and enough dry fallen timber to fuel their fires.

"We'll build a lean-to as temporary camp first, then start our winter quarters," Snow directed.

With the three of them working, and Snow giving directions, the women built the lean-to while Jacob unloaded the packhorses. Snow had the cooking fire going and a nice bed of coals by the time the lean-to was finished. Blue Flower and Willow soon had the evening meal prepared.

"Tomorrow we start on the winter cabin," Snow said.

The next morning, Snow marked out an area that represented the outline of the structure they were going to build. He gave Blue Flower and Willow a pick and shovel with instructions on what he wanted them to do.

Jacob was surprised that the women were expected to do such manual labor, but kept his mouth shut. He realized he still had a lot to learn about frontier life. Hearing Snow give his instructions in Shoshone made Jacob realize he was going to have to learn how to speak the language or he would never know what the women were telling him. He didn't like to be left out when the three of them started jabbering.

Snow had Jacob get an axe while he unpacked the crosscut saw. Then they set out to search for trees that could be used for the walls of the shelter. Snow marked several trees, then set Jacob to notching the first one.

When Jacob had cut a fourth of the way through the tree, Snow dragged the saw over to it. Using his good arm, Snow took

Jacob's Promise

hold of one end of the saw and helped Jacob saw until the tree fell. With the tree on the ground, Jacob went to work chopping off the branches to make a smooth log.

They felled fifteen trees the first day and were dead tired at suppertime. Snow's little son, Spider, who had helped his mother all day, fell asleep in her arms before he had finished eating. Willow brought Jacob his meal and sat and ate with him.

She tried to talk to him with hand signs and the few English words she knew. These conversations often ended with Willow leaning against Jacob giggling at their failed communication. In the beginning this closeness made Jacob uncomfortable, but it wasn't long before he started looking forward to their meals together. There was something about being near Willow that gave Jacob a feeling he had never had before.

Snow and Blue Flower watched approvingly as the two youngster's friendship deepened.

CHAPTER 38

Pink and Dulucky, along with the new driver Lem Crocker and the Flanagan boys, got to Independence during the first week in November. The trip back had its usual problems, but fortunately they had no run-ins with the Indians.

They left their wagons and animals in Independence and had the furs loaded onto the riverboat for the trip down river to St. Louis. They wouldn't get paid until the furs were secure in the warehouse there.

When their boat docked, they supervised the loading of the furs onto wagons and accompanied them to the warehouse. A warehouse clerk counted and accepted the furs.

He invited Pink and Dulucky into his office for coffee while he wrote them a receipt and got money from the safe to pay them their wages. They sat for half an hour drinking their coffee and talking about the trip.

"It's nice to be back where we can sleep under a roof and not have to worry about being wet and cold," Pink said.

"We didn't hit the rainy weather until we were almost to Independence," Dulucky added.

"You're just the folks I need to talk to," the clerk said. "My wife and I are planning to leave for Oregon come spring, and I'd like to have some idea of what we're going to face on the trip. We have a little girl traveling with us."

Jacob's Promise

"Well, mister, if you're traveling with a wagon train, the Indians shouldn't be a bother," Dulucky said. "They may try to steal some animals and sometimes they try to collect a bounty for crossing their land," Dulucky said. "But I don't think you have much to worry about."

"I saw three names on the inventory sheet," the clerk said. "Pink Hays, G. Dulucky Sanders, and Lem Crocker, but only two of you came with the furs."

"Lem has a woman in Independence and decided to stay a bit. You can send his pay up to him," Pink said.

The warehouse man counted out the money the company owed them and when he finished counting, he said, "I'm sorry I didn't introduce myself. I'm William Copple. I don't want to sound like a greenhorn, but I'd like to know a little bit more about what we might face headed west.

"When I tell my wife I talked to someone who has made the trip, she'll have a million questions. She's worried sick about a young niece and nephew wandering around out there somewhere searching for her," William said.

Pink looked over at Dulucky and said," There must be a lot of separated folks out there. We picked up a young man out on the prairie, looking for his sister. Name was Jacob Hesser. He ended up driving a wagon for us to Fort Bridger.

"Oh, my God! That's my wife's nephew. What about his sister," William asked.

"There wasn't any girl with him," Dulucky said. "He told us he was looking for his sister cause, they'd been separated by some no good travelers they had joined up with."

"Don't tell me anymore now," William said, "Let me give you the address of where we're staying. I want you to come to our place for supper tonight so my wife can hear your story. There's no use in you having to tell it twice."

William ushered the two men out of his office, threw on his coat, locked the door, and galloped to the dress shop to tell Ruth the news. At the dress shop he related what he had heard.

"We'll celebrate with steaks tonight," Ruth said almost dancing with joy. "Now go back and finish your work."

Ruth was so nervous that her work began to suffer. After hearing the news, she found herself tearing out as many stitches she put in the fancy dress she was working on.

"Ruth, why don't you go home? You're no good to me here. You've been as fidgety as a water bug ever since William brought you the news about your nephew." Olive shook her head sympathetically at Ruth's fumbling.

"Oh, thanks, Olive. I promise I'll make up for it tomorrow." Ruth hurried into her coat and helped Mary Ann, who came every day after school, with hers. Ruth flew out the door with the little girl scrambling to keep up.

Pink and Dulucky showed up at the house that evening. William poured them a drink of whisky while they waited for Ruth to call them to the table. She was anxious to hear their tale but refused to let them tell it until the meal was over.

She poured them a final cup of coffee then sat and listened intently as Pink and Dulucky alternated telling the story. Dulucky finished the tale by relating how Jacob was spending the winter trapping beaver with a mountain man. named Snow.

"It's hard to believe Jacob is trapping beaver. I don't think he knows much about trapping outside of the little he did on the farm," Ruth said.

"Snow has a bad arm and needed someone to help him, and Jacob wanted to make enough money to be able to buy horses and supplies to get to Oregon." Dulucky said.

"Jacob's with a real good man," Pink added.

"You say he's going to wait on South Pass to check wagons headed for Oregon, but did he say how long he was going to stay there?" Ruth asked.

"He didn't say. He just said he was planning to get there in August at about the time the first wagons from Independence arrive," Pink said.

"Everyone going to Oregon has to go over South Pass, and if your wagon train gets there in August he'll probably be there," Dulucky said, trying to sound encouraging.

"I can't believe the news about Jacob. I wish we knew more about Beth Ann," Ruth said wringing her hands. "I'm worried about her alone with those people Jacob didn't like."

CHAPTER 39

Joe had gotten to know a number of people in town while he was recuperating from leg amputation and was able to help Beth Ann get a job as a cook in the hotel. She agreed to work six and a half days a week so she could make money for the trip to Oregon. After she cooked the noon meal on Sunday, she had the afternoon off and spent it with Joe.

Joe had settled Beth Ann in the same rooming house where he was staying. He intended to head out of town and go to his wife's village before the snow started flying, but Beth Ann's arrival had complicated his plans.

He longed to see his wife and daughters, but he didn't want to desert Beth Ann. He had to remind himself that she was only sixteen years old and still naive, even with her two close calls at being kidnapped.

In some ways, Beth Ann's showing up had made Joe more aware of his disability. He could go to his wife and live the rest of his life in her tribe. He knew they would welcome him, but he would be an extra mouth to feed.

How could he hunt with only one leg? He could no longer do the physical things trapping required, especially with Two Bears gone. The more he thought about it, the more depressed he got.

Beth Ann noticed how quiet he had become and questioned him about what was bothering him. Finally, he admitted he was worried about how he was going to support his family.

"Get your family and come with me to Oregon," Beth Ann urged. "My uncle's opening a big store out there and after he hears all you've done for me and Jacob, I'm sure he'll find a job for you in his store."

Joe mulled this over. The idea of being cooped up in a store was repugnant, but with a steady job he could have his family with him all year, and his daughters would be able to go to school in a white settlement.

One Sunday afternoon in early October as they sat on a bench along Main Street enjoying the sun, Beth Ann noticed Joe kept looking at her and then looking away.

"Joe, do you have something you want to say to me? If you do, I wish you'd spit it out".

"I been thinking about what you said about Oregon," Joe said. "I've wrestled with it for two weeks now. Dang it, I've decided that come the first part of March, I'll ride up and get my wife and girls and bring them back with me.

"Tomorrow I'll start talking to some wagon builders about what we'll need. I still have most of the money from the furs I sold in St. Louis. They can have it done, and we can start out for Oregon sometime in May."

Beth Ann threw her arms around Joe and pressed her cheek against his. "You keep coming to my rescue when I need help the most, I don't know how I can ever repay you," she said.

"You don't owe me a thing so forget thinking about it," Joe said, barely able to control his emotions.

Beth Ann saved every penny she could from her earnings as a cook. She wanted to be able to contribute her share for the trip. She had a steady stream of young men interested in courting her, but she let each know by her cool response to their overtures that she wasn't interested. She was not going to let anything interfere with her goal of heading for Oregon.

The first week in March, Joe started out on his quest to get his wife and daughters. He met an old arthritic Indian who wanted to get back to his people in the Pawnee nation, but didn't have a horse or supplies to get there.

Joe took him along as a helper and a companion. He figured he was probably saving the old man's life by getting him away from the white man's liquor. Joe hated to admit that part of the reason he wanted the old Indian along was his fear that he wouldn't be able to manage by himself.

March and April were lonely months for Beth Ann as she waited for Joe's return. She became even more anxious when she saw Willie and Simon Copper ride into town one afternoon. She knew they hadn't gotten on the boat, but she thought they had decided to ride overland back to St. Louis. She wished Joe would hurry back.

In the middle of the following week, after the noon meal was over, Beth Ann took a break from her kitchen duties and sat at a table by the window drinking coffee. She sat there each day hoping to see Joe come galloping down the street.

Her dreamy thoughts were slow to focus on the appearance of two people on horseback riding toward the hotel. She blinked and could hardly believe it when she recognized Joe riding one of the horses with a little girl perched in front of him.

Beside him rode an Indian woman with another little girl. Beth Ann jumped up, spilling her coffee onto the table, and ran out into the street to greet them. She got to the hitching rack just as Joe pulled his horse to a stop.

He handed his little girl down to Beth Ann before he dismounted. The child's black eyes studied Beth Ann for a moment before a smile spread across her face.

"Beth Ann," the small voice asked.

"Yes, yes," Beth Ann squealed, as she hugged the girl close to her and did a spinning dance of pure joy out into the road. Joe's wife rode up and looked down at the dancing pair. In Arapaho she said, "This must be the girl you talked about. She is a happy one."

"That's Beth Ann," Joe said. "Looks like she's stolen one of our girls."

Joe tied his wife's horse to the rail and lifted his other daughter to the ground before helping his wife to dismount. Beth Ann rushed over and picked up the second girl, then with both laughing girls in her arms turned to face Joe and his wife.

"Beth Ann, I want you to meet my wife, Little Bird, Two Bears' sister. I call her Birdie and you can too. The girl in your left arm is Moon Star and the other one is Sparrow. I think we're going to have to come up with some more American-sounding names for the girls. They'll want to have American names when they start school in Oregon."

Beth Ann shifted each girl to a hip and studied the handsome face of Birdie. A pair of shining black eyes stared back at her. A warm smile spread across Birdie's full lips. "I see why Joe like you."

Standing in the shadows on the other side of the street Willie and Simon watched the reunion with interest. "Why we still hangin' around here," Simon whined. "Thought you said we was just stayin' long enough to make money for boat fare back to St. Louis."

Willie turned in disgust and spit tobacco juice at Simon's feet. "Damn it, Simon, will you quit complainin'? I told you I think they lied about Jacob bein' dead just ta get shed of us. Willie snapped. "I think they know where he is and by God, we're gonna watch 'em 'til we find out fer sure."

Jacob's Promise

CHAPTER 40

The day for leaving St. Louis for Independence had arrived. Ruth hugged Olive and said her goodbyes while William waited with Mary Ann in the carriage he had hired to take them to the boat dock.

"Come on, Ruth, or we'll miss the boat. Everything we own is already on board," William called.

William had sent an order to Independence last fall for a wagon to be built and ready for them when they arrived. All they had to do when they got to Independence was to buy the mules and supplies they needed for the trip. William didn't want anyone else picking out the mules they would be depending on. The wagon train they signed with was due to leave on May 15th.

The Missouri River was high and over its banks when the boat pulled away from the landing to start the journey west. Ruth worried every time William had to help clear a snag. When she closed her eyes, she could still see Ralph struggling as he was pulled under the swirling water.

Ruth enjoyed the warm spring sunshine that fell on the bow of the boat, as well as, Mary Ann's company. She entertained Mary Ann by teaching her the names of the birds they saw along the river. She viewed each bend in the river and each tree they passed as a milestone of the trip west.

A loud tooting on the boat whistle announced the sighting of

Independence. Ruth hurried Mary Ann back to the cabin and tucked the last pieces of clothing into a suitcase. As soon as the boat was secured to the wharf, William jumped off and hired a livery to carry them and their luggage to the hotel.

He rushed to get them settled in their rooms and then had the driver take him to the shop where his wagon was being constructed. He inspected the wagon then went to the stockyards to look over what was left of the last shipment of mules.

"I was told there would be some quality mules in Independence, but this lot looks worn out," William said.

"I got a new bunch, I'm sure you'll like, coming in next week, fresh out of southern Missouri," the stockman said. "I'll send word to the hotel the minute they come in."

On returning to the hotel William gathered his family and led them down the wide staircase to the hotel dining room. Ruth and William were both famished and made quick work of their food. Mary Ann had cleaned every morsel off her plate and pleaded for a second round of cherry tarts.

"Please tell the cook how much we enjoyed the food," William told the waitress.

"We do have a good cook," the waitress said. "It's amazing that someone as young as she is can cook as well as she does. "

"Well, she prepared a fine meal. I'll leave a tip for you and will you please take another one back to the kitchen and give it to the cook?" William said as he handed her two large silver coins.

After clearing the table, the waitress took the dirty dishes back to the kitchen. "Beth Ann, a customer thought your cooking was so good he sent you a reward. That's the first time I can remember anyone sending the cook a tip."

"Good heavens!" Beth Ann said. "I've got to see what this man looks like." She headed for the dining room.

"He's the one with the red headed woman and the little girl," the waitress said.

Beth Ann cracked the door open and looked out, but she didn't see any family of three at any of the tables.

"I guess they left. Maybe they'll be back for breakfast and I can point them out to you then," the waitress offered.

Her workday over, Beth Ann walked to the small house Joe had rented. She had promised Birdie she would help make dresses for the little girls. She was also secretly making two dresses for Birdie.

She knew how proud Birdie was of the fine beadwork on the buckskin dresses she made, but if Birdie was going to travel with white folks and live in Portland, she was going to need clothes that would help her fit in.

Beth Ann stayed later than she should have that night, watching the girls play and sewing with Birdie. The next morning, she had to drag herself out of bed at her usual 4 A.M. She sat on the edge of the bed and sighed.

This would be her last week of getting up at this early hour to go stand over a hot cook stove. Next week she would be moving with Joe's family for the first organizational meeting of the wagon train. She informed the hotel manager that Friday would be the last day.

At breakfast, the waitress rushed into the kitchen to tell Beth Ann that if she wanted to see the man who had tipped her, he was in the dining room.

"Where are they sitting?"

"They're the second table, next to that big fern plant just right of the door."

Beth Ann walked over to the dining room door and pushed the door open a crack. She saw the man and the little girl, but the woman had her back to her. The little girl dropped her fork on the floor, and when the woman bent down to pick it up, Beth Ann saw her profile. With a scream of joy, Beth Ann burst into the room.

The scream startled Ruth, as it did every other diner in the room. She twisted in her chair to see what had happened, then jumped to her feet, knocking over her coffee, and dumping her napkin on the floor.

The two women rushed into each other's arms, both trying to talk through sobs. Little Mary Ann sat, wide eyed, not understanding what was happening.

When her emotions were finally under control Ruth turned to William. "Beth Ann I'd like you to meet my husband, William. William, I want you to meet my niece, Beth Ann Hesser."

Beth Ann looked questioningly at her aunt Ruth.

"Your uncle Ralph was killed in an accident a year ago and I have remarried."

Bill Heyduck

After a moments silence Beth Ann said, "I'm sorry to hear bout Uncle Ralph, but happy you found someone."

They stood holding each other's hand as if they were afraid one of them might suddenly disappear. The reunion was interrupted when a waitress approached the table and whispered to Beth Ann.

"Customers are getting upset because their food isn't being served."

"One more thing before you go back to work." Ruth held on to Beth Ann's arm. "Jacob is alive,"

Beth Ann's breath faltered, and new tears welled up in her eyes, "I knew it. I knew Mark Whipple lied. I should have made the poison stronger."

"Poison," Ruth gasped. "Who got poisoned?"

"I have to go. I'll tell you all about it after I get off work tonight."

As Beth Ann got up to leave the table, she became aware of Mary Ann for the first time. "And who are you?" Beth Ann bent down face-to-face with Mary Ann.

"Oh, where are my manners? Beth Ann, I want you to meet Mary Ann, William's daughter. "

"Don't let us frighten you with all our tears, Mary Ann," Beth Ann said. "They're tears of happiness." Then turned and scurried back to the kitchen.

Two tables away behind a large potted fern Willie and Simon were enjoying one of their rare days of eating a breakfast of something other than a campfire mush meal. When they heard the emotional meeting of Ruth and Beth Ann.

Willie peeked around the fern to see what the commotion was. He was surprised to see Beth Ann rush into the arms of the red headed woman they had met at the broken-down stagecoach in Illinois. As the women talked, he pulled his head back out of sight, but stayed behind the fern and listened.

When Beth Ann returned to the kitchen, Willie turned to Simon with a smile on his face. "I told ya he was alive."

"Who," Simon asked.

"Jacob, you idiot. Who did you think I meant? I Just heard the redhead tell Beth Ann he was alive, but she didn't say where he was. We have to be ready to move when they do."

Jacob's Promise

Simon's shoulders slumped. "I don't know, Willie. We don't have enough money to get home now. We both got jobs. We go any farther and we may never get back home. We can tell Pa Jacob's dead. How will he know different?

"You fergittin' what he did to our brothers? Well, I ain't, and you better not either."

Beth thought the workday would never end. As soon as the last customer left, she hurried up to her aunt's room. There were emotional hugs all over again before they settled down to talk. William excused himself and went down to the hotel bar for a drink.

Ruth spent the next hour telling Beth Ann everything she knew about Jacob.

Beth Ann couldn't believe that Jacob was still alive. She had almost begun to believe the Whipples' lies about the Indians killing him. By ten o'clock, the long hours of wakefulness caught up with Beth Ann and her eyelids began to droop.

"I'm sorry, Aunt Ruth, I can't keep my eyes open. I have to be at the hotel at four-thirty in the morning and I have to get to bed."

"We have months ahead of us to talk. Go home and get some sleep. You have to be up early, and I don't, so scoot," Ruth ordered.

Walking home in the cool of the night air Beth Ann's head cleared and a jarring thought came to her. Aunt Ruth had talked about them traveling together to Oregon and Beth Ann promised Joe and his family she would go with them. What in the world was she going to do? How was she going to tell one of them she couldn't go with them?

The next morning at breakfast, Beth Ann went out to their table to tell them about her promise to go west with Joe's family. William got a surprised look on his face when she said Joe's name.

"I think I saw that name on the list of people traveling in our train." He produced a list of those who had signed on to the wagon train and pointed to Joe's name. They would all be traveling together after all. Her problem was solved.

"Tonight, I want to take you all out to meet my friend Joe and his family," Beth Ann announced. "Joe's traveled the road we'll be taking out to Laramie, and I am sure William will want to talk to him. Why don't I meet you in the lobby after I get off work at seven o'clock?"

"It looks like you've been adopted by two families," William said. "I'm looking forward to meeting this Joe you've told us about."

At seven o'clock Beth Ann met them in the hotel lobby and led the way to Joe's house. Birdie had finished brewing some herbal tea a few minutes before they arrived and served them all a cup as soon as they were seated.

"The tea's delicious," Ruth said. "I've never tasted anything like it."

Before Birdie could thank her for the compliment three noisy girls came running through the house laughing.

"In about two weeks, Mary Beth will be speaking Arapaho and the other two will be speaking English, if I know anything about how youngsters pick up language," Joe said.

CHAPTER 41

Jacob adjusted the last rawhide hinge and tested the door to see that it opened and closed without dragging. Satisfied, he announced the cabin was officially finished. Blue Flower and Willow moved everything from the lean-to and started a fire so the cabin would be warm and the floor dry by bedtime.

The cabin didn't look like any cabin Jacob had seen in Illinois, but then again, it was only a temporary shelter. The bottom half of the cabin was dug out of the earth and only the top half was made of logs. At its peak on the inside, it measured only five feet and even Willow couldn't stand up to her full height.

The door was three feet high, and it was necessary to enter feet first and leave headfirst. Because there were no windows, the only light came from candles or by the fire in a fireplace.

They celebrated their first night in the cabin with a feast of steaks from the elk Jacob shot the day before. Willow sat next to Jacob as they ate. She and Jacob had been working side-by-side for the last few weeks and Jacob had gotten over his shyness.

The touch of her arm rubbing against his no longer brought a blush to his face. He didn't blush, but other strange feelings had stirred within him when she looked at him and smiled.

To add to the festivities, Snow pulled out a bottle of brandy he had hidden in the packs before they left Fort Bridger. "I only brought one bottle, so we'll have a sip of it on special occasions."

Snow poured a fourth of a cup for Jacob and then one for himself. He held his cup up in the air and said, "To a house well built, to good trapping, to good health, and to good women."

Jacob had never tasted liquor, and the first sip made him gasp for air. Snow told him to sip it slowly until he got used to it. After a few more sips, Jacob saw what Snow meant about getting used to it. The brandy seemed to make his body glow. The warm spot it made in his stomach radiated out to the very tips of his fingers and, in the end, made him sleepy. He moved off to the corner of the cabin he had chosen for his bed and began to undress.

"Get a good sleep, boy. Tomorrow is going to be a busy day." Snow said before heading for his own bed on the other side of the cabin.

Jacob crawled under the buffalo robe, a gift from Wounded Bull and felt the first vestiges of sleep creep over him.

Blue Flower and Willow went out to bury the garbage and rinse the tin plates. When they came back, they snuffed out the candles. Only the flickering of the fire dancing on the underside of the roof remained.

Jacob was jarred out of his half sleep by a cold breeze hitting his backside as the corner of the buffalo robe was lifted. The next thing he knew, Willow had slipped under the robe and was pressing her naked body against his back.

"Am I your woman? Blue Flower and Snow say I your woman," Willow whispered in Jacob's ear.

Jacob lay motionless as Willow glued herself spoon fashion against his back. He had never heard Willow say this much in English. She had always been there to help him when he needed it, but she had answered his questions with one or two syllables, not sentences. When Jacob turned to question what she said, his arm fell naturally over her waist and his hand rested on her bare back.

"I now Jacob's woman," she said again, as she pulled herself tightly against him and searched for his mouth with hers.

In Jacob's past world, this familiarity would never have happened. The young people back in Illinois didn't do this sort of thing until they had married. Up until this moment, he had only thought of Willow as a friend. His body told him it was more than friendship Willow was offering. As if his hands had a mind of their own, they timidly began to explore her body.

Jacob's Promise

Her smooth naked skin against his brought an instant physical reaction that Jacob had never experienced before. In the dark of his corner bed, Willow had suddenly become a woman, and he wanted her.

The next morning Willow was gone from his bed when he woke. He rolled over and saw her pouring fresh coffee into a tin cup by the fireplace. She hung the coffee pot back over the fire and brought the steaming cup to Jacob.

"I now your woman, yes?"

Jacob hesitated for just a moment before he nodded and said, "Yes, you're my woman."

A smile spread across Willow's face. Then she turned and went back to fill a bowl with stew for Jacob's breakfast.

Snow and Blue Flower had been lying in bed watching the two youngsters with both relief and satisfaction. "The joining of those two will make for a happy camp the rest of the winter," Snow whispered to Blue Flower.

Spider interrupted their quiet discussion with a scream as he jumped into their sleeping pallet with them. After a few minutes of horse play, they joined Jacob and Willow in front of the fire for breakfast.

After eating, Snow and Jacob climbed out of the cabin door and went to their old shelter where their trapping gear was stored. As they gathered up the traps, stakes, and bait, Snow said, "We'll just take ten traps today because I want to take my time showing you how to pick where to set a trap. You have to learn to think like a beaver if you expect to catch one."

They tramped for half an hour through a light snow that had fallen the night before. Snow stopped by a stream to show how and where to set his trap. By the time the last trap had been set, Snow knew Jacob could be trusted to go out on his own to run the line of traps.

"In a week or two when my arm's better we'll place all the traps. Tomorrow we'll go out and check the ones we set today, and I'll show you how to skin a beaver without damage to the pelt. You cut the pelt and it isn't worth dragging back to the fort to sell."

On the walk back to the cabin Jacob was silent, but his mind was churning with questions about what had happened last night. Finally, he blurted out, "About Willow...."

Bill Heyduck

Snow cut him off before he got another word out, "Jacob, you're not back in Illinois now. Out here the rules you lived by in Illinois don't work. Out here a man needs a woman to help him and comfort him during the long winter of trapping.

"A woman needs a man to provide for her, protect her, and to comfort her each night. You learn to depend on each other. You're equal partners. Willow's a good young woman and a good match for you. That's why I brought her along. Be good to her, Jacob, and she'll be good for you."

"You mean it was your idea to bring her? I thought you said she was kicked out of the lodge by her brother-in-law."

"Just a little white lie. Her brother-in-law would never have kicked her out. She was family. If I'd told you my real reason, I'd have had an argument with you. I knew a camp with two men and one woman was a camp that could lead to trouble, so I decided to bring Willow along. I'm glad it's worked out the way I thought it would."

In some ways Jacob was a little put out at what Snow had done, but these thoughts evaporated the minute they entered camp, and he saw Willow smiling at him.

Jacob crawled into his pallet that night and waited to see if Willow would once again join him. When she came, he greeted her not with questions as he had the night before, but with a welcoming embrace.

Life had suddenly changed for Jacob. A loneliness he had felt since being separated from Beth Ann was now filled by something new that he couldn't fully explain. Willow had become a part of his life. He didn't know exactly how it had happened, but he felt it in his very soul. She was the first person from outside his family he knew he was destined to share his life with.

Once Snow's arm was strong enough to run his own trap line, he stopped accompanying Jacob. Beaver hides began to pile up in the old shelter. Willow became Jacob's teacher in how to skin a beaver without harming the pelt. While they skinned, Jacob taught Willow new words in English. Her effort to teach Jacob Shoshone was less successful.

The grass for the horses near the campsite was nearly depleted and a new pasture had to be found. The dry feed they had packed with them would not last if they didn't have some grass to supplement it. Snow found a small valley near their camp, sheltered from the heaviest of the snow, and with a good supply of dry grass.

They built a fence of twigs and rope across the narrow mouth of the inlet to the valley to hold the horses. The women now had the additional chore of checking the fence during the day while Snow and Jacob were gone. The horses were a treasure they couldn't afford to lose.

In the middle of March, Snow caught a bad chest cold and started running a fever.

Jacob was afraid it would turn into pneumonia and insisted that Snow stay in the cabin. "With Willow's help I can run all the traps while you rest," Jacob insisted.

Some days he and Willow ran both trap lines and spent the night away from camp. Sleeping under the stars with Willow by his side was a welcome escape from the stuffy cabin, where privacy was impossible.

On one of these overnight trips after they retired, Willow loosened the blanket wrapped around them and moved away from the warmth of Jacob's body. She tilted her head and looked into Jacob's face. "It will soon be spring. Trapping will end. What you do then?"

"I don't know." Jacob dodged the questions. "I need to talk to Snow."

These were things Jacob had not let himself think about. He knew that in the weeks he and Willow had been together she had become a very important part of his life, but he hadn't thought about what he going to do when trapping season ended.

A frown creased Willow's brow, but she accepted Jacob's answer and didn't ask again.

Jacob and Willow had been gone two days and had skinned a hefty load of beaver pelts. The following morning, they tied the beaver pelts to backpacks and headed back to the cabin at daybreak, hoping to get back in time to share the noon meal with Blue Flower and Snow.

Nearing camp Jacob opened his mouth to call out, but the call died in his throat when he heard the sharp report of a rifle followed by a loud scream, then silence.

Bill Heyduck

Jacob and Willow ducked off the trail, slipped off their backpacks, and crept forward until they could see the cabin. Jacob froze when he saw Blue Flower lying face down on the ground. Near the cabin door he saw an Indian slumped against the wall, with blood oozing out of a hole in his chest. Two other Indians were creeping along the side of the wall toward the cabin door.

Jacob motioned for Willow to stay behind him as he moved forward. He pulled a hatchet out of his belt and checked the load in his rifle. Willow pulled out her skinning knife and knelt behind him. Jacob moved forward to the edge of the tree line and stopped.

Twenty feet in front of him stood the nearest Indian. Jacob stepped out of the trees and threw the hatchet. It made two turns in the air and with a sickening thud buried itself in the back of the Indian's skull. The second Indian turned at the sound, but Jacob fired before the he could lift his rifle. The breast plate of bones the Indian was wearing shattered leaving an ugly hole.

Jacob rushed over to Blue Flower, knelt down and turned her onto her side. Blood ran from a wound in her chest. Her eyes were wide open, but they were blank. Jacob gently rolled her over on her back and closed her eyes.

He was still on his knees when he was startled by a noise behind him. He turned to see an Indian with his war club raised over his head ready to strike. Instead of striking him, the Indian stood wide-eyed, as if paralyzed. His arm holding the club went limp, and he pitched forward, bouncing off Jacob before hitting the ground. Willow stood looking down at Jacob, holding a bloody knife in her hand.

"Be careful, there may be others," Willow whispered.

Jacob knew it was dangerous to enter the cabin, but it had to be done. Snow was in there and he was sick and maybe helpless. He slowly pulled the door open and waited. No sound came from inside. He slipped his head inside the door and waited for his eyes to adjust to the faint light from the candles and fireplace.

The first image he saw was an Indian sprawled, face down, in the middle of the floor. Looking deeper into the gloom he sighted a second Indian crumpled across Snow's bed. Snow, his head covered with blood and his hand still gripping the Indian's hair, lay dead in a twisted ball of covers beside the Indian.

Jacob crawled over to Snow and looked down into his

unseeing eyes.

Willow called softly from the doorway. "Come, Jacob, there will be at least one watching the horses. We cannot let him get away."

At the edge of the clearing they found tracks in the snow and followed them back into the woods. They had gone a short distance when they heard a horse snort. Jacob spotted a lone Indian watching the path. Jacob's bullet hit him before he could get the war club out of his belt.

"They are Utes," Willow said. "We are on their land."

"Help me with the horses," Jacob said. "We don't want there to be any possibility of them wandering back to a Ute village."

"Spider! Did you see him in the cabin?" Willow asked.

"No. I didn't even think about him. We'll ride back. It'll be faster."

At the cabin they secured the horses and began calling Spider's name. They went inside and called but got no answer. Their fear was that Spider had been killed and thrown someplace out in the woods.

Standing quietly trying to get up the courage to search for Spider's body they were startled by a whimpering coming from inside the cabin. Rushing inside they heard the small cry again.

It seemed to be coming from the rumpled buffalo robe on Blue Flower and Snow's pallet. They peeled back the robe and found Spider hiding under the buffalo robe, trembling with fear. Willow grabbed him and held his shivering little body in her arms.

With Willow carrying Spider they went outside. Jacob turned to Willow and whispered, "Keep him occupied. I don't want him to see Snow and Blue Flower."

"No! He will see Blue Flower and Snow buried. It is good for him to know that death is part of life and that we will never lie to him."

CHAPTER 42

Fort Laramie was a big disappointment to Beth Ann. She was expecting to see a bustling city, but all she saw was a rundown fort and trading post. The storekeepers sold overpriced supplies to the travelers that hadn't been smart enough get all their necessities in Independence. Fortunately, Joe had overseen supplying their wagons, and they spent very little in Laramie.

Joe led the wagon train far out to the west of the fort before he picked out a campsite. He wanted to put some distance between them, and the Indians camped all around the entrance to the fort.

Even camped away from the fort, a few Indians came by wanting to be fed. One Indian they turned away came back in the night and stole one of the mules. The owner of the mule wanted to charge into the Indian camp to retrieve his mule, but Joe stopped him.

"You try that, and we'll have a fight on our hands that'll get a lot of people hurt. You want to take the chance of getting your family killed over a mule?"

A week out of Fort Laramie, they met a group of Indians blocking their trail demanding pay for crossing their tribal land. They wanted rifles and ammunition as the toll. Joe went out with the wagon master to talk with them. William tagged along. Through signs and a few words in the Sioux language Joe told them they would not pay with rifles but offered them an ox.

Jacob's Promise

The Indians refused the offer and insisted on receiving rifles. With rapid hand signs Joe let them know it was the ox or nothing. After lot of arguing and threats the Indians grudgingly accepted the ox and let the wagons pass.

Each night Beth Ann and Ruth held school for Mary Ann, Moon Star, and Sparrow. They drew the letters of the alphabet in the dirt by the campfire for the girls to repeat aloud. Using the sounds of the letters they slowly built words.

This was material Mary Ann already knew, but she enjoyed helping the Indian girls say the strange words. Before long they were taking turns reading aloud from a book of bedtime stories Ruth had purchased in Independence.

Joe's two girls were quick to pick up English from their days of play with Mary Ann. It made teaching them to read much easier than Ruth had expected. William discovered the exchange of language worked both ways when he heard Mary Ann conversing with Birdie in Arapaho.

A week into the trip they passed a lone wagon, sitting by the river, seemingly deserted. Joe thought it was strange to see a lone wagon and stopped the train to investigate.

"Everyone wait right here," Joe said after they were stopped. "We don't want to get too close. Let me go have a look first."

"I don't see what we could have to fear from a lone wagon," William said.

"Just the same, you wait here until I have a chance to go have a look."

Joe rode up to the wagon without seeing anyone, so he called out, "Stranger coming into camp."

No one answered. Then Joe saw a grave about thirty feet out behind the wagon. When he rode around the wagon, he saw a man sitting on a stool with a blanket wrapped around his shoulders. A woman was lying on a blanket in front of him with skin as white as snow. The man looked up at Joe with watery, blood shot eyes.

"She just died this mornin', and I ain't had the strength ta dig a hole and bury her. The fever took our youngest three day ago and the second yesterday. Guess I'll be next."

"Where's the wagon train you were traveling with?" Joe asked.

"It left the day the first child got the fever. Said we 'd have to trail along a mile behind them. Then my wife and other baby got sick and I had ta stop to take care of 'em."

"I'll be back to dig the grave for your wife," Joe said and rode back to where William was waiting.

"They've all been stricken with the cholera. The man's the only one left, and he's sick," Joe said. "Take the wagons a good way on up the river before you stop. We don't want to take a chance of this spreading to us."

Beth Ann overheard Joe telling William to go on and leave the sick man to fend for himself. "Joe, you can't just leave a sick man," she protested. "If no one else will go, I'll do it."

"Beth Ann, I can't stop you from doing something stupid. But I will tell you this. As much as I care for you, if you so much as touch that man, you'll not be allowed to return to our wagons. I won't take the chance of you infecting us with the fever."

Beth Ann was startled by Joe's harsh words. He had never talked to her like that before. "I don't think I'll ever get used to the brutal ways of surviving out here. I can at least warm some stew and set it out for him," Beth Ann replied.

Joe untied a shovel from the side of the wagon and returned to the baby's grave and began digging another by its side. "The graves dug," Joe said and backed away.

Struggling, the man dragged his wife over to the grave. He wrapped the blanket around her and rolled her into the hole. Joe waited while the man said a silent prayer, then shoveled dirt over her body.

"I'm sorry, I can't do more for you, mister. I can't take the chance of carrying the fever back to my family."

"I can see how you feel. Maybe you should dig another hole. I'll sit on the edge and just fall in when my time comes." He paused and took a labored breath before going on. "Thanks fer yer help and if 'in ya catch up with the other wagon train, tell 'em that none of Elmer Higgins family survived."

"Well, Mr. Higgins, you never know what'll happen. Maybe you'll be able to shake this off and make it to Oregon after all."

Joe rode back to camp and had William call a camp meeting for that evening after supper. He stood before the group and cleared his throat.

"I know some of you are upset we didn't help that man. It

seems an unchristian thing to do, but the welfare of this wagon train was at stake. Touching any of their belongs could have brought the fever into our camp. Do you want to be in the wagon that has to be left behind to travel alone?"

The crowd was silent.

"We may see another wagon from that same wagon train before the week is out because the fever may not have stopped with just one family. We won't even stop.

"If I see any of you get near a stopped wagon, you'll have to fall back a mile behind us. You will not be allowed to camp with us for at least two weeks. If that sounds harsh, I'm sorry, but that's how dangerous the fever is."

That night they camped by the Sweetwater River where the grass was fresh and green. The stock experienced the first good grazing they had had for the last hundred miles. Joe suggested they rest a couple of days because the trail on the other side of Devil's Gate was going to be a tough one.

Just as Joe predicted the next part of the trip was worse than they had imagined. The trail was covered with boulders that ranged in size of apples to the size of a one room cabin. Almost half of the wagons encountered some sort of a mishap.

With each passing day Beth Ann's patience grew shorter. South Pass wasn't that far in front of them, but at the rate they were traveling, it would be September before they got there. Surely Jacob would be long gone by then.

The day Joe told her they had reached the wide-open, rocky slope of South Pass, Beth Ann could hardly contain her desire to gallop up ahead. Joe cautioned her that they still had a long way to go to get over the pass, and the wagons had to take it easy on the long pull. Beth Ann looked up the steep incline with both fear and hope in her heart.

A mile to the rear Willie and Simon stood on a raised mound and watched the wagons start up the slope. Simon had become more unhappy with each passing mile.

"I think we heard wrong. That's the start of the mountains, and we ain't seen hide nor hair of Jacob." Simon kicked at a rock in disgust.

"You might as well get over your little fit, cause we're too far out to turn back now."

Bill Heyduck

"Shit," was all Simon could say before remounting his horse.

CHAPTER 43

They had stayed in the cabin overnight. The next morning Willow was up early to build a fire and make breakfast. When Jacob rolled out of bed, she handed him a gourd bowl filled with breakfast stew, then ran to the cabin door, and crawled outside.

Wondering what had gotten into her, Jacob set his bowl down, and rushed out after her. He stuck his head out the door and found her ten feet away bent over, gagging.

"Why didn't you tell me you were sick? Is it something you ate?"

"It is your son's fault,"

"What son? You mean Spider? What did he do?"

"Not Spider. Your son. The son I am carrying in my belly."

Jacob stared at Willow not understanding. Then his jaw dropped. His face must have shown his shock when he finally understood what she had said.

"You are not pleased. I can see it in your eyes." Willow held still with downcast eyes.

"No, that's not true. I'm just surprised. How long have you known?"

"A week. Maybe two."

"When will it come, I mean be born?"

"It will be many moons before that happens. The medicine man will know."

"You say my son. How do you know it'll be a boy?"

"I know, the spirit has spoken to me in my sleep."

A broad smile. Spread across Jacob's face. "Will Beth Ann ever be surprised." He chuckled then went to Willow and folded her in his arms.

"Jacob, we must not stay here. The Utes will soon come looking for their brothers."

"I've worried about that too. I planned to get the rest of the hides off the stretcher today and then head back to your people."

After breakfast Jacob left the cabin to get the horses from their valley pasture. He had a real chore tying them all together in a long string. The Utes' horses were harder to handle than his pack animals. He saddled two horses, one for Willow and one for himself. Spider rode bareback on one of the gentler horses. Willow went first leading the packhorses, next came Spider and last Jacob leading the wilder Indian ponies.

Days later as they neared the Shoshone village an outrider saw them and rushed off to report that riders were headed for their camp. Wounded Bull jumped on his horse and rode out with the others to see who they were. His heart sank when he saw Jacob, Willow, and Spider, but not Snow and Blue Flower.

"Where are Snow and Blue Flower?" Wounded Bull asked fearing the answer.

"Dead," Jacob answered.

Wounded Bull didn't question the weary travelers about what had happened until they had rested and eaten.

Jacob let Willow tell the story of the Utes attack and the death of Snow and Blue Flower.

"Willow, will you tell them what I say? I want to be sure they understand." Jacob turned to face Wounded Bull.

"As Willow's oldest male relative, I want to request you give me Willow in marriage. I have six fine Ute horses to exchange for her." Jacob had learned from Snow that giving horses was the proper thing to do when a brave asked for a woman in marriage.

Willow's face turned red and she hung her head as she repeated Jacob's words. She wasn't sure until now that Jacob would take her for his wife.

"The sisters of my wife seem bent on marrying white men." Wounded Bull smiled. "If that is Willow's choice then I accept your gift of six horses and offer Willow to you. Now what of the boy, Spider? He is of my wife's blood and is welcome in my lodge. I will raise him as my own son."

When Willow translated this for Jacob, he looked at Wounded Bull for a moment before he shook his head.

"Tell him we'll take Spider as our son. Snow treated me as his son when he took me as his trapping partner and taught me the things a father teaches a son. I'll treat his son as my own."

Willow's face broke into a wide smile. She also looked upon Spider as her son.

"Jacob has claimed me for his wife and has now claimed Spider for his son. My heart is filled with happiness," Willow whispered to herself.

The next night the tribe gathered for the joining of Willow and Jacob. Jacob stood nervously watching as logs were placed into a double-layered stack in the sacred fire circle of the packed earth surrounded by teepees.

Willow whispered, "Seven kinds of wood from special trees have been chosen by the tribe's holy man for our wedding. The large stack of wood in the center represents the creator and the holy union of two people."

She pointed to two smaller stacks of wood, one on the north and one the south. "Those stacks of wood represent us."

The Shaman approached the couple and sprinkled tobacco, sage, sweet grass, and corn over their heads and shoulders. He turned and chanted a song as he walked to the sacred circle and dusted the stacked wood with tobacco, sage, sweet grass, and corn. Two braves moved forward to light the two small piles of wood on the north and south of the circle.

Willow nodded to Jacob and whispered in English, "Go push your pile of burning wood into the center pile."

After seeing that Jacob understood, she went to her fire and started pushing it toward the center of the fire circle with her foot.

Careful not to get burned, Jacob began pushing his small fire. After the fires were joined the Shaman announced that the two lives were now merged into one holy union.

Jacob understood only half of what was said but was convinced this ceremony was just as binding as any wedding in a church.

Bill Heyduck

After spending two weeks in Wounded Bull's lodge Jacob announced he was going to Fort Bridger to trade furs for supplies for the trip to Oregon. He figured he could easily get to Fort Bridger, finish his business and get to South pass in twenty days.

Willow started to pack, but Jacob stopped her.

"I think you and Spider should stay here with your family while I'm gone. I'm going to be at the Bridger trading post for a few weeks, and I don't think it's a good place for a family."

Willow got a sinking in her chest. Was she just a winter bride? Was Jacob planning to leave for Fort Bridger and not come back until fall?

"Wounded Bull can bring you and Spider to South Pass in August. I'll wait for you there."

Willow tried not to show her relief when she heard Jacob include her and Spider in his plans.

Jacob knew he was leaving Willow sooner than he needed to, but he was restless in the village, and didn't feel he was earning his keep. At Bridger's he thought he might get some work to occupy his time until he left for South Pass.

"We also have furs to trade," Wounded Bull said. "You will not have to travel alone."

Wounded Bull secretly told Willow he was sending the braves with Jacob to make sure he didn't get lost or get his furs stolen before he got to the trading post.

When Jacob and the Indians reached South Pass the braves pointed out the camping site where Jacob would meet Wounded Bull and Willow.

Jim Bridger was standing in the doorway of his trading post when Jacob and the Shoshone braves rode through the gate to the fort.

"Where's Snow?"

"Killed by Utes," Jacob answered.

"Climb down and come inside and tell me how it happened." Bridger led Jacob to the back room of the fort and closed the door. Once inside he turned to Jacob and said, "Watch what you say when you're outside this room. There are Utes here and if they heard you say you killed some of their brothers you could end up with your throat slit."

Jacob's Promise

Bridger listened to Jacob's story of the fight with the Utes and when the story ended, he went to the packhorses to inspect Jacob's furs.

"You have some fine pelts, Jacob, and I'll see that you get quality trade goods for them."

Jacob was thrilled when the trading was done and surprised at how much the furs had gained him. He was now well-supplied for the trip to Oregon.

The Shoshone braves stayed two days trading, gambling, and racing their horses against members of other tribes. On the third morning they told Jacob they were leaving.

Jacob gave them some glass beads for Willow and a tin whistle for Spider. He assured them he knew his way back to where he was to meet Wounded Bull. He had traveled the trail three times, once with Pink and Dulucky, once with Snow and then with the Shoshone braves.

Jacob, bored with his idleness at the fort, began to miss Willow to warm his bed each night and Spider's happy laughter. Life at the fort wasn't any more agreeable than life with the Shoshones had been.

Bridger watched Jacob mope around the fort for a week before he decided to intervene and offered him a job caring for the livestock. Maybe that would shake him out of his lethargy and bring some life back into him.

Jacob worked with the horses a few days, but his mood didn't change and without warning one morning he started packing up to leave for South Pass.

"Leaving a little earlier than planned, I see," Bridger said.

"I can't sit here any longer. If I'm going to have to sit and wait, I'd rather do it out at South Pass where I might catch an early wagon train. One of them may have gotten itchy feet and left earlier than usual. "

"You be careful out there alone. Don't make your camp too obvious or you might attract the wrong kind of attention."

"Thanks for all your help, Mr. Bridger. I won't forget it." Jacob heaved himself into the saddle. He turned his mount and leading two packhorses left the fort.

Along the trail he met a few other travelers with furs to trade, headed towards Bridger's. A couple of nights he camped with mountain men who had known Snow and had even spent one season trapping with him. The trapper wanted to hear all about Snow and how Snow had met his end.

A day later, halfway to the meeting place on South Pass, Jacob's horse developed a limp and Jacob had to walk. He led his lame horse, with the packhorses trailing behind. It was a good thing he left early, he thought, because walking extended the time it took him to get to South Pass.

Even at his slow pace he arrived ahead of Willow and Spider. Thinking of Spider brought a smile. He and Willow were going to have to find an English name for him once they got to Oregon.

The days dragged as he waited for the first wagon of the season to come into sight. Late one afternoon he saw a group of Indians come over a crest in the distance. Taking Bridger's advice, Jacob moved behind s group of boulders, out of sight. When the distance shortened, he was able to pick out Willow and Spider riding with them

He couldn't contain his joy. He moved out into the open and began to wave his arms wildly. Willow galloped forward, slipped off her horse, then stood bashfully waiting for Jacob to come to her.

Wounded Bull helped Spider down, and the boy ran forward screaming, "Jacob, Jacob." He leaped into Jacob's arms and hugged his neck.

Wounded Bull and the braves stayed for the night exchanging stories. Many of Wounded Bull's stories were about the adventures of Spider learning to hunt.

"Spider will be a good hunter if all the deer are deaf," Wounded Bull laughed.

Jacob thought he saw a bit of sadness in Wounded Bull's eyes as he poked fun at Spider's exploits.

CHAPTER 44

Jacob built a shelter under overhanging rocks out of sight of anyone coming up the slope of South Pass. He wanted to be able to observe any passing traveler, but wanted his campsite hidden. He was worried that there might be Utes using the trail.

They had been camped two weeks before they heard the first wagon train come creeping up the slope. Jacob stepped out onto the trail and studied each wagon and driver as they drove by. He described Beth Ann to people in each wagon, but no one recognized her name.

The men nodded and answered his questions, but the women and children remained silent and just stared at the man in buckskin and his Indian woman and child.

"White people find our family strange, I think," Willow observed. "See how they all stare at us?"

"Maybe it's because we look so well fed," Jacob said. "A lot of them sure look ragged and hungry." Jacob didn't want to upset Willow by telling her that the people might be staring because they disliked seeing an Indian woman and a white man together.

Jacob and Willow waited days between wagon trains, and they all had the same answer when Jacob asked about Beth Ann. No one remembered any one fitting her description. The waiting made Jacob restless. After the third train passed without any word of Beth Ann the inactivity got the better of him. He rose early one morning and saddled his horse.

"We need fresh meat, I'm tired of eating jerky. I'll be back before dark. Stay out of sight unless you see a wagon train, then be sure to ask each wagon about Beth Ann."

Willow played games with Spider to keep him entertained, but he tired and after the noon meal he lay down in the shade of a boulder to sleep.

Late that afternoon, Willow saw a wagon train lumbering up the slope toward her. She shook Spider awake as the wagons approached and moved out where she could be seen. When the first wagon drew up beside her, she called out, "Do you know Beth Ann Hesser?"

To her great surprise, the man pointed back the way he had come. At the next wagon the same response was given. Willow became more excited with each passing wagon.

When the eighth wagon drew up beside her, Willow was beginning to think they were playing a joke on her. But she again stepped forward and called, "Beth Ann Hesser?"

A woman with flaming red hair stood up in the wagon and jumped over the side before the wagon came to a stop. The wild look on the woman's face startled Willow. She took a step backward and asked questioningly, "Beth Ann Hesser? I am Willow Hesser, wife of Jacob Hesser.

Ruth stood dumbfounded when she heard the girl say she was the wife of Jacob Hesser. She looked down and saw Spider hugging Willow's leg and thought, *that can't be Jacob's child.*

The women stood facing each other, neither saying a word. William broke the silence when he called down from the wagon, "Ask her where Jacob is. She seems to understand English."

"Jacob is hunting." Willow answered. "He will come soon."

Beth Ann was riding near the back of the wagon train and saw Ruth standing beside the wagon talking to an Indian woman. Joe saw the same thing, and both headed in that direction. Beth Ann got there first and called out to Ruth.

"Who's the Indian girl?"

"She says she's Jacob's wife," Ruth replied.

"I am wife of Jacob Hesser," Willow said proudly.

Beth Ann almost fell off her horse when she heard Willow say she was Jacob's wife. She slipped out of the saddle and confronted

Jacob's Promise

Willow. "Where's Jacob?"

"Jacob is hunting, he will be here soon." Willow frightened by the two white women facing her. "Are you Beth Ann or is it the one with fire hair?" Willow asked.

"I'm Beth Ann, and you say you're Jacob's wife?" Beth Ann asked again, a little shocked at what she had just heard.

"I am Willow, the wife of Jacob Hesser. I speak the truth," Willow replied, stubborn pride showing in her voice.

"Jacob's alive," Beth Ann shouted. She grabbed the surprised Ruth around the waist, lifted her off the ground, and twirled her around laughing hysterically as she repeated over and over, "I can't believe it. I can't believe it. To finally know for sure."

"Put me down, Beth Ann. You're scaring the girl and the little boy to death."

This was the first time Beth Ann had noticed the little boy. She set Ruth back on the ground and looked down at Spider. "Who is he?" She was still shocked at Willow's declaration that she was Jacob's wife.

"He is our adopted son, Spider," Willow answered.

"Your brother has been a busy boy since you last saw him." Ruth shook her head.

Beth Ann studied Willow. She noticed the defiant look on Willow's face when she stated she was Willow Hesser, wife of Jacob Hesser. That look convinced Beth Ann that she indeed had a new Indian sister-in-law.

Carefully Beth Ann took what she hoped was a non-threatening step toward Willow, smiled, and reached out to take Willow into an embrace.

Willow gave a sigh of relief and returned the hug.

Willie and Simon had stopped a mile back down the trail when they saw the wagon train come to a standstill and watched. "What you figure's goin on up there?" Simon asked.

"Probably a break down." Willie saw the other wagons going by the one that had stopped.

Willie and Simon had followed a mile or so behind the wagon train all the way from Independence. Close enough to pounce if they saw Jacob, but far enough back that they wouldn't be recognized.

Simon tapped Willie on the shoulder and pointed toward the tree line. "Someone's movin' in that tree line up ahead of us. Better be ready it might be Indians."

They watched as a buckskin clad rider emerged from a line of trees. An antelope and rifle draped in front of the saddle.

"Looks like one of those mountain men we heard about," Simon said. "Think he's part of the wagons?"

"He ain't dressed like them others. I think he's a loner," Willie answered. "Why don't we go see if he'd like to give us a piece of that antelope?"

"Antelope steak sounds good, but what are you gonna' do if he says no?"

"Two guns against one says he'll be happy to give us a steak or two."

As he rode toward the man Willie pulled his rifle from its scabbard and laid it along side of his leg out of sight. He studied the buckskin clad stranger. Long blond hair streamed out from under his hat and half covered his face. If the hair hadn't been blond Willie would have thought it was an Indian.

"Hey, stranger wait a minute. I'd like a word with ya," Willie called.

The rider turned at Willie's call.

Recognition was slow to come, but when it did Willie jerked his horse to a halt and leveled his rifle at the rider. A smile spread across his face. "Well, I'll be damned. Hey, Simon, say hello to the murder'n bastard who killed our brothers."

It wasn't until Willie spoke that Jacob realized it was the Cooper brothers. The scraggly beards and mustaches had hidden the faces he remembered.

"We've come a long way ta find ya, Jacob."

Jacob's unflinching eyes bore into Willie. "I killed two of the murderers of my parents, and I got no apologies for doing it. Are you cowards ready to admit what you did?"

"I ain't admittin' nothin'. All I aim ta do is make things right for my pa. Ya got a prayer, ya better start sayin' it." Willie eased the rifle up with the barrel pointed at Jacob's head. "Look at the coward, Simon. He can't even look me in the eye."

Jacob wasn't worried about eye contact. He was watching Willie's finger as it slowly tightened on the rifle's trigger. A split

Jacob's Promise

second before the rifle fired Jacob dropped over the side of his horse, taking his rifle with him.

The bullet buzzed just inches from his left ear. Jacob intended to keep one leg locked over the horse's back like the Shoshone braves did, but instead he slipped and hit the ground. He broke his fall with the butt of the rifle and rolled onto his back.

A satisfied smile creased Willie's lips when he saw Jacob fall out of the saddle and hit the ground on the far side of his horse. The smile faded when he saw Jacob's rifle rise and fire. The smile died as Jacob's bullet hit Willie in the middle of his chest, knocking him to the ground.

Heart pounding, Jacob dropped his rifle and using the horse as a shield pulled his ax from his belt. He drew the ax back ready to throw and stepped around the horse's rump. Instead of facing a blast from Simon's rifle he saw Simon on the ground bent over Willie. Cautiously, Jacob walked toward Simon, the hatchet still poised to strike.

Simon lifted his head and saw Jacob ready to strike. He covered his face with his hands and cried, "Don't hurt me. Please."

"Give me one good reason why I shouldn't kill you."

You've killed all my brothers, ain't that enough? I'm not the one who wanted to come after you. That was Pa's idea. I told Willie in Independence we shoulda' turned back, but he wouldn't do it."

Jacob watched the unsteady form of Simon and knew he didn't have the heart to kill him. He lowered his ax and laid it against his leg. "I should kill you for all the sadness you've caused."

"Please let me go," Simon begged. "I promise I'll never bother you again."

Jacob sucked in a trembling breath and put his hatchet back in his belt. "Go home, Simon. Tell your pa the killing is over," Jacob said.

"I ain't goin' home. I'd never make it alone."

"Then bury your brother, and go wherever you want, but if I see you again, I may change my mind. There's a trail up ahead that branches off to Fort Bridger, you best take it."

Jacob picked Simon's rifle, pointed it straight up, and fired it. He didn't want to take chance that Simon might change his mind and shoot him in the back. Jacob mounted his horse and without turning back rode off up the trail.

Half a mile up the slope he noticed the wagon. His heart surged. Could that be Beth Ann? He jammed his heels into the horse's flanks and galloped up the slope.

Willow stood, bewildered. The many voices speaking English overwhelmed her. They each asked questions but didn't give her a chance to answer. Everyone talked at once. Willow was ready to scream for them to stop when she heard two gunshots come from back down the trail.

Everyone stopped talking and looked in that direction. They could barely make out two men and a group of horses. One man suddenly fired a rifle toward the sky then mounted his horse and started up the slope toward them.

Joe pulled his rifle from its scabbard and watched the approaching rider. A broad smile creased Willow's face. She reached out and touched Joe's arm.

"There will be no danger from that rider."

Beth Ann was the first, after Willow, to recognize Jacob and raced down the slope, her feet flying over the rocky ground.

Jacob jumped off his horse just before she reached him and was almost bowled over when she threw herself into his arms.

"You look like a mountain man except you don't have a beard," she cried.

"Willow doesn't like hair on my face," Jacob answered, a lump forming in his throat. He struggled but was unable to stop the tears from welling up in his eyes.

"What was all the shooting about down there," Joe asked.

Jacob looked down at Beth Ann before he answered. "I bumped into the Cooper brothers."

Beth Ann gasped. "The Cooper brothers? I thought we left them in Independence."

"They must have followed you, hoping you would lead them to me," Jacob said. "They won't be a bother anymore. After Simon buries Willie, he's going to head for the Fort Bridger cutoff. He's been warned not to follow us."

"I can't wait to hear how you got here," Beth Ann said hanging onto Jacob's arm. Willow moved up beside Jacob and clasped his other arm possessively. Spider clung to Jacob's leg bewildered by the noisy strangers.

"There'll be plenty of time for you to get acquainted and exchange stories tonight," Joe said. "Right now, we have to catch up with the rest of the wagon train.

"We can't stand out here on the side of this slope all day and gab." Joe race ahead to catch up with the main part of the wagon train. He needed to find a level place for the train to camp for the night.

Beth Ann stayed behind to help Willow and Jacob pack up their camp. She bubbled with happiness. It had been an eventful day. She was reunited with her long-lost brother and had gained a sister-in-law and a nephew. Life was sweet again.

ABOUT THE AUTHOR

One of Bill's grade school report cards had a side note, 'day dreams instead of working'. Later his day dreaming turned into young adult novels. Day dreams along with his experiences as a boy scout, a pilot at sixteen, four years in the Marine Corps, work as a carpenter, a truck driver, a bulldozer operator, a TV scenery designer, a public school teacher, a potter, and a college professor became fuel for day dreams and story plots.

Bill lives, day dreaming and writing in rural east central Illinois.

Made in the USA
Monee, IL
28 January 2021